Natural SATISFACTION

An Naturel Trilogy, Book Three

ANNA DURAND

JACOBSVILLE BOOKS · MARIETTA, OHIO

ISBN: 978-1-949406-45-0 (paperback)
ISBN: 978-1-949406-46-7 (ebook)
ISBN: 978-1-949406-47-4 (audiobook)
Library of Congress Control Number: 2020923323

Manufactured in the United States.

Jacobsville Books
www.JacobsvilleBooks.com

Publisher's Cataloging-in-Publication Data
provided by Five Rainbows Cataloging Services

Names: Durand, Anna, author.
Title: Natural satisfaction / Anna Durand.
Description: Marietta, OH : Jacobsville Books, 2021. | Series: Au naturel trilogy, bk. 3.
Identifiers: LCCN 2020923323 (print) | ISBN 978-1-949406-45-0 (paperback) | ISBN 978-1-949406-46-7 (ebook) | ISBN 978-1-949406-47-4 (audiobook)
Subjects: LCSH: Nudism--Fiction. | Nudist camps--Fiction. | Romanies--Fiction. | Man-woman relationships--Fiction. | Oregon--Fiction. | Romance fiction. | BISAC: FICTION / Romance / Romantic Comedy. | FICTION / Romance / Contemporary. | GSAFD: Love stories. | Humorous fiction.
Classification: LCC PS3604.U724 N38 2021 (print) | LCC PS3604.U724 (ebook) | DDC 813/.6--dc23.

Praise for Anna Durand's Books

"[*Natural Passion* is] hilariously funny, irreverent. and steamy."
Debbie Orazi, Goodreads reviewer

"Wow! I'm so happy I picked up [*Natural Passion*]. [...] Refreshing, funny, and sexy, with a unique twist on a vacation spot. [...] Another author to add to my favorites list, and I can't wait for Ollie and Mara's story in *Natural Impulse*."
Sharon Clayton, The Eclectic Review

"Anna Durand adroitly sets the stage for a fun romantic comedy [in *One Hot Roomie*]. Durand's two main characters are perfect foils for each other; both are conflicted and for good reason. Seeing as they try to make being roomies for two weeks work is priceless entertainment."
Jack Magnus, Readers' Favorite

"[*Notorious in a Kilt*] is the book I have been waiting for! A great second-chance romance and one of my favorites in this series."
The Romance Reviews

"I loved the Scottish in Ian and the strength of Rae, but the love of one little girl makes [*Notorious in a Kilt*] something to behold."
Coffee Time Romance

"I have enjoyed this whole series, but Emery and Rory [from *Scandalous in a Kilt*] have stolen my heart and are now my favorites!"
The Romance Reviews

"An enthralling story. [...] I highly recommend the writing of Ms. Durand and *Wicked in a Kilt*, but be warned you will find yourself addicted and want your own Hot Scot."
Coffee Time Romance & More

"*Dangerous in a Kilt* by Anna Durand delivered! [...] It was the journey, characters, and smoking hot sex scenes that kept me turning the pages."
The Romance Reviews

"There's a huge hero's and heroine's journey [in *Dangerous in a Kilt*] that I quite enjoyed, not to mention the hot sex, and again, not to mention the sweet seduction of the Scotsman who pulls out all the stops to get Erica to love him."
Manic Readers

Other Books by Anna Durand

Brit vs. Scot: A Hot Brits/Hot Scots/Au Naturel Crossover Book
Natural Passion (Au Naturel Trilogy, Book One)
Natural Impulse (Au Naturel Trilogy, Book Two)
One Hot Chance (Hot Brits, Book One)
One Hot Roomie (Hot Brits, Book Two)
One Hot Crush (Hot Brits, Book Three)
The Dixon Brothers Trilogy (Hot Brits, Books 1-3)
One Hot Escape (Hot Brits, Book Four)
One Hot Rumor (Hot Brits, Book Five)
Dangerous in a Kilt (Hot Scots, Book One)
Wicked in a Kilt (Hot Scots, Book Two)
Scandalous in a Kilt (Hot Scots, Book Three)
The MacTaggart Brothers Trilogy (Hot Scots, Books 1-3)
Gift-Wrapped in a Kilt (Hot Scots, Book Four)
Notorious in a Kilt (Hot Scots, Book Five)
Insatiable in a Kilt (Hot Scots, Book Six)
Lethal in a Kilt (Hot Scots, Book Seven)
Irresistible in a Kilt (Hot Scots, Book Eight)
Devastating in a Kilt (Hot Scots, Book Nine)
Lachlan in a Kilt (The Ballachulish Trilogy, Book One)
Fired Up (standalone romance)
The Outlands Shifter (standalone romance)
The Mortal Falls (Undercover Elementals, Book One)
The Mortal Fires (Undercover Elementals, Book Two)
The Mortal Tempest (Undercover Elementals, Book Three)
The Janusite Trilogy (Undercover Elementals, Books 1-3)
Obsidian Hunger (Undercover Elementals, Book Four)
Willpower (Psychic Crossroads, Book One)
Intuition (Psychic Crossroads, Book Two)
Kinetic (Psychic Crossroads, Book Three)
Passion Never Dies: The Complete Reborn Series

Chapter One

Heidi

Today, I have returned to the scene of the crime, or rather, the scene of my worst humiliation. After making a complete fool of myself a few months ago, when I'd thrown myself at Ollie Jackson repeatedly, I let my friends convince me that coming back to Au Naturel Naturist Resort was a good idea. Face my fear, that was the mantra. Prove to the world I'd moved past my shame.

Easier said than done, as the saying went.

I was the girl who loved to have fun, who never let anyone or anything drag me down. But I did the dragging all on my own. Ollie and I had dated for, like, five minutes last year—then I dumped him so I could reconcile with my cheating ex. Later, I'd returned to Au Naturel and tried to win Ollie back, even though he'd been with Mara Severins by then. Had I really wanted Ollie? No, not really. I realized that on my last day at the resort. I hadn't wanted to admit I gave up a good man because I thought I didn't deserve him.

I stared out the window of the big, pink RV my friends and I always drove whenever we headed for the naturist resort. And yeah, naturist meant nudist. We always wore T-shirt dresses when we arrived at Au Naturel so we could whip them off the second we exited the RV.

But today, I wore cargo pants and a loose-fitting T-shirt.

My friend Shelby sat down beside me, wearing her standard concerned look—mouth tight, brows lowered, gaze targeted on the object of her cheering-up campaign.

That would be me. Heidi Mackenzie, the most upbeat member of the Kitten Brigade, had become the girl who needed cheering up. I didn't feel like I belonged in the Kitten Brigade anymore. The wonderful people at the naturist resort had given us that nickname because we were young and carefree, always ready to cut loose and have a good time. I didn't feel like doing any of that anymore.

So I ignored Shelby and kept staring out the window.

My friend poked my arm. "Time to start talking, Heidi. You've been Ms. Silent Treatment for the whole three-day trip to Oregon."

"You guys insisted I come along, so I came." I would've rather stayed home in Nebraska, doing my boring job and avoiding my parents.

Shelby poked me again. "But you've said, like, ten words since we left home. Come on, girl, this is our vacation."

I eyed her sideways. "We went to the resort a few months ago. This trip is strictly so you guys can convince me I need to get laid."

Yeah, they'd been saying that for a while now. Get back out there, get laid, get something. They weren't pushing me to have anonymous sex. They just wanted me to act like the girl I used to be. But I couldn't do that. No more silly, self-centered Heidi. I was a mature woman with a serious job, not a sorority slut.

"Heidi." Shelby almost whined my name.

I sighed. "I'm not trying to ruin you guys' vacation. But we are going back to the place where I made a total ass of myself. I'm having trouble getting excited about that."

"Sure, I understand. But things will get better."

"Uh-huh." I didn't see how that would happen anytime soon, but I wouldn't contradict her. She and the rest of our group needed to believe in happy endings. I'd stopped believing in those a long time ago.

Shelby threw her arms around me, squeezing hard. "I love you, Heidi."

"Yeah, I love you too."

My friend pulled away, giving me a sympathetic smile. Then she rejoined the rest of our group where they'd gathered at the front of the RV.

As the vehicle turned onto the gravel driveway that led to the resort, I dug a baseball cap out of my duffel bag and stuffed the hat onto my head. Sometimes I missed wearing girlie clothes, but I'd made a vow to become a mature adult. No more skimpy dresses. No more shrieking with joy at every little dumb thing. I was a grown-up now, not a goofy kid.

The closer we got to the resort, the more acid churned in my stomach.

And when we broke out of the woods into the large clearing around the resort buildings, I got so nauseous that saliva filled my mouth, a sure sign I was on the verge of vomiting. I took several slow, deep breaths until the nausea faded away.

You can do this. Breathe, girl.

I obeyed my own commands, and though I wasn't about to barf anymore, I still suffered from a creeping unease that made my skin itch.

Jane, who had driven the last leg of our journey, parked at the end of the driveway near the little house occupied by Eve and Val Silva, the owners of the resort. Eve and Val weren't the ones I dreaded seeing.

Through the RV's windshield, I spotted Ollie Jackson and his fiancée, Mara Severins.

Ugh. Why couldn't they have taken today off? Well, I'd have to see them eventually. Sure, Mara and I had become friends, kind of, and we talked on the phone and texted sometimes. But virtual friendship was nothing like the in-person kind.

Mara was such a sweetheart. She would never do the idiotic things I'd done.

Jane opened the door, and my friends tumbled out of the RV, grinning and laughing.

I heaved my butt off the seat and scuffled out of the vehicle. The sun seemed a lot brighter than it had a few minutes ago. I hunched my shoulders, letting my gaze wander over the people who had gathered to greet us. Eve and Val, of course, stood in front. Ollie and Mara waited just behind them, and Ollie had his arm around his fiancée. Behind them, on the big lawn, senior citizens played miniten in the nude. The game was based on tennis, but designed for and invented by naturists, aka nudists. Instead of tennis rackets, they had wedge-shaped boxes over their hands. Thugs were a bizarre addition to the sporting world, though not many people who weren't nudists knew about miniten.

No miniten for me. I used to love the game, but I wouldn't play it anymore because Mature Heidi did not jump around with a wooden box on her hand.

My friends whipped off their T-shirt dresses and flung them high into the air, whooping with joy.

Part of me still wanted to join them, to be like them, but I couldn't. Revamping my life meant revamping myself too.

So I hid out near the front bumper of the RV and watched them.

While Eve, Val, and Ollie greeted the Kitten Brigade, Mara walked up to me.

"There you are," she said. "I'm glad you came, Heidi. Welcome back to Au Naturel Naturist Resort."

"Uh, hi." I shoved my hands in the pockets of my cargo pants. "It's nice to see you again, Mara."

"Don't be nervous. We're friends, and all that stuff that happened months ago doesn't matter anymore."

"You honestly are the nicest person on earth. I can see why Ollie loves you."

Mara moved closer, smiling a little. "I get that you're embarrassed about what happened last time you were here, but everything's different now. Think of this as a new beginning."

"I want it to be a fresh start, but crawling back to the scene of the crime doesn't feel like a new beginning."

Mara's smile grew bigger. "But it is, Heidi. Au Naturel is your home away from home, and we're all so happy you're with us again."

She pulled me into a firm hug.

When she let go of me, I tried to smile but only managed to kind of sneer or something. I didn't mean to, but my lips just wouldn't form a real smile.

Mara patted my arm and left.

Eve and Val were helping my friends carry their tents and bags to the camping area on the other side of the clearing. I'd arranged to stay in the guest house, which had disappointed the Kittens. They didn't understand my new outlook on life, but they accepted my decision.

Mara joined Ollie where he was chatting with his best friend, Damian Petrescu. Or, as Damian called himself, the Ludar prince. He claimed to have gypsy ancestry or something, but he was just another arrogant man who thought he was God's gift to women. He hadn't tried to give me that gift yet, but if he made a move, I'd have to disappoint him. My new outlook came with a new dictate—no dating, no sex, nothing but self-reflection until I'd gotten my head screwed on straight again. Men, especially hot ones, had no place in my life right now.

And yeah, Damian Petrescu was hot.

I let my gaze travel up and down his body, taking in his gypsy-chic outfit—black jeans, a long-sleeve black shirt with the top three buttons unhooked, and big black boots with bronze clasps. A necklace that looked like intricately braided rope hung around his neck, and a chunky silver ring glistened on his right hand. Damian hadn't been dressed like that the last time he'd been at the resort, but Mara and Ollie had told me Damian quit his job and joined the team at Au Naturel as concierge and resident gypsy. He did palm readings or whatever and had a "gypsy wagon" parked behind the guest house. That was his home base for peddling hooey to tourists.

But damn, that man was fantastic eye candy. Val Silva had the most ripped body I'd ever seen, while Ollie had a more normal type of muscular physique. Damian was somewhere in the middle. He boasted muscles, a fact I knew because I'd seen him naked. Ollie's best friend had dived right into the naturist lifestyle on his first visit to the resort a few months ago. And okay, maybe I'd loved admiring his sexy bod. With that olive skin and dark hair, he looked every bit the gypsy prince. He'd let his hair grow out some since the last time I'd seen him, so now wild curls framed his masculine face.

I did not have the hots for Damian Petrescu. He was man candy, for sure, but also a player. I couldn't verify that assessment with facts, but I sensed it. Having hooked up with one too many players, I'd developed a sixth sense for detecting them.

Tearing my gaze away from Damian, I retrieved my duffel bag from the RV and headed into the guest house. Once I got inside the building, I froze at the bottom of the stairs. My room was on the second floor, but suddenly, I couldn't make my feet budge another inch. A fresh start? How would I get that when I'd come back to the place where I'd always behaved like a foolish flirt? I tipped my head back, staring up at nothing. Maybe coming here had been a huge mistake.

I should go home. Catch the next flight out.

Had seeing Damian again triggered this sudden anxiety? No, of course not. I was not afraid I might succumb to his charms and revert to my old ways. That was just dumb.

"Hey. Remember me?"

I startled, swerving my gaze to the man who'd sneaked up behind me. "Oh, it's you. Damian, right? You're Ollie's friend."

Why was I acting like I barely remembered his name? So he wouldn't get the wrong idea and decide I might be his next target, that's why.

"Yeah, but I don't think we were ever properly introduced." Damian held out his hand. "Damian Petrescu, proud Rom and descendant of the Ludar line."

I shook his hand cautiously. "Right. I remember now. You're the guy who loves to put on gypsy airs. I'm Heidi Mackenzie." I raked my gaze over his entire body, and my tongue darted out to moisten my bottom lip. Not because I was attracted to him. No way. "Why are you dressed like Dracula's low-rent cousin?"

"Women love the way I dress." He smirked. "You do, that's for sure. I can tell by the way your pupils dilated when you saw me and the way you licked your lips."

"My lips are dry, and it's kind of dark in here. It makes everybody's pupils get bigger."

"Have dinner with me."

I blinked slowly, my brows hiking up. "Excuse me?"

"You heard what I said. Have dinner with me. I give awesome dating."

Oh yeah, this was exactly how I expected Damian to behave. *Player alert.* "Yeah, I'm sure you think you're awesome at everything to do with women. But I'm not interested."

He leaned against the bottom post on the staircase, cocking his hip. "I bet you'll change your mind after a date with me. What have you got to lose? I'll buy you a nice meal, we'll have some laughs, and then you can decide how badly you want to get me naked."

"Oh please. Does that kind of talk really work for you?"

"Usually." He slanted toward me and lowered his voice. "I can give you the best time of your life, and I'll even talk dirty if you beg me for it." He grinned. "Actually, you won't have to beg. I love whispering filthy things into a woman's ear."

"I'm not into that." It was a lie, but sometimes a woman had to deceive a man to protect herself. I crossed my arms over my chest. "I'm not interested in dating or sex at all."

"Come on, you must be joking. Aren't you the girl who loves to be naked and loves to suck every ounce of marrow out of life?"

Hearing him say the word suck sent a hot shiver through me. But that did not mean I wanted to sleep with him. Even if I did want that, I would not do it. "I'm not a silly, wild girl anymore. I've changed, for the better."

"Don't you miss having a good time?" he asked. "I guarantee I can make you feel good."

Oh God, that sounded amazing. Even before I made my celibacy vow, I'd gone without sex for months. A steamy, meaningless fling sounded perfect.

No, it did not. *Focus, Heidi.*

"I'm not having sex with you," I said.

"We can start with a date, then."

I shook my head, trying to frown but not quite succeeding. "You really are persistent, aren't you? Maybe I'm not being clear enough. I'm done with men, at least for a while."

"Have you defected to the other side?"

"What?" For a second, I had no idea what he meant. Then it hit me. I shook my head again, almost smiling. "Oh, I get it. I'm not a lesbian. I'm taking a break from dating, that's all."

"Hmm." Damian inched closer. "We can start with getting it on, and upgrade to dinner once you're over this no-dating thing."

"Do you have concrete for brains?" I made exaggerated lip movements to match my exaggerated enunciation when I informed him, "I am celibate. No sex. No dating. No men, except for platonic friends. Get it?"

"I can read lips, you know. You could've just mouthed all that, and I would've understood."

"You're so pigheaded, I figured you needed extra emphasis."

"How about a kiss?"

"No, Damian." Jeez, why was he so determined to get in my pants? I wore baggy clothes so men wouldn't pay attention to me. That tactic had worked out so well, hadn't it? "We can be friends—platonic, which means no sex, no kissing, no fondling—but that's it."

He sighed with no small measure of sarcasm. "Have it your way."

"Thank you."

"We'll be friends, until you drag me into the woods and ravage me."

I couldn't help it. I smiled. "You're going to be a handful, aren't you?"

"Oh yeah. I always am."

He kissed my hand and walked away.

That man was trouble with a capital T, two exclamation points, and a double underline.

Chapter Two

Damian

I loved my job. Working at Au Naturel Naturist Resort was the best thing that had ever happened to me, and I had my best friend to thank for it. Ollie had convinced me to quit my old job, since I was bored out of my ever-loving mind there, and join him here. He'd been pestering me about it for almost a year, ever since he quit his tech job to move to Oregon. I kept saying no. I mean, a nudist resort? How could I ever concentrate with all those hot, naked girls prancing around? Then I came here for a visit and suddenly understood.

Not that many hot girls on the premises. Well, except when the Kitten Brigade was here. I'd met those girls twice so far, including today, but most of our guests were families or senior citizens.

So yeah, no hordes of nubile hotties to distract me.

Too bad, but also good. I loved women, but this was my job now, not a sexy vacay at an adults-only nudist resort in the Caribbean. But today, my focus had been shattered by the arrival of one woman—Heidi Mackenzie.

She was the sexiest woman on earth, even in cargo pants and a baggy T-shirt with a baseball cap covering all that lush blonde hair. I'd seen her naked, but I had never so much as shaken her hand. We got introduced on my first trip to the resort a few months ago when I showed up for a surprise visit so I could hang with my best friend. Turned out Heidi was Ollie's ex, though they dated for such a short time they barely had a chance to blink before it was over. She still had a thing for him and tried to seduce him away from Mara. It didn't work. Heidi felt humiliated and sneaked out with her tail between her legs.

I would've loved to get between her legs, but no way in hell did I want to become the rebound guy. That sucked, a fact I knew from experience.

While Heidi's girlfriends disrobed and got the party started, I snagged Ollie and Mara so I could get more info about the hottest member of the Kitten Brigade. I already knew they'd been given that nickname because those girls loved to have fun and flirt with any eligible male on the premises. They didn't do anything raunchy—a damn shame, I said—but they did spice up the place.

My polite inquiries about Heidi resulted in Ollie informing me that I should "leave her alone" and "give Heidi some space." Ollie had also told me Heidi needed all the friends she could get.

Well, if sexy little Heidi needed a friend… I volunteered for the job. As long as it came with benefits.

I knew underneath those layers of khaki she had a killer body. Though she'd covered her head with a baseball cap, I knew those long, golden-blonde waves usually tumbled over her shoulders. Every time I'd seen her, I wanted to fist my hands in that hair while I fucked her. She was hiding her curves, but I'd seen every inch of that body the first time we met. She had spectacular breasts and a toned physique, but those curves softened her figure so she didn't look like a bodybuilder.

Christ, I wanted to explore that body from head to toe.

But Heidi had told me to buzz off. Not in those exact words. But yeah, I got the point.

Fortunately, I'd never been that easy to discourage. The way Heidi licked her lips and her pupils enlarged when she looked at me, I knew she felt the same lust I did. But like I'd told Ollie earlier, I wasn't a total dick. I could sense when a woman needed some space, and for now, I'd give it to her. Ollie wouldn't tell me everything about Heidi, like why she threw herself at him when they'd only dated briefly. I'd ask Heidi about that sometime.

Since I couldn't seduce Heidi yet, I decided to watch the naturists playing miniten. They kept trying to get me into their games, but I couldn't see past the wedge-shaped wooden boxes on their hands. They called those things "thugs." Now there was a friendly, fun-sounding word. The thugs looked like medieval torture devices designed to help the guy who wanted to lop off your hand get his ax lined up right. Not that I thought people actually did that with thugs.

I kicked back on a lawn chaise so I could observe the miniten game. Most of the players I knew, like the senior citizens who came here often. Ruth and Sylvester Norris had basically taken up residence at the resort, and Eve and Val let them have a permanent lock on the bungalow behind the guest house. Anyway, I watched while Ruth and Sly led their team, the Silver Foxes, to victory despite the younger crew giving it their all. The old farts had stamina and the killer instinct, but the guests who were my age always underestimated the Silver Foxes.

Heidi emerged from the guest house a few minutes after the miniten game ended.

Unfortunately, that was right when I had to go to the office on the second floor of the guest house to perform my concierge duties. Guests left notes in the box beside the office doorway or they submitted their requests on our mobile app. Yeah, we had one of those now. Ollie created the app himself since he had all the computer creds required to do mind-numbingly boring stuff like that.

So I schlepped up to the office and snagged the few pieces of paper that were in the request box, then I sat down at the desk and accessed the app. Not much going on. Nudists were surprisingly easy-going. They didn't have prima donna demands, which meant I had more free time than I suspected the average concierge at a normal resort might have had. I changed into my uniform and took care of every request, delivering bottles of sunscreen and insect repellent, dropping off extra towels and pillows, and finally, helping a guy my age get his locked suitcase open. The dude lost his key. Luckily, I knew a thing or two about picking locks.

Strictly in case of an emergency. I wasn't a criminal or anything, though I did learn lock-picking from a pro. He was behind bars, but I didn't hold that against him.

After completing every concierge task, I headed out to the lawn again.

The Kitten Brigade was about to play volleyball, and one of Heidi's friends seemed to be trying to convince her to participate. Heidi hunched her shoulders and kept shaking her head.

I remembered the last time the Kittens had visited. Heidi played every game with gusto—miniten, tennis, volleyball, whatever—and she didn't wear a sports bra. I'd followed the movements of her bouncing tits instead of the bouncing ball. Man, she had fabulous jugs. It was weird that I'd seen her completely naked, many times, but I had never so much as kissed her cheek.

That was nudism. Hot girls on display, but no touching allowed.

Heidi's friends gave up and started the volleyball game without her. Heidi shuffled over to an Adirondack chair, the one farthest away from the game in progress. Her chair sat under the bows of a large pine tree, so she had plenty of shade. Since nobody else was on that side of the lawn, she had privacy too.

I marched over there and dropped onto the chair beside hers. "Thought you liked sports. Why aren't you playing with your friends?"

She raised her brows. "You really don't believe in easing into a conversation, do you? It's straight to the intrusive questions."

"Why not answer? Maybe I'll go away if you satisfy my curiosity."

"Doubtful. You seem like the kind of guy who has an insatiable curiosity about things that are none of your business."

I might've thought I'd annoyed her if not for the calm, almost sultry tone of her voice. Her lips curled up a touch too. And her blue eyes sparkled, even though the sun didn't hit them directly.

She was beautiful. Was it any surprise I wanted to seduce this girl?

"You're right about one thing," I said, leaning over the arm of my chair to get closer to her. "I am insatiable."

"Hmm." She roved her gaze over my entire body. "Why aren't you dressed like a Dracula knockoff anymore? Thought that was your shtick."

"I'm not a knockoff of anyone. I'm an original. Johnny Cash always wore black, you know, but he wasn't a vampire."

She turned slightly sideways, toward me. "You like country music? I would've thought you'd be more into death metal."

Her lips curled up even more when she said that. Heidi was teasing me. *Score one for the Dracula knockoff.*

"I like good music," I said. "Don't care if it's country, classical, or jazz fusion. What about you?"

"What music do I like?" She shrugged. "Not into music except at parties. Then I don't care what it sounds like as long as I can dance to it."

Now there was the Heidi Mackenzie I expected to see. Except I wasn't seeing it. She told me she loved to dance, but she sat there

in an Adirondack chair wearing khaki cargo pants and a baggy
T-shirt. She still had that baseball cap on too. Carefree Heidi was
still in hiding.

I jumped up and held out my hand to her. "Let's dance."

"What?" She drew her head back like she thought I might've
been concealing metal spikes in my palm. "There's no music. And
nobody else is dancing."

"Let's be trailblazers. Maybe we can inspire other people to get
off their asses and do the rumba." Not that I had one single clue
how to rumba, but that wasn't the point. "Come on, Heidi. Have
a little fun."

She shook her head. "I don't dance anymore."

"Why not? Did you join one of those cults where every guy has ten
wives and the women have to wear ugly brown dresses?" I glanced at
her clothes. "Or maybe the cult uniform is cargo pants."

"I am not in a cult." She gave me the once-over, puckering her
lips like she was trying not to smile. "You're the one who usually
looks cult-ready. You probably want to sleep with me just so you
can make me your satanic sacrifice."

"People wear uniforms at work. It's not a cult thing."

"I was talking about your fake-gypsy outfit."

Fake gypsy? She was trying to annoy me, but I wouldn't fall for
it. "Relax, Heidi, I'm not into sacrificing beautiful women. I might
bite your neck, though, and suck on various parts of your body."

"Celibate, Damian. I've told you already there will be no sex, no
kissing, no anything that you're thinking about right now."

I chuckled. "You read thoughts? That's supposed to be my shtick."

"Don't need a crystal ball to know what you're thinking."

How could I convince Heidi to have fun? Maybe I should've
been asking myself why I cared if she didn't have any fun. It was a
challenge, I supposed, and I'd always loved those.

"Okay, no sex," I said. "But let's at least go for a walk. That'll be
a lot more entertaining than sitting around watching other people
have fun. And besides, I have a secret place to show you."

"A secret place?" She said that like she thought I was going to
drag her off to my satanic-sacrifice lair.

"You'll like it, I promise." I held out my hand again. "Come on,
Heidi, it's just a walk."

She chewed on her lip for a few seconds, then she placed her
hand in mine. "Okay. Show me your secret place."

Chapter Three

Heidi

Damian led me around the edge of the lawn, where my friends were playing volleyball, and along the tree line until we came to a narrow trail that headed into the woods. He strode down that path. I'd never seen this trail before, despite having visited the resort many times over the years. Had I somehow missed it every single time I came here?

The path might've been narrow, but we still managed to walk side by side. I didn't mind that. Company was nice, even if my new "friend" wanted to get me naked. He hadn't said anything overly suggestive since he tried to talk me into dating with a possible upgrade to sex.

Damian was hot, but I had a plan and I would stick to it. Maybe it was more like penance than a plan. I had some serious penance to do to make up for all my mistakes.

So yeah, no sex. Not with Damian. Not with anyone. No kissing either. And absolutely no flirting, not even if Damian started it.

"Where are we going?" I asked. "I've never seen this trail before."

"That's because it didn't exist until recently. I talked Eve and Val into starting a pilot program for something new we can offer to our guests. It's still in the developmental phase."

"I hope you're not taking me to your secret sex house."

He chuckled. "Interesting that your mind went straight to sex. But no, this is G-rated entertainment."

"Okay. That's good." I considered him for a moment while we kept strolling down the trail, and my brain kept dreaming up questions I wanted to ask him. Before I did that, I needed to decide if I wanted to be friends with Damian. If not, then I didn't need to ask him personal questions. But my curiosity was pushing me to find out more about the man who liked to dress like a sexy vampire. Not that I would ever admit to him that I liked his Dracula-gypsy shtick.

Right now, he was wearing his work uniform. But damn, he looked hot in that too.

Stop thinking about how hot he is. No sex for six months, remember?

"You look like you want to say something," Damian told me. "Go on, I don't mind. You might've noticed I'm not shy. Shameless might be a better description."

"No kidding? I never would've guessed, Mr. I Love to Talk Dirty."

"Would you want me to lie and say all I want to do is hold your hand and recite sonnets to you? I'm honest and upfront about what I want. You can feel free to slap me if you don't like it."

Feel free to slap him? Damian was the weirdest man I'd ever met.

"No thanks," I said, "count me out. Emotional torture is more than enough for me to handle."

He raised his brows. "Torture? I don't want to do that."

"Oh. Good." Maybe he meant that, maybe he didn't. I had no idea. But my brain kept urging me to ask questions and satisfy my curiosity, so I gave in. "What did you do for a living before you took a job here?"

"I was a corrections officer at a state prison in Idaho."

My feet stopped moving. My eyes refused to blink. I stared at him for several seconds, trying to digest his response. Damian seemed like the type of guy who would be a massage therapist or the owner of a cigar shop, not a prison guard. Maybe I had misjudged him.

"Wow, that sounds crazy stressful," I said.

"It could be, but there were never any incidents at the facility where I worked." He smirked. "You expected me to have some kind of sleazy job, didn't you?"

"No, I was thinking either massage therapist or cigar shop owner."

"Hmm. That's better than what most people assume I would do for a job." He swept his gaze over me from head to toe and back again. "What do you do? For work, I mean."

"I'm a pharmacy technician."

"Really? I never would've guessed that."

He didn't sound disappointed like most men were when I revealed my career choice to them. They often responded by lamenting the fact they'd hoped I was a model or a stripper.

Damian studied me again, tipping his head to the side. "I would've guessed geologist."

"Ha-ha."

"Not joking. You seem smart, and the last time you were here, I noticed you kept picking up pebbles on the beach and examining them like you were figuring out what kind of rock they were. Everybody else was swimming in the lake or relaxing on the beach, but you were busy with rocks."

He noticed that? Weird. Either he'd been stalking me or... I didn't want to think about the other option. It meant he was interested, and I didn't want to attract anyone's interest right now.

"I do love rocks," I said, "but it's a hobby, not my job."

The fact that he assumed I had a serious job instead of being a stripper gave me an odd sensation in my tummy. Not quite fluttering. Something similar, but not that. It didn't mean I liked him.

"Here's the deal," Damian said. "I'm attracted to you, Heidi, but I won't push it. You made it clear you think you don't want to date, so I'll respect that. But we can be friends. Right? Just friends."

"Um, okay. Friends might be nice."

"Awesome. Now, let me show you my pilot project."

Damian wasn't a jerk who only cared about what his dick wanted. Huh. I never would've guessed that, but I supposed my checkered past with guys had colored my outlook. Having a new friend sounded kind of nice.

I could keep my libido in check. No problem.

He reached for my hand, then pulled his away. "Sorry. Force of habit."

"Don't worry about it." Wasn't I the one who said no sex, no kissing, no fondling? Now I'd just excused him for attempting to touch me. Well, hand-holding wasn't exactly a felony offense. But it did imply intimacy, so yeah, he shouldn't do that. I might've been flip-flopping on the whole touching thing. Not on the dating thing, though. No way. So no touching either, just to be safe.

But I had always loved going for walks hand in hand.

Cut that out, girl.

I followed Damian down the trail, trying very hard not to stare at his ass. Men's tushes had never been my favorite part of the male anatomy, but I'd seen Damian's naked rear a few months ago when he'd first visited the resort. He walked around in the nude for a long, long time. Even while I'd been insanely determined to win Ollie back, I couldn't stop myself from admiring his best friend's bod. I mean, I was a heterosexual woman and Damian was a hot man. He must've worked out. Not so much that he had giganto muscles like Val Silva. Damian's physique was somewhere between Ollie's subdued muscles and Val's totally ripped body.

His ass flexed under his pants with every leisurely step he took. The fabric clung to his glutes, accentuating every movement of those muscles.

Why did I say I wouldn't have sex for six months?

Because you don't want to make a fool of yourself again, you idiot.

Right. I had this plan that involved celibacy. But I could still ogle Damian's tush. No harm in that.

Damian moved to the side as we entered a grassy clearing that was ensconced in the forest. Two horses grazed inside a large field that had a wooden fence around it and a metal gate. Part of the field nearest to us had been fenced off to form a small, round paddock.

"What is this?" I asked.

"My pilot project." He swept his outstretched arm to indicate the entire clearing. "I want to offer riding lessons and horseback tours. Val and Eve suggested I try it out first to make sure having horses out here is feasible, and to make sure I really want to do this. I know I do, absolutely, but I respect their opinions. That's why I started my pilot project."

"You ride horses?"

"Of course. I'm a gypsy, after all." One side of his mouth ticked upward. "Oh wait, that's wrong. I'm a low-rent Dracula knockoff."

"I'm sorry I said that."

He shrugged. "I've been called worse. Dracula's cool, anyway. Must be, considering how many movies have been made about him and his kind. Vamps are supposed to be very erotic and enticing to women." He bared his teeth. "Want to find out if it's true? I'd love to bite your neck and suck on it."

"There you go again, mouthing off. And I was just starting to think you might be a nice guy after all."

"It was a joke. I'm not a total dick, you know."

"Doesn't change the fact that I'm celibate. No kissing, fondling, or neck-sucking."

He sighed. "Is this no-sex thing permanent? Or can I make a reservation to seduce you on the day your celibacy plan ends?"

I rolled my eyes, but I couldn't help laughing. "Is this how you prove you're not a dick? It's less than convincing."

"Okay, I give. Let's go play with the horses."

My gaze shifted to the horses out in the field, chomping on grass and swishing their tails. They looked serene right now, but I tried to steer clear of the big four-legged beasties. My history with horses wasn't pleasant.

"I'd rather not," I told Damian. "Horses and me... We don't get along."

"These two are sweethearts. You'll like them."

Staring out at the horses, I suddenly realized I was hugging myself.

"Are you afraid of horses?" Damian asked.

"Um...maybe. A little." I forced myself to lower my arms, and instead, I stuffed my hands in my pants pockets. "I got bitten by a horse when I was eight."

"You're with me this time, and I won't let anything happen to you."

I might've thought he was being arrogant when he said that, but his tone of voice belied that. He sounded like he genuinely meant to protect me. Once upon a time, I'd loved horses and wanted to learn to ride. After the biting incident, I hadn't gone near a horse ever again, not even a miniature one.

"How about this," Damian said. "I'll go in there and catch the boys, then bring them over here so you can pet them over the fence. We can call it a soft launch for your riding lessons."

"What's a soft launch?"

"A limited preview before a product launches."

"Oh." I bit my lip, studying the horses. Didn't I want to change my life? Become a better person who wasn't terrified of being alone or making bad decisions? Facing one of my fears might kick-start that plan. I cleared my throat and straightened my spine. "Okay. Let's do the soft launch."

"Awesome."

He walked over to a small shed I hadn't noticed before. It was made of wood and almost the same color as the tree trunks around it. Plus, shadows darkened the area, making the little building blend in even more. Damian pulled out a key ring and unlocked the shed, then retrieved two halters and lead ropes from inside it.

"Be right back," he said as he went through the gate and closed it behind him.

I watched Damian sauntering out into the pasture. Hunching my shoulders, I wondered if I was ready for this. What, I could stalk Ollie but I couldn't pet a horse? Sheesh.

Time to face my fears—starting with horses.

Chapter Four

Damian

I caught the horses and put their halters on, then led them back to the fence where Heidi was waiting. She was biting her lip pretty hard and gripping the wood fence like it might fly away. I got that she was anxious around horses, but I also had a feeling she'd get over that faster if she faced her fear instead of hiding from it. Heidi Mackenzie didn't strike me as the cowering type. But facing fears could be hard, so I'd take it easy with her.

Not just with the horses. But with dating too.

Heidi took one step away from the fence when I brought the horses up to it.

"Meet Lenny and Georgie," I said. "They're geldings, which means they've been castrated so they won't be big-time assholes like stallions can be. These guys are laid-back. That's what makes them great riding horses."

"Okay," Heidi said carefully, eying the horses like they might leap over the fence to maul her.

"Georgie and Lenny are lovable. Give them a chance, and you'll see." I held both leads in one hand and stretched my arm out to Heidi, offering her my other hand. "Come on, it'll be okay. They won't stampede over you."

She took a baby step toward me, just enough that she could grasp my hand. "Isn't this close enough?"

"You can't pet them from there. Come a little closer." I gently pulled on her hand until she tiptoed to within a foot of the fence. "Good. Now just reach out your hand to touch Georgie's neck."

I patted him with my free hand, trying to show her Georgie wasn't a wild beast. He nuzzled my cheek.

Heidi almost smiled.

"Give it a try," I said. "He won't bite, I promise."

She moved closer, inches from the fence, and slowly raised a hand, stretching it out toward Georgie's neck. Her fingertips grazed him, but she pulled her hand away.

"It's okay," I said, "try again. Take all the time you need. You're not the first horse-o-phobe I've met. Ollie hadn't been super comfortable around horses—got kicked once on a pony ride at a county fair—but I talked him into letting me teach him how to ride. Not long after, we started going on trail rides whenever he visited me. If Ollie can get over the fear, so can you."

Heidi glanced at me, surprise in her eyes, but she quickly diverted her attention to Georgie. She touched her fingertips to his neck again, but this time, she moved her fingers in a faint petting motion. After a minute or two of that, she laid her palm on his neck and glided it up and down.

"Look, he's smiling," I said. "That means he likes you."

"How can you tell he's smiling?"

"Ludar lidar."

Her lips kinked into a slight smile. "Yeah, I remember your Ludar lidar. It told you Mara wasn't the right woman for Ollie."

"No system is perfect."

She kept petting Georgie, running her hands along the length of his neck, while she looked at me. "What is Ludar lidar, anyway? Doesn't sound very gypsy-ish."

"Lidar is like radar, except it uses lasers instead of microwaves. I just thought Ludar lidar sounded cooler than Ludar radar." I realized I was still holding her hand, but I didn't want to let go. She seemed to have forgotten her hand was still in mine, or maybe she knew but didn't care. "When I say I'm using my Ludar lidar, it just means that I have an intuition about something."

"I get it." Heidi skimmed her hands up to Georgie's ears to scratch behind them, which he loved, though I wasn't sure she knew she was doing that. "I might've been wrong about you, and I'm sorry."

"No need to apologize. I know I can come on kind of strong. It's my way."

"The Ludar way?"

I winked. "Wouldn't you love to find out?"

Heidi laughed, the sound soft and delicate. Georgie nuzzled her arm with his lips, and she laughed again. "He's a real sweetie."

"Yep. And I think he's smitten." I nodded over my shoulder. "Want to try petting Lenny too? Mara and Eve both say Lenny has a muzzle as soft as velvet."

Heidi moved sideways to get closer to Lenny, but she kept holding my hand. That meant she had to angle her other arm across me to pet the horse, but I didn't mind. I liked having her hand in mine. Heidi stroked Lenny's neck and scratched behind his ears.

"Look," she said, "his bottom lip is hanging down."

"Means he's relaxed and happy—and he likes you."

How could any male, human or beast, not like Heidi Mackenzie?

After a few more minutes of watching Heidi pet the horses, I decided she'd probably had enough immersion therapy for today. She just got here a few hours ago, so she must've been tired from the long ride in an RV. I had to let go of her hand to take the halters off Lenny and Georgie, and I didn't plan on trying to reclaim her hand while we walked back to the resort.

But Heidi slipped her palm into mine.

What happened to "no dating"? Holding hands felt like dating behavior to me, but I wouldn't complain about it.

Once we reached the lawn, Heidi and I went our separate ways. But before we did that, I stopped us at the edge of the lawn.

"Are you any less afraid of horses now?" I asked.

"Yeah, your idea helped. Thank you, Damian."

"We can do more horse therapy anytime you want. Just call me or come find me."

She kissed my cheek. "You're not as much of a player as I used to think."

"Thanks." I'd take any compliment from Heidi, even a half-assed one. "I'll be in the gypsy wagon if you want a palm reading. I give great readings."

"I bet you do."

She started to walk away, but I caught her arm to stop her. When she glanced at me, I said, "For the record, I don't think I'm awesome at everything. I suck at geometry. Squeaked by with a C minus in high school."

Heidi's brows tightened as if I'd confused her.

Then she headed for her girlfriends who were relaxing on chaises, while I went back to the office to change into my gypsy uniform.

I spent the next two hours doing my shtick, reading palms and tarot cards, though I didn't gaze into any crystal balls. Maybe I couldn't prove my tarot and palm readings were accurate, but even I didn't stoop to crystal-ball bullshit. The big crystal orb in my wagon was there strictly for show. Tourists loved the way I'd decorated the interior, and they loved my gypsy routine, though I was sure ninety-nine point nine percent of them realized it was just for fun.

At lunch, I looked for Heidi in the dining hall but didn't see her, so I ate in my wagon. Ollie, Mara, Eve, and Val wanted me to join them in the caretaker's house, but I preferred to have lunch alone. It gave me time to think—about Heidi, of course. I wanted her, and I liked the side of her I got to see when we visited the horses, but I didn't know if I should pursue anything with her. She claimed she didn't want to date or have sex, so I guessed what I wanted didn't matter.

Maybe I was arrogant and persistent, but I never tried to push a woman into being with me.

Just as I went back into the guest house to check on my concierge duties, my cell phone rang. I dug it out of my pocket, but before I could say hello, my mom started speaking.

"Damian, are you still slumming it at the nudist camp?"

"No, I'm working at a naturist resort. It's beautiful here, Mom, not a slum." Which I'd told her many times over the past couple of months, but she didn't listen any of those times. My mom wasn't a snob, not really. She just didn't understand my desire to live and work at a nudist resort. "Ollie works here too, you know. Your 'precious, sweet little Oliver' is a nudist."

I didn't say that like I was offended by how much my mom loved Ollie. It didn't bother me. She loved me too, but Mom had always had a soft spot for my best friend. Seemed like the geek thing actually worked. Even mothers fell for it.

But Heidi Mackenzie liked my gypsy thing.

She also crushed on Ollie for a while, so I probably shouldn't have gotten smug about the way Heidi almost drooled over me. Yeah, I did not want to be the rebound guy.

"Maybe we should come there," Mom said, "to see what our boy is doing in the wilderness with a bunch of hippies."

Yep, my mother thought hippies were gauche, but being a gypsy was high class. Where did I get my Ludar prince routine? From my mother. She liked to dress up as "Ileana the Ludar queen" and do highly entertaining palm and tarot readings for our neighbors at birthday parties, weddings, bar mitzvahs, whatever. People loved it.

And they knew it was bullshit. My mom was born and raised in Brooklyn, and her real name was Monica.

"You don't need to come here, Mom," I said. "Unless you're suddenly itching to get rid of your clothes. A lot of the naturists here are your age or older, so all you codgers can commiserate about how your asses hurt while enjoying a little nude sunbathing."

She huffed. "I'm fifty-six, not eighty. Don't lump me in with the codgers just yet."

"I know, Mom, it was a joke."

"But I was serious about visiting you. I need to make sure my sweet Ludar prince hasn't gotten himself into trouble."

Maybe I had gotten myself into trouble—just a little, with Heidi the celibate sex kitten—but it wasn't anything I couldn't handle. Definitely nothing my mom needed to know about. I was an adult, not a dumb kid.

I'd just reached the bottom of the stairs, about to climb up to the second floor. "Gotta go, Mom. Say hi to Dad."

"Be careful, Damian."

We hung up.

Of course my mother couldn't say "have a good day." No, she had to tell me to be careful. I didn't know if Mom would ever accept the idea that I lived and worked at a nudist resort, I loved it, and I would never quit. This was my dream job.

So yeah, I might've been crazy. But in a good way.

After I took care of the concierge requests, I resolved to find Heidi. Probably a bad idea, but then, I'd always enjoyed a challenge—and a dirty-hot bad idea.

Chapter Five

Heidi

I lay on the bed in my room, staring up at the ceiling, counting the little acoustic balls stuck to it. I kept losing count, though. The balls had no pattern to follow, so I was pretty sure I counted the same ones five or six times. What did it matter? Why was I staring at the ceiling?

Because of Damian Petrescu, that was why.

The man was trouble. I didn't care how sexy he was, or how surprisingly sweet he could be, I would never, never, never sleep with him. Six months of celibacy. I'd made that vow, and I refused to break it on my first day at the resort. I had willpower. Somewhere. Probably buried way down under a lot of hooey like all that silly stuff I used to love to do.

No more chasing butterflies. No more playing miniten in the nude with no sports bra. And absolutely no more flirting with every guy who walked past me. Time to dig out that willpower because Damian would push me to the limits of my self-control. I wasn't blaming him, not directly. After I told him I planned to be celibate, he hadn't pushed me at all. He'd barely flirted with me after that. But our time at the horse pasture had shown me a side of him that left me stunned and confused. Sweet, patient Damian didn't jibe with the Ludar prince who offered to "upgrade" me to dating if we had sex first. Or maybe he had said he'd upgrade me from dating to sex. Ugh, I couldn't remember. Didn't matter since I was never going to get naked with him.

Avoiding Damian seemed like the best solution to the problem of my MIA willpower.

Someone knocked on the door.

I moaned like a miserable coward. "Who is it?"

"Damian."

Oh shit. Why had he appeared two seconds after I thought about him? Maybe he did have Ludar lidar or whatever the hell it was. And what on earth did Ludar mean? He explained lidar, but that other word was a mystery to me, one I did not need to solve.

"Are you going to open the door?" he asked. "I brought you a surprise."

Great. He probably brought me lingerie.

I moaned again and heaved myself off the bed to trudge over to the door. Taking a deep breath, like that would quell my lust at all, I opened the door.

Damian stood there wearing his gypsy outfit. He held out his hand. "Give me your phone."

"Excuse me?"

"It's for your surprise. I promise I'm not trying to hack your phone. Ollie would know how to do that, but I haven't got a clue." He kept holding his hand out, and when I didn't move a muscle, he gave me an amused smile. "Trust me, Heidi. You'll like this."

Grumbling, I got my phone from the bedside table and gave it to him.

His thumbs flew over the screen, and his focus was zeroed in on whatever he was doing. After a minute, he handed the phone back to me. "There you go. Jams to lift your spirits, everything from Mozart to Miles to Minogue."

"Huh? I know who Mozart is, but the rest made no sense."

"Miles and Minogue." Damian chuckled. "That means Miles Davis, the jazz musician, and Kylie Minogue, the Australian pop singer."

"Oh, right, I get it."

"I was trying to be clever with my alliteration, but I guess my efforts tanked."

"No, it's not you. I'm still feeling kind of off-kilter." Why did I tell him that? Since I didn't want to date him, he didn't need to know. But he had suggested we could be friends. Maybe it was okay to blab that stupid confession to him.

"Being back at the resort is weird for you," Damian said. "I get that. After the stuff with Ollie the last time you were here, I'm sure it'll take time for you to get comfortable."

"Yeah, I think so."

"Don't hide in your room all day. Listen to the music I gave you, then take a chance and get out there with your friends."

I couldn't understand why he cared about making me feel better. We didn't know each other, not really. But he did care, and that gave me a strangely comforting sensation of warmth on my skin. "Thank you, Damian. It was so sweet of you to give me this music."

"No problem. I'll leave you alone, but I hope you'll come outside later."

He turned to walk away.

And for some reason, I grabbed his arm to stop him.

Damian raised his brows. "Something wrong?"

"No." I let go of his arm and bit my lip. "Would you, um, like to talk?"

"About what?"

I hunched my shoulders. "Anything, I guess. When we talked earlier, it was nice."

"Sure, I can hang with you for a while. I promised Ollie I'd take the new guests out to the pilot project later, since they've got a horse-crazy kid, but I've got some time to kill."

He sat down in the chair by the window while I relaxed on the bed—sitting up this time, not lying flat on my back staring at the ceiling balls.

"What does Ludar mean?" I asked. "You called yourself a Ludar prince, and you mentioned your Ludar lidar."

Damian rested his feet on the bedside table, his ankles crossed, and clasped his hands over his belly. "The Ludar people came from Eastern Europe, mainly Bosnia but also Romania. My mother is descended from that line. My dad is of Rom heritage, which means Eastern Europe and Russia. Both Ludar and Rom are known as gypsies. We call ourselves that, but I think it's mostly because that's easier for most normal people to remember. Rom, Ludar, Romnichels, it all gets kind of confusing."

"Okay. So you are a genuine gypsy."

"By heritage and by choice, yeah, I am. But nobody in my family has ever been to the old country. We're all Americans who love football and apple pie." His mouth slid into a sexy smile. "But we do have gypsy powers. Want me to read your palm?"

I didn't know how he did it, but he managed to make that simple question sound erotic.

"You don't actually believe you have psychic powers or whatever, do you?" I asked. "The gypsy thing is cool and fun, but you can't actually divine my thoughts."

"No." He winked. "Or maybe I can."

He planned to keep up this "I'm a mysterious gypsy thing" for as long as possible, didn't he? Maybe he was teasing me, but I couldn't tell for sure. Did I want him to tease me? Friends could do things like that, so it wouldn't necessarily mean he was trying to seduce me.

I felt a twinge of disappointment when I realized that.

No, I didn't. *Get a grip, Heidi.*

So what if Damian looked extra sexy in that black outfit, kicking back in a chair like he owned the place. I didn't even care that the way he'd smiled a minute ago made my tummy flutter. I had willpower, if I could ever find it.

"Do you speak Romanian or whatever language the Ludar speak?" I asked.

"I don't know much Romanian, not like my mom. She's fluent. I took French in high school, but I don't remember anything except how to ask where the bathroom is."

"Yeah, I took Spanish, but I've forgotten all of that too. Can't even ask where the bathroom is."

He smiled, and even though he wasn't trying to be sexy, he was.

And my tummy fluttered again. Dammit.

"Where does your family live?" I asked.

"St. Paul, Minnesota. My mom was born and raised in Brooklyn, my dad too, but they moved to St. Paul when I was in eighth grade. Dad got a job there. My brother and his wife and kids live there too."

"How did you wind up in Idaho?"

He smirked. "You mean how did I wind up in the potato state working at a prison. It's simple. After college, I wanted an adventure, so I joined a circus run by gypsies, mostly Ludar and Rom. By the time we got to Idaho, I'd had enough of the vagabond lifestyle, so I applied for a job as a prison guard. They hired me, and I kept that job until Ollie convinced me to work here instead."

Damian had told me that part this morning, but he hadn't mentioned his circus job.

"What did you do in the circus?" I asked.

"I was an animal trainer. Horses, mostly, but I also helped out the elephant and monkey trainers whenever they needed it." He sighed like he was remembering good times. "I also did some palm reading, though it's my mom who's the best at that stuff. Our friends and neighbors always love it when Ileana the Ludar Queen entertains them."

How was I supposed to reconcile all these different sides to him? Circus trainer, prison guard, concierge at a nudist resort, gypsy showman. Damn, this guy was confusing.

Surprising was a better word.

"What about you?" Damian asked. "Tell me about your family."

"My parents are divorced. Bitterly divorced. Holidays are lots of fun, with my parents griping at each other and my grandmother smacking her spoon on the table to make everyone shut up. Last Thanksgiving, Mom threw a big lump of mashed potatoes at Dad."

Damian's face went blank. He just looked at me like that for a long time.

Finally, he took his feet off the table and sat forward. "Christ, Heidi, I'm sorry. That must be awful. And here I was telling you how awesome my family is."

"I'm glad you have parents like that. And I don't need any sympathy. I'm used to Mom and Dad acting that way. They got divorced when I was ten."

"Do you have any brothers or sisters?"

"Only child."

He watched me with a strange expression that I couldn't figure out. Pity? Sympathy? Disgust? I had no idea.

Damian got up and walked to the bed, sitting down near my feet. "I think I'm starting to understand you—your behavior, anyway. You've got scars, don't you? Lots of them, I'd say."

"Yeah. Doesn't everybody?"

"Most people don't have as many as you seem to." He patted my leg. "Scoot over. I'd like to sit next to you if that's okay."

"Um, sure." I scooted over to make room for him.

Damian sat beside me, though not touching me. "Don't take this the wrong way, but you seem like you could use a hug."

How did he know that? Because yeah, a hug would've been awesome. But I shouldn't let him do that. He might get the wrong idea—or I might. Sitting this close to him, I started to feel warm again, but not in the comforting way I'd experienced earlier. I felt warm in a completely different way, one that skirted dangerously close to desire.

"Guess that's a no to the hug," Damian said, not sounding annoyed, just mildly disappointed.

"Actually, a hug would be nice." Why had I said that? My mouth insisted on telling him the truth, even while I tried to deny it in my own mind.

He draped an arm across my shoulders, tugging me closer until I could've rested my cheek on his shoulder if I'd wanted. God, did I want to, but I fought the urge. Fought it like crazy. He smelled good, like woodsy cologne or potpourri or something.

Damian stroked my upper arm with his fingertips.

I couldn't stop myself. I rested my cheek on his shoulder.

We sat there like that for several minutes, not speaking, just enjoying the easy intimacy of the moment. I'd told him about my family. Ollie didn't know about that. Even my ex, the one I'd gone back to over and over despite his cheating, never met my parents or asked me about them. So I never told him. But today, I'd needed to tell Damian.

He cleared his throat. "Sorry to cut this short, but I need to do my job for a while. I'd much rather stay here with you, but..."

"I get it. You can leave, it's fine." I lifted my head to look at him. "Besides, I've got those jams you gave me, the ones you promised will make me feel better."

"Guaranteed to lift your spirits."

We gazed into each other's eyes. It wasn't a conscious decision on my part, and I didn't think it was for him either. Our gazes gravitated to each other all on their own, like our subconscious minds craved the connection. He still had his arm around me. I was still leaning into him. Our faces hovered a foot apart at most, and suddenly, I needed to be closer, needed to feel his lips on mine.

I couldn't make myself move or speak. Just as well since I *really* shouldn't kiss him.

But God, I wanted to.

Damian slanted his head down, leaning in a touch, bringing his mouth to within millimeters of mine. His breaths ghosted over my lips, tantalizing my skin with a sultry warmth. I couldn't tear my focus away from his eyes, couldn't catch my breath, couldn't make myself pull away.

"I want to kiss you," he murmured. "But only if you want it too."

Oh yes, I wanted that. But my voice wouldn't work, so I gave my consent the only way I could. I closed my eyes and pressed my mouth to his. Damian's lips were soft and warm, and I couldn't stop myself from moaning with pleasure. He kissed me back, tugging me closer with the arm he'd draped around me. I laid a hand on his shoulder, sliding it up to his neck, and moaned even more deeply when he slipped his tongue between my lips. Heat rushed through me from head to toe, settling in my lower belly, igniting a fire between my thighs. He explored my mouth with leisurely strokes of his tongue while I thrust my hand into his hair to pull his head even closer.

No one had ever kissed me like Damian did, like he had endless lifetimes to spend doing nothing but kissing me.

When he pulled away, he was breathing harder, like he couldn't catch his breath either. "As much as I'd love to keep kissing you…"

"Guests need you. It's fine. I'm fine, promise." After that kiss, yeah, I felt fantastic. "Go do your horse whisperer thing."

"I don't whisper to them." He slid off the bed and winked. "Don't need to. I've got Ludar magic, remember?"

Oh, he definitely had some kind of magical powers, at least when he kissed.

Damian walked out the door.

And I listened to the music he'd given me, but I didn't need songs to lift my spirits anymore. Making out with Damian had erased all my worries.

But I still wouldn't sleep with him. We shared one hot moment, that was all. My Damian cravings would be gone now, for sure. One hundred percent gone.

Until I saw him again, at least.

Chapter Six

Damian

Heidi kissed me. Sure, I had suggested it, but I expected her to remind me again that she's celibate and there would be no dating or sex. Instead, she kissed me. Damn, I'd loved kissing her. I hadn't meant to do it, hadn't meant to say I wanted to do it, but our conversation had made me feel the need to comfort her. And that somehow turned into a lip-lock.

Not that I was complaining. No way. Feeling her lips on mine, tasting her… That had made me crave Heidi even more.

I managed to focus on my job for the rest of the day, but once I clocked out, the urge to find Heidi and kiss her again got stronger. Okay, I didn't actually clock out since we didn't have time cards or even strictly set hours. But anyway, I was done for the day. And I needed to see Heidi.

The dining hall was packed, as usual, full of naturists enjoying the buffet and conversation. All those voices chattering away might've made the dining hall a noisy place, but people who loved to go nude could be surprisingly polite. Out in the wider world, most people weren't that thoughtful. Another reason I loved it here.

I spotted Heidi sitting at a table near the back with Ollie, Mara, Eve, and Val. I would've expected Heidi to hang out with her girlfriends, but she surprised me again. I noticed an empty chair at the employees table where the five of them sat. They weren't eating, didn't even have plates yet. Were they waiting for me? Was Heidi waiting for me?

Yeah, suddenly I'd become a girl, worrying about whether my crush had a crush on me too.

Ollie saw me and waved, urging me to go over there.

I jogged across the dining hall and sat down beside Heidi. Had she saved this chair for me? Christ, I really had become a girl.

"Hey, guys," I said to the others. Then I glanced at the sexy woman sitting beside me. "Hey, Heidi. How was your afternoon?"

"Good. How was yours?"

"Fine." What a nice awkward conversation we were having. I never felt weird around a girl after I kissed her. I never got nervous around girls either. The awkwardness had the bizarre effect of making me spout inane things. "Hey, uh, you can visit the horses anytime you want."

"Thanks. Not sure I'm ready for a solo visit yet."

"Yeah, I get it."

I glanced around and realized the other two couples at the table were staring at me and Heidi. Ollie smirked. Val seemed vaguely amused. Mara and Eve both smiled with their lips sealed and their cheeks dimpled.

"Aw," Mara said, "you two are so cute together."

"We're not together," Heidi said.

She didn't have to say that quite so fast, did she? Like she needed to make sure everyone, including me, knew we weren't dating. Was it my imagination, or had she almost shouted that statement?

I needed to have sex with her soon, before my balls shriveled up and I actually turned into a woman.

"Let's get our food," Ollie said. He got a sneaky look on his face and added, "Damian and Heidi better stay here to make sure nobody steals our table. We'll bring you guys some food."

All the guests were already here and already seated at other tables, so I knew he was full of crap. Since when did he try to play matchmaker? Ollie had hated it when my mom tried to set him up with the daughter of one of her friends. But now he was trying to maneuver me and Heidi into…something.

True love, marriage, and babies. That was what my best friend had suddenly decided I needed.

Once the others had hurried off to the buffet, Heidi and I enjoyed the most awkward silence in history. Yeah, I was pretty sure not even cavemen and cavewomen who spoke in grunts ever suffered through a silence as awkward as this one. I scratched my neck. Heidi clasped her hands on the table. I cleared my throat and set my hands on my thighs. She toyed with one of her little stud earrings.

Those little studs were blue like her eyes. Staring at her earring made me want to look into her eyes since they were almost the same shade, but she kept staring at the wall.

Finally, I couldn't stand the cavepeople awkwardness anymore. "We had a good talk earlier, so this shouldn't be so hard now."

Heidi swerved her gaze to me but kept her head aimed straight at the wall. "I know, but it is weird. We, you know, kissed."

"Yeah, I remember." That kiss was something I would never forget, not even when I got old and couldn't remember how to zip up my pants.

"About what happened earlier," she said, "it can't ever happen again."

"You kissed me."

"A gentleman wouldn't point that out."

Now I wasn't a gentleman? Because I let her kiss me? Jeez, this girl was wound up even tighter than I'd realized.

"I'm sorry," I told her. "I wasn't trying to be a dick. But you're acting like it's my fault you kissed me."

"Well, it kind of is. You said you wanted to kiss me."

"But I didn't—"

I stopped myself before I argued more with her about who instigated that kiss. We shouldn't have been fighting about this, but clearly, our kiss had unsettled her. I didn't know everything her ex had done to her, though I knew the story about how she kept going back to the cheating jerk over and over. Heidi had told me about her parents, and I got the feeling their hostile relationship had affected her in ways even she probably didn't understand.

That meant I needed to be gentle with her. Not my strong suit.

"Listen," I said, "I don't want to argue about it. The kiss happened, but it doesn't matter who started it. I won't try to kiss you again unless you tell me that's what you want, and I'll do my best not to flirt with you either. Honestly, I'm not that good at stopping myself from flirting, but I promise to try."

She stared blankly at me, without blinking, for several seconds while all around us people were talking and laughing, having a good time.

Maybe I said too much. Or not enough. Either way, all I could do was wait.

Heidi sighed and glanced down at her lap, then aimed her baby blues at me. "Sorry I got mad at you. I don't mind the flirting. Actually, I kind of like that. It's the intimate stuff that freaks me out. You know, kissing and dating and…other stuff."

"By 'other stuff,' you mean sex."

"Not just that." She wriggled on her chair and hunched her shoulders, seeming like she couldn't get comfortable. "Relationships too. That's 'other stuff,' I mean."

"Oh, right. I get it."

"We don't know each other that well, but I'd like it if we could be friends."

"Thought we already were. I suggested it this morning, and you said being friends might be nice."

She almost smiled. "Forgot I said that. So we are friends already."

"Yep." I reached out, intending to touch her leg, but then I realized that was a bad impulse. She might've taken it as a come-on, though that wasn't what I meant. I started to pull my hand away.

Heidi grasped my hand and laid it on her thigh.

"Uh, what are you doing?" I asked.

"Putting your hand on my leg."

"But you just said—I'm confused, Heidi. What the hell do you want me to do or not do?"

"I…" She pushed my hand off her leg, and I swore her cheeks turned faintly pink. "That was completely inappropriate. I'm sorry."

She jumped up, clearly about to flee.

"Where are you going?" Mara asked as she and Ollie returned to the table. "Heidi, we brought you food."

Mara held up the two plates she had in her hands. Ollie held up two plates too.

Heidi hurried around to the other side of the table. "I'd rather sit by you and Eve. You know, girls on one side, boys on the other. Doesn't that sound like fun?"

Though Mara seemed less than convinced by Heidi's announcement, she carried her two plates to the opposite side of the table, setting one down in front of Heidi. Mara sat down with her plate.

Ollie scrunched up his eyebrows, clearly confused.

Yeah, I was right there with him.

Mara gave Ollie a stern look, nodding her head in a gesture I was pretty sure meant she was ordering him to sit down on the boys' side of the table.

Ollie shook his head and took the chair beside me, handing me a plate. He leaned toward me and whispered, "What did you do?"

"Nothing. I think Heidi's got a Jekyll-and-Hyde thing going on."

"I told you to leave her alone."

"She's an adult, Ollie. Neither of us gets to tell Heidi what to do or who to do it with." Not that I'd done much of anything. She kissed me, and somehow, I became the bad guy. "Chill out, man. Let me worry about Heidi. We're friends now."

"Friends?" Ollie said, sounding way too baffled by that idea.

Was it so bizarre for me to be friends with a woman?

I gave up trying to explain myself to Ollie just as Eve and Val came back to the table. We ate our meals and talked, though not about much of anything. Pointless small talk seemed to be all any of us could manage. After dinner, I went to my room and Heidi went to hers.

For hours, I tossed and turned in bed, trying to figure out what to do about Heidi Mackenzie.

I had no frigging idea.

Chapter Seven

Heidi

I behaved like a completely insane person at dinner last night. Damian had been so nice, but I freaked out because our friends conspired to push us together by abandoning us while they went to get the food. Seriously? That was the best plan four adults could come up with. Well, at least their ineptitude made me feel better about my screwy behavior.

Why had I freaked when Damian got confused by me putting his hand on my leg? Why had I grabbed his hand, anyway? Jeez, I was a mess.

But I had an inkling of why I kept acting like a crazy person around Damian.

I liked him. I was attracted to him. My celibacy vow had made perfect sense until I saw Damian yesterday, right after I'd stepped out of the RV. He'd kind of flirted with me months ago when I first met him. But now, he'd ramped up the flirtation to a whole new level. Damian didn't do anything obnoxious. He was surprisingly sweet underneath the cocky exterior. But I'd been fooled before by a man who convinced me he wasn't a jerk, and I'd been dumb enough to keep going back to him. Grant never helped me face my fear of horses, though, and he never told me he wanted to kiss me but then waited for me to say it was okay.

Not that I had said that. I kissed Damian instead.

Maybe I was having such a hard time because I kept fighting my true nature. I'd always loved flirting with guys, loved the build-up to the first kiss, loved that free-fall sensation when I realized I had feelings for a guy. I hadn't experienced the free-fall with Damian—jeez, I hardly knew him—but I had enjoyed the flirtation. And when we sat on my bed and he said he wanted to kiss me...

I hadn't felt anticipation like that in years.

After a fitful night's sleep, I didn't feel like showering or brushing my teeth, or changing out of my pajamas. When had I become a slob and a coward? Cargo pants were one thing, but loafing in my PJs... That was an alternate universe version of me. So I made myself get clean, get dressed, and go out into the world. I'd chosen jeans and a loose-fitting blouse with short sleeves and a flower print. My blue sneakers matched the flowers on my shirt. For too long, I'd been wearing frumpy stuff like cargo pants and baggy T-shirts. It had been a way to kind of punish myself for my past transgressions, I guessed. Today, I suddenly wanted to wear something feminine again.

But that impulse had nothing to do with Damian.

Seriously, nothing.

The second I stepped into the dining hall, Mara ran up and hugged me. "Heidi, you look beautiful this morning." She stepped back, grasping my upper arms. "Are you wearing makeup?"

Yeah, maybe I had put on a teeny bit of eye shadow and mascara, and my lip balm had a slight tint to it that made my lips look pretty. For about half a second, I wondered if Damian would like the way I looked today, then I resisted the urge to smack myself on the forehead for thinking about that—about him.

So of course, Damian walked into the dining hall right then.

He had to squeeze past me since I was standing a foot inside the threshold, but he didn't stop to flirt with me. He nodded and said hello to me and Mara, then he wandered off toward a table where some of the Silver Foxes were eating.

Damian wanted to eat with the senior citizens?

"Are you okay?" Mara asked.

"Huh? Yeah, I'm fine." The fact that I'd kept staring at Damian until she asked me that question didn't mean a thing. I was confused by his decision to dine with the seniors, that was all.

Mara glanced toward the self-proclaimed Ludar prince. "If you like Damian, go for it. You don't need anyone's permission, and he's a good man."

"Not interested in Damian. He's weird. Besides, I barely know him."

"That didn't stop me. I slept with Ollie the day after we met." She grinned. "And look how that turned out."

"Uh-huh." I couldn't think of anything meaningful to say. Why did my eyes insist on making me look at Damian? I'd done it again when Mara told me he was a good guy, and I was doing it again right now. *Get hold of yourself, woman. No man is so hot you can't keep your eyes off him.*

Except Damian kind of was.

I ate breakfast with Mara, Ollie, Val, and Eve. They did not pester me about Damian, thank goodness, and kept the conversation limited to everything else not related in any way to the gypsy who had the softest lips I'd ever felt.

After breakfast, I headed outdoors to hang out with the Kitten Brigade. Every single one of them was naked. They had decided to play miniten, Kittens versus Kittens. Shelby tried to talk me into playing, but I wasn't up for that yet. Sure, I felt better. Not better enough to strip naked and shove a wooden box over my hand. Nudity was required for miniten, at least according to my friends. So instead, I relaxed on a chaise and watched them having a good time.

The first game ended with Shelby and Allison beating Jane and Heather. Leah rushed over to me, pleading for me to join them so the other Kittens could play a match, but they needed one more person since each side had two players.

"Not a nudist anymore," I told Leah. "Get Mara or Eve. They love miniten."

"But we want you, Heidi. You're the best player, our reigning champion."

I'd won my fair share of miniten matches, but I couldn't participate now. Maybe never. At least, not until I figured out why I kept screwing up my life.

Leah glanced past my chair, and her lips stretched into a slow, sneaky smile. "Oh, I've got a fabulous idea."

She ran away before I could ask what her idea was. Honestly, I doubted I wanted to know considering her sneaky smile. She and the rest of the Kittens gathered in a huddle like they were football players or something. After a minute, they pulled out of the huddle.

Leah shoved two fingers into her mouth and whistled. The sound echoed off the buildings and the trees. "Listen up, naturists. We're playing a miniten mixed doubles match. We need two hot guys to volunteer. Come on, studs, man up! Or are you afraid the girls will make you look like wusses?"

Sylvester Norris, one of the Silver Foxes, jogged up to Leah. "I'm in. But you know I like to play aggressive."

Leah laughed. "Oh yeah, we all know how you old farts get about miniten." She looked at someone further away, someone I couldn't see. "Come on, join the game. You know you want to."

Damian traipsed past my chair, flashing me a sexy smirk and winking. He stopped in front of Leah and stripped naked.

Her jaw dropped. Not an exaggeration. Her eyes bulged, and her mouth fell open while she ogled Damian's body, making no attempt to disguise her appreciation.

Sylvester was already naked, but Leah hadn't gaped at him like that.

I could see only his backside, but wow, that man had gorgeous glutes.

He turned sideways to follow Leah's hand movements while she explained something. Probably which team would take which side of the grass court.

Oh my God. From this angle, I had a perfect view of his dick, the way it hung slack between his hips. His cock was sleek and thick, but not too thick, just right for closing my mouth around it. Damn, I wanted to feast on that beefstick for hours. Months ago, I'd seen Damian naked and felt only the slightest sexual interest in him. Today, I couldn't stop staring at his naked body, and I experienced a wave of heat that stole my breath for a few seconds. The muscles on his chest made me want to lick a trail over every single one of them, moving lower and lower while I kissed his defined abs and inched my way closer and closer to that beautiful dick.

I wanted to fan myself, but I didn't have a fan. Not even a piece of paper I could fold over and use to cool myself down. That wouldn't work, anyway. The only thing that might cool me down was sex with Damian. I couldn't do that. Wouldn't do that. *Celibacy vow, remember?*

But I hadn't been with a man since before my stalking-Ollie nonsense.

No sex with Damian. No way. So what if he had the hottest body I'd ever seen? No sex, no way, period.

Sylvester and Taylor took one side of the court while Damian and Leah took the other. They started batting the tennis ball around in the laid-back way most people played miniten. Nudists liked the game because it wasn't as strenuous as tennis, though sometimes guests got a little overexcited—guests like Sylvester. He and his wife, Ruth, could turn a laid-back game into a death match. Nobody minded, though. They never did anything lewd or got too aggressive.

Damian leaped up to whack the ball.

And his dick flapped.

I usually thought men's flapping members were silly, but I found myself getting tingly and slick while I watched Damian's manly bits waving around with every graceful, athletic move he made to hit the ball. His muscles flexed, from his thighs to his biceps and everywhere in between.

Leah missed her shot—on purpose, it looked like—and stumbled, holding her knee like it really hurt. "Timeout. I twisted my knee."

Damian rushed over to check her supposedly injured knee, but Leah shooed him away. "I just need to sit down for a while. It's fine, I swear." She glanced at me. "Heidi can fill in for the rest of the match."

I groaned, though I doubted she could hear it. "For the umpteenth time, I am not a nudist anymore."

"We'll make an exception to the nakedness rule for you." Leah fake pouted. "You can't let us lose the match. You're the best player."

"Yeah," Sylvester said. "Get in there and show 'em how it's done, kiddo."

The entire Kitten Brigade looked at me with hopeful expressions.

How was I supposed to say no when they looked like that? I could keep my clothes on, though I'd be playing alongside Damian the naked gypsy.

Leah clasped her hands under her chin and grinned at me, hopping up and down on her tippy toes.

Oh jeez. She'd be so disappointed if I didn't do this, they all would, but I knew Leah had faked hurting her knee as a means to push me and Damian together. Did everyone think I liked him? Or had Mara told Leah—

For heaven's sake, what was wrong with me? Now I was thinking like a teenager. I was an adult, and I could handle playing miniten with Damian, even if he was buck naked.

I pushed up out of my chaise and headed for the miniten court.

Leah handed me her thug as I walked past her.

And we played miniten.

Sylvester and Taylor had skills, but Damian played the game like he'd been born with a thug on his hand. I'd been playing for years, but he hadn't tried the game until recently. With all those muscles, he had the equipment to rock miniten. And rock other things too. Naked, sweaty, dirty things.

I missed my swing. The ball shot past me, but Damian whacked it over the net.

Never in my life had I gotten so distracted by lustful thoughts that I couldn't concentrate on winning a game of miniten.

Taylor hit the ball over the net, but when I raised my racket, my foot slipped. I fell down, landing on my side.

Damian knelt to sling an arm around my waist and hoist me up. "You okay?"

"Fine, thanks." That was a lie. I hadn't injured myself, but I was nothing close to fine with my body crushed to his naked muscles.

He let go and picked up my racket, handing it to me.

We ended up winning the game, but I couldn't concentrate on that fact. The feel of his body, his arm around me, his dick pressed against me... It had made me almost lightheaded. He hadn't been aroused, not at all, but I could still feel his dick. Watching Damian play miniten had been the most erotic thing I'd ever seen, but not because he did anything unseemly. He played like a gentleman—a determined, focused gentleman. Maybe it was his attitude and his determination that got me so hot and bothered. Whatever the cause, I'd gotten so turned on I could feel the slickness between my thighs. It had drenched my panties, and my clitoris throbbed every time I glanced at him.

Oh yeah, miniten had been the worst idea ever. I should've gone back to my room before Damian took his clothes off.

He walked up to me, took my hand, and kissed it. "You're an expert player, Heidi. We won because of you."

That was baloney. I'd been distracted most of the time—by his body.

"You did most of the work," I said. "How did you pick up the game so fast? I thought you hadn't played until you came here."

"I hadn't, but it only took a few weeks to understand the rules and strategy. Ollie and Eve took turns teaching me."

He hadn't let go of my hand, and now he rubbed the back of it with his thumb.

I resisted the urge to clear my throat because I didn't have any reason to do that. It was a dumb impulse. But standing here with naked Damian inches away from me and his hand holding mine, I couldn't think straight.

He kissed my hand again, this time letting his lips linger on my skin. "I have to get back to work, but I'll see you at lunch."

Damian sauntered away.

And I went back to my room. I tried to watch TV, even listened to some of the songs Damian had given me, but I couldn't relax. My thoughts kept returning to Damian in the nude, whacking a tennis ball around with a thug, his muscles flexing and his dick bouncing.

My body thrummed with a need I could not quench. Not with Damian. But I could do something to alleviate this craving.

I unzipped my jeans and slid my hand inside them, inside my panties, until my palm rested over my mound.

My mind conjured a vision of Damian naked, sweat drizzling down his skin.

I pushed my longest finger between my folds, into the hot slickness there, and began to brush that finger up and down in an easy rhythm. While I fantasized about Damian's muscles and imagined his body positioned over me, his hips thrusting, I slid another finger down there to rub myself harder and faster. God, I was getting wetter. Every time I pictured Damian on top of me, I got so hot I could barely breathe. Panting, gasping, I worked myself into a need so intense I thought I'd go insane if I didn't come soon.

Another vision flared in my mind, of Damian kissing me.

My back bowed into the mattress, my head snapped forward, and every muscle in my body went rigid—except my fingers. I couldn't breathe, but I couldn't stop rubbing and rubbing until the climax overtook me. My mind wouldn't let me stop picturing Damian thrusting into me, and I came so hard I would've cried out if I'd had any breath left. My free hand fisted in the blanket. I kept scraping my fingers over my clit until the last wave of my orgasm faded.

Wow. I hadn't experienced a climax like that in… I wasn't sure I'd ever come that hard before.

And Damian hadn't even touched me yet.

I would keep quenching my lust the solo way. It was the safest sex. Getting involved with Damian would only lead to more humiliation and heartbreak.

Chapter Eight

Damian

I stood outside the door to Heidi's room with my fist raised like I was about to knock. I had been about to do that, but I stopped when I heard strange noises coming from inside her room. After about two seconds of listening, I'd realized what those noises were.

Heidi was masturbating.

Really enjoying it, by the sound of things. All her gasps and groans made me want to barge in there and take over for her fingers or her vibrator, whatever she was using to get off. The bed creaked faintly, which made me picture that bed thumping and creaking like crazy while I fucked her.

Just when my brain decided to divert all the blood in my body to my cock, the noises stopped. I could still barge in and—

No, I wouldn't be that kind of asshole. I might've been a bit of an ass sometimes, but I wasn't a complete jerk. Still, I couldn't decide whether to knock or leave and pretend I hadn't heard anything. If I knocked now, it might've been obvious I'd been hovering outside her door. Plus, I had an erection, so she'd notice that for sure.

I'd come here to invite Heidi to the picnic Eve and Val had organized for the guests. Some people preferred to eat lunch in the dining hall, but others loved the idea of eating alfresco in the most natural way imaginable.

Well, now that I'd been standing here like a moron for several minutes, I supposed Heidi wouldn't know I'd overheard her. So I knocked, then held my linked hands in front of my groin, casually, like I was doing that for no reason.

The door opened, and Heidi's eyes went wide. "Damian? What are you doing here?"

She sounded slightly panicked. Oh great, had she somehow guessed I must have heard all those hot noises she made? Her gaze flicked down to my groin, and her eyes flared wider for a heartbeat. Then she looked at my face, though not my eyes. She seemed to be staring at my nose.

"Eve and Val organized a picnic for lunch," I told her. "Wanna come? We're going to the lake."

"Um…" She bit her lip, and her gaze traveled down my body and back up again, hesitating at my groin. "Think I'll eat in my room."

"Are you sure? It's a beautiful afternoon. About a dozen guests are joining the picnic, so this isn't a trick to get you alone."

"I never thought it was."

Why had I said that? Trying to convince Heidi to come along on the picnic, while I had the hardest hard-on ever, was messing with my head and making me say stupid things.

She looked so damn good in those jeans and that flowery shirt.

"The guests will probably be naked," I said, "but you can keep your clothes on. I'll keep mine on too. That way, you won't be the only non-naturist."

"I don't know…"

"You can hang out with Val and Eve the whole time. I won't be offended if you'd rather not talk to me." I held out my hand, palm up. "Fresh air is good for you, Heidi."

How stupid had that sounded? Had I actually said "fresh air is good for you"? Christ, she must've thought I'd suffered a head injury during the miniten game that turned me into a ninety-year-old grandpa.

She took a deep breath, making her breasts rise and fall. "Okay. I'll go on the picnic."

"Great. Eve made sandwiches with her secret sauce on them."

"Ooh, I love that." She slipped her hand into mine. "And I'm starving. Ravenous, actually. Miniten burns more calories than I realized."

Ravenous. I wish she hadn't said that word with so much…hunger. I was doing my damnedest to get rid of my erection, but the way she said that word had sent more blood rushing south.

Heidi didn't seem to care that I had a hard-on.

The feel of her hand in mine wasn't helping matters. I couldn't stroll down the trail to the lake, surrounded by a dozen other people, while I had a raging stiffy. I needed to alleviate the problem somehow. Since I was pretty sure Heidi wouldn't let me get naked with her right now, I went for the only feasible option.

When we got to the bottom of the stairs, I said, "Need to use the restroom. I'll meet you outside."

Before she could say anything, I ran to the restroom and slammed the door, locking it. Being an employee had its perks. I could lock the door to keep everyone else out.

Maybe I should've checked to see if anyone was in here first.

Peeking under the stall doors proved I was alone.

I leaned against the wall beside the sinks, unzipped my pants, and pulled my dick out. My mind went straight to a fantasy of Heidi touching herself, writhing and moaning. I closed my hand around my cock and glided it up and down, over and over, while I imagined sneaking into her room late at night when she was getting off on her own. I'd take over that task with my mouth on her clit, gorging myself on the luscious flavor of her cream.

"Fuck," I growled, working myself faster.

My fantasy escalated to Heidi thrashing, grasping my head, and bucking her hips while she screamed my name.

I slapped a hand on the nearest sink, gripping its edge so hard my fingers hurt. I couldn't breathe, and the only part of my body I seemed to have any control over was my hand pumping my cock. The pressure mounted, ramped up by the hottest fantasies I'd ever had. Heidi writhing, screaming my name while I gave her the best orgasm in history. I came so hard and fast that my knees almost buckled.

Only when I'd finished did I realize I'd, um, spewed all over the sink.

"Shit," I muttered, then I yanked a bunch of paper towels out of the dispenser on the wall and did what I could to clean things up. The janitor left all the cleaning supplies in a locked cabinet in the corner, so I used my master key to get out some disinfectant. Once I'd cleaned everything up, I finally remembered to zip my pants.

When I walked out of the restroom, I looked reasonably normal. My uniform wasn't even wrinkled.

Heidi stood just outside the restroom door.

I froze. Did she know what I'd done? I didn't care. So what if I jerked off after hearing her do the same thing? I was a man, not a robot. Of course I got turned on by overhearing her orgasm, and of course I needed to relieve the pressure. I had no reason to feel embarrassed.

So why was I scratching the back of my neck and avoiding her gaze?

"Are you okay?" Heidi asked. "You ran off so fast, I was worried you were having some kind of…medical problem."

Was that a euphemism for jerking off? I'd never heard anyone call it a "medical problem" before.

"I'm fine," I told her. "Just, uh, really needed to go."

Not exactly a lie. I had needed to "go," just not in the way people usually meant when they said that.

"Better get a move on," I said. "Everybody's waiting."

We walked outside and met the rest of the gang on the lawn. Ollie carried a big picnic basket, but Val carried two of those. I offered to take one, and though Val didn't seem to mind lugging both baskets, he let me help out. I was reasonably sure Val could bench press a small car. Maybe a midsize sedan. He didn't need help with two picnic baskets, but I would've felt like a jackass if I hadn't offered to take one.

Guests had blankets slung over their shoulders or arms. I hadn't thought to bring one for Heidi. Damn.

I must've looked annoyed with myself because Ollie sidled up to me and said, "Got an extra blanket for you and your new girlfriend." He lifted the blanket he had over his arm, revealing another one underneath it. "So relax, you're covered. Got condoms too."

Luckily, he said that too softly for Heidi or anyone to overhear.

Condoms? I'd barely kissed Heidi, and she had way too many hang-ups for me to seduce her today.

"Guess you're planning to do your fiancée in the woods," I told Ollie. "Those condoms aren't for me, that's for sure."

My best friend smirked and wagged his eyebrows.

I had no idea what that was supposed to mean.

We all enjoyed our picnic by the lake, though I didn't see any couples sneaking off to have a little alone time in the woods, not even Val and Eve who were the two horniest people I'd ever met. They loved to make noise too. I couldn't count how many times I'd heard them getting it on in the caretaker's house. They lived there, so they had every right to be doing whatever the hell they wanted in their own home. I'd stumbled onto them at the hot spring last week too, and that was one awkward moment.

But I now knew Eve had great tits.

Heidi decided to hang out with the Kittens instead of having a private picnic with me. I lay on the blanket Ollie had brought for me, gazing out across the lake. I did not fall asleep, though Ollie shoved me once to make sure I was awake.

"Don't want you to get sunburned," he'd told me with a smirk. "Heidi doesn't go for guys who look like roasted pigs."

"I used sunblock, Ollie. That means I won't burn even if I do fall asleep."

"Oh-ho, you know what that means. You do care what Heidi likes in a man."

"Go jump in a lake." I pointed toward the water. "It's right over there."

Ollie kept smirking, but he went back to his own blanket with his own girl and didn't harass me about Heidi anymore.

I did notice Heidi watching me even while she was hanging out with her friends. She was wearing sunglasses, so I couldn't tell for sure if she was ogling me. I had stripped off everything except my boxer shorts. Maybe I'd told Heidi I wouldn't go naked as some kind of solidarity thing, but I hadn't been lying. Boxers were clothes. Promise kept.

Once, I glanced in Heidi's direction just as she lifted her sunglasses to look at me. She roamed her gaze over my entire body and licked her lips. When she noticed me noticing her, she lowered her sunglasses again and turned back to her friends.

Everybody tromped back to the resort, then split off to do their own thing.

I jogged to my room to change into my other work outfit, what Heidi said made me look like "Dracula's low-rent cousin." Her sort-of insult hadn't bothered me in the least. I could tell she liked my Ludar prince costume. But I wasn't wearing it to impress Heidi. I had actual work to do—in my gypsy wagon, for paying customers who loved my palm readings and all that other stuff average people expected from a gypsy.

Trotting out to my wagon, I opened the padlock on the door and went inside to get set up for the afternoon's entertainment.

Maybe Heidi would take me up on my offer for a palm reading.

I wouldn't hold my breath.

Chapter Nine

Heidi

What was I doing on this beautiful afternoon? Sunbathing? Having fun of any kind? Nope. My friends had wanted me to play Monopoly with them in the entertainment room, but I couldn't get into the idea. I loved board games, but I was too distracted to enjoy it right now. So instead, I was lying on my bed again, staring up at the ceiling balls again, thinking about Damian again. For two hours.

Yes, it was entirely his fault I couldn't have fun.

How could I think about anything except him when he stretched out on a towel on the beach wearing nothing but a pair of boxers? Honestly, the man had no shame. I mean, sure, other guys had gone naked—including Ollie and Val, two super hotties—but I couldn't have cared less about them. My eyes insisted I had to gawk at Damian. Damn, he had the kind of body any woman would drool over. Not that I drooled. Maybe my mouth had gotten a teeny bit overly salivated, but that did not mean I wanted to get naked with the Dracula knockoff.

Maybe I should've stopped thinking of him that way. Vampires were hot, after all. I'd watched enough movies and read enough romance novels to understand the allure of a man in black. Even Johnny Cash was kind of hot in that color. But Damian Petrescu… He could set the entire state of Oregon on fire just by stripping naked on the beach.

He hadn't gotten naked, though. He'd worn those boxers, which only made me want to go over there, rip those shorts off, and drag him into the woods.

If Damian were a player, like I'd always assumed, I wouldn't want him this much. He just had to go and be a nice guy. *Damn him.*

Laughter outside my window made me sit up. I'd left the window open to get some fresh air, so I could hear whatever went on out there. My room was on the backside of the guest house, and there wasn't much out there except for the bungalow where Ruth and Sylvester slept. Well, that and Damian's gypsy wagon.

More laughter echoed off the trees.

I slid off the bed and leaned out the window.

Shelby and Heather stood just outside Damian's wagon. Leah was descending the steps. All three of my friends laughed some more, grinning.

Damian followed Leah out of the wagon.

Heather kissed his cheek. Shelby squeezed his biceps and pretended to swoon. At least, I thought she was pretending. Damian kissed Leah's hand, and she giggled. The girls trotted around the guest house, out of sight. What had those three been doing in Damian's wagon?

Damian saw me and waved.

I waved back.

He made a come-hither gesture.

No, I would not go down there. Considering how much I liked the way he looked in that black outfit, I knew I'd only get myself into trouble if I went downstairs and climbed into his wagon. What did he have in there? Chairs? Cushions on the floor? I would've loved to lie on a pile of pillows while Damian—

Oh no, I would not go there, not even in my fantasies.

I shut the window.

For twelve minutes and thirteen seconds, I stopped myself from rushing out there. Finally, I couldn't stand it anymore, what with my curiosity prodding me to go to him. I didn't rush, though. I walked.

Damian wasn't outside anymore. A sign on the wagon's door said, "Knock, please. The spirits appreciate politeness."

Oh yeah, that sounded like a Damian thing to say.

I knocked on the door.

Damian swung it open a split second after I knocked. His lips curved into an enticing smile. "Glad you came, Heidi. Welcome to my lair."

He stepped back enough to make room for me and offered me his hand.

I accepted it, and he helped me into the wagon, shutting the door.

Whatever I'd expected to find in here, I'd been dead wrong. The space was cozy and homey, but with an elegant gypsy style that made it intriguing. The entire interior was composed of wood in warm, rich shades of honey, from the floor to the walls to the ceiling. A blue velvet curtain cordoned off the front section, the part furthest from the door. The rest of the space featured a padded bench upholstered in shades of gold, blue, and green, as well as a small round table fashioned from honey-colored wood and topped with a gold tablecloth. I saw shelves of knickknacks too, everything from a crystal ball to little figurines of magical creatures. A long window behind the bench let in the natural light, but I saw a lamp and an overhead light fixture too.

The table sat low to the floor, surrounded by pillows.

Earlier, I'd fantasized about Damian and a stack of pillows, but this was nothing like what I'd imagined. These pillows clearly served as seats.

"Sit down," Damian said. "The bench or the pillows, whichever you prefer."

I settled onto the bench, loving the cushy padding. "What's behind the curtain?"

"The Great and Powerful Oz, of course."

"Cute. But seriously, what's back there?"

Damian walked to the curtain, hunched over a little since the wagon wasn't as tall as he was. He pulled back one side of the curtain, revealing a bed accessed by wooden steps. Cream-colored sheets and a scarlet blanket covered the bed, with cream-colored pillows scattered across the length of it up against the wall. Sunlight shined through a small window at the center of the wagon's back wall.

"Your love nest?" I asked.

"The wagon came this way. I didn't ask for a bed." He let the curtain fall shut. "I do occasionally sleep in here, but I've never seduced a woman on that bed—or anywhere in this wagon."

I shouldn't have cared whether he had done that or not, but I felt bizarrely relieved to hear him declare he hadn't. "You seduce women outdoors, then? Or in your room?"

"No, Heidi, I don't. I haven't had sex since before the first time I came here."

He'd been celibate? Why? Damian seemed like the kind of passionate man who would never go without sex for long. But it had been months for him?

"I shocked you," he said, sitting down at the table, cross-legged on a royal-blue pillow. "You've been assuming I'm the kind of guy who screws a woman every night, haven't you? I'm not like that."

"Yeah, I, um, can see that now. Sorry I leaped to that assumption."

"Don't worry about it. What other people think doesn't matter to me." He folded his hands on the tabletop. "Except for you."

He cared what I thought. That was weird and slightly disturbing.

But it also made me feel warm all over like I'd drunk a glass of brandy. Yeah, Damian was intoxicating—and I hadn't even slept with him yet.

Not that I would sleep with him.

"Did you want a palm reading?" he asked. "Or maybe tarot? You must've come here for a reason."

"I wanted to see your wagon, the inside of it." I glanced around to admire the lush surroundings again, then I ran my palms over the velvet cushions beneath me. "It's beautiful. Very cozy."

"No other reason? Just wanted to get a look at my secret den of mystical sorcery?"

He smiled with his lips sealed, the expression sexy and mysterious, worthy of the Ludar prince he claimed to be.

And God, I wanted him.

"I should go," I told him. "You must have paying customers waiting for you."

"My gypsy hours are over. I'm all yours." He patted the pillow next to his on the floor. "Come over here, Heidi. Let me read your palm."

His voice had gotten lower and rougher, so enticing that I couldn't stop myself from sliding off the bench and crawling onto that cushion. I sat cross-legged like he did. No more than a foot separated us, and the proximity sent a warm tingle of excitement rushing over my skin. The hairs on my arms shivered erect. So did my nipples.

"Are you right-handed or left-handed?" he asked.

"Right."

"We'll start with the left, then. It can tell me more about your character and personality than your dominant hand. Though I don't need to read your palm to know what kind of woman you are." He held out his hand, palm up. "Trust me, this won't hurt."

I wasn't worried about that. If he touched me, even my hand, I didn't know if I could stop myself from kissing him again. I should've walked out the door, but I couldn't move except to hold out my left hand to him.

He turned it palm up and cradled my hand in his. "Ready?"

"Uh, sure. Never done anything like this before."

"I'd love to be the one who pops your palm-reading cherry."

Why did he have to phrase it like that? Spoken in his sexy rumble, those words sounded like the most erotic come-on ever.

With my hand cupped in his, he bowed his head and lifted his free hand to skim his fingertips over my palm, moving them slowly, focused on the task of…whatever it was he was doing. The sensation of his fingers on my skin elicited a shiver of the sensual kind. I'd been acutely aware of him before this moment, but now, my body awakened in ways I'd never experienced before. I swore the touch of his hand and his fingers reached beneath my skin, like he was already inside me, thrusting with leisurely strokes of his cock while his skin brushed over my entire body. The memory of kissing him replayed in my mind. The heat of his mouth. The softness of his lips. The sensuous way his tongue coiled around mine and flicked out to taste me. I loved kissing him, and I hungered to do it again, right here, right now.

Damian turned my hand over and began caressing the backside.

I couldn't catch my breath. Everything between my thighs tingled and ached, desperate for his touch. God, I needed him to fuck me, like I'd never needed anything before—and he'd only touched my hand.

He turned it palm up again, gazing up at me without lifting his head. "You have long palms and fingers, and your skin is silky soft. That means you have water hands, Heidi. Souls like yours are full of compassion, imagination, and curiosity. You're also sensitive, emotionally."

"Yeah, I'm a flake. I already knew that."

"Being sensitive isn't a bad thing. Unless you get too wrapped up in the emotion of every moment and forget to take care of yourself."

He must have guessed that based on the things I'd told him earlier. Palm reading was hooey, right? But the feel of his skin on mine made it hard to breathe or think or do anything except watch him while he examined my palm.

Damian swirled his longest finger over the center of my palm, then glided it up to the base of my index finger, massaging the fleshy spot there. "Your Mount of Jupiter is hard to figure out. It's not large, but not sunken either. You have confidence, but sometimes you forget that, and you have a connection to the spiritual world."

"Are you talking about ghosts?"

"Not necessarily. There are many forms of spirits." He moved his fingertip to the base of my middle finger and skated it in a circle. "Your Mount of Saturn is average, I'd say, but it shows you have integrity." He shifted to the next finger over and glanced up at me, his head still bowed. "The Mount of Apollo signifies optimism and the strength of your life essence. Your vitality burns inside you like a smoldering fire, just waiting for a chance to erupt."

I cleared my throat, unable to make my vocal cords work. My breasts felt heavy, my skin tight, and the strength of my lust for him made my breaths shallower and faster.

"Ah, the Mount of Mercury," he said, his tone hushed and so damn sexy as he moved his finger to the spot just under my pinky. "This one is well-developed, which tells me what I already knew. You're a smart, capable woman."

He dragged his finger across the center of my palm, teasing the most sensitive part and making me suck in a sharp breath, then he slid it toward the bottom of my hand, below my pinky. He rubbed that area with his thumb in gentle circles until my skin grew so sensitized to his touch that I bit down on my bottom lip to stave off a whimper.

"Just like I thought," he said, "you have incredible compassion and imagination, though you don't harness that power to its full potential. Not yet."

"Oh." That syllable was partly a reply to what he said, but mostly it was my breathless response to the way he touched me. How could massaging my hand feel so sensual that I'd lost all capacity for thought? With anyone else, it wouldn't. I knew that, though I couldn't explain how.

"And now, the Mount of Venus." He glided his thumb over to the base of mine and massaged that fleshy area while he spoke. "Can you guess what this region signifies?"

"I...don't know." My brain shut down a few minutes ago, so yeah, I had no clue about anything. "Tell me, please."

He leaned toward me, still massaging the base of my thumb, bringing his face to within inches of mine. "Passion, sensuality, attraction, and magnetism." He gazed straight into my eyes. "You have all of those qualities. That's why you're so anxious these days, isn't it? Because you're fighting your natural instincts, the ones that drive you to indulge your desires."

Indulge my desires? I used to do that, too much, and it got me into trouble. Maybe I did burn to indulge my lust for Damian, but it was a horrible idea. Another round of humiliation wouldn't do me any good. Still, I couldn't stop myself from gazing into his eyes, letting myself sink into the depths of this heady desire for him. His mouth hovered so close to mine that I could've kissed him if I slanted in a touch.

"You're a special woman, Heidi," he murmured. "Don't hide behind cargo pants and a baseball cap. Let your inner goddess come out to play."

Oh God, I wanted to do that. Strip naked, crawl over his entire body, take his cock into my mouth and—

No, not again. No, no, no, no. I was tumbling head over heels into another mistake, and this time, I didn't know if I could claw my way out again.

I jumped up. "Sorry, I can't—This is—I just can't."

"Take it easy. I didn't mean to upset you, but I got a little carried away. I apologize." He patted the cushion I'd been sitting on. "Come on, don't leave yet. Please."

"No, I can't. Sorry. It's me, not you."

I staggered to the door and flung it open. As I clambered down the steps, Damian called out to me.

"We haven't even gotten to Mars or the lines yet."

No idea what that meant, but it didn't matter. I ran to the guest house, heading for my room.

Chapter Ten

Damian

What was that about? Heidi panicked and bolted, all because of a palm reading. I'd stuck to the principles of palmistry, but okay, maybe I got a little too invested in the process. Touching Heidi felt so good I couldn't stop myself. She smelled good too. And looked good. I should have kept my head down, focused on the reading, instead of looking into her eyes. Her pupils had gotten bigger, a sure sign of desire, and she kept licking her lips, though I was positive she didn't realize she was doing that.

I didn't see Heidi for the rest of the afternoon or in the evening. She must've been hiding in her room. Ruth Norris told me Heidi had "skulked" into the dining hall to grab some dinner, then took her meal somewhere else to eat it. Her room, I was sure. This was my fault, though I couldn't quite figure out why. I hadn't done anything more salacious than massaging her hand and talking about the mounts, those fleshy little mounds on her palm. Maybe the word mount had freaked her out. Could she have thought I meant I wanted to "mount" her right there in my gypsy wagon?

No, she was too smart not to realize "mount" had other meanings unrelated to sex. I did want to use that word in its dirty meaning, but not until Heidi got comfortable with the idea of sleeping with me. Maybe she'd panicked because I talked about the Mount of Venus and how it represented passion and sexuality. I hadn't invented that stuff to get her horny. It was a genuine part of palmistry.

I could drive myself crazy trying to figure out why Heidi ran away, so I stopped trying.

Eve and Val were hosting a staff dinner at their place tonight, and I never missed those, even though I kind of felt like a fifth wheel. Eve and Val, Mara and Ollie, they'd coupled up big time. Me? I couldn't convince Heidi not to freak out when I massaged her palm. So yeah, I attended the staff dinner as the obligatory fifth wheel stuck at the end of the table. Both couples sat side by side, exchanging loving glances and affectionate smiles while I pushed food around on my plate and tried to talk my stomach into wanting noodle omelet and spinach.

Vegetarian wasn't my thing. But mostly, I couldn't work up any enthusiasm for food because I kept thinking about Heidi.

"What's wrong with you tonight?" Ollie asked. He was sitting beside me, though he faced across the table instead of facing me.

"Nothing's wrong."

"You've been frowning at your food and moving it around like you think an alien creature will burst out of your noodle omelet any second to strangle you."

"Shouldn't you be making goo-goo eyes at your fiancée? She's probably feeling neglected since you haven't looked at her in at least ten seconds."

Ollie's brows hiked up. "Since when do you get grumpy? Something's definitely up with you tonight."

"I am fine," I said, emphasizing each word so maybe he'd believe me. Yeah, sounding grumpy might not have been the best tactic to refute his claim.

"Did you and Heidi have a fight?"

"We're not dating, so we can't have a fight. Not the kind you mean."

I suddenly realized everyone was looking at me. Looking and listening. Damn.

Eve, who sat opposite Ollie, touched my hand. "We all saw Heidi fleeing from your gypsy wagon this afternoon. Seemed like you must've had a fight."

"Why can't any of you grasp the concept that Heidi and I are not a couple?"

"But you like her a lot. Don't you?"

I did like Heidi, but this wasn't the kind of thing I wanted to talk about at the dinner table with Eve, Val, and Mara. Ollie was my best friend, so I would've talked about it with him. It shouldn't have been a group discussion, though.

"Can we talk about something else?" I asked.

Eve patted my hand. "Go talk to her. You two can work things out, I know."

My first impulse was to remind Eve, and everyone else, that I was not dating Heidi Mackenzie. But more grumpiness would only convince them I had a thing going on with Heidi. Maybe I did, sort of. I couldn't force her to want to have a thing with me.

She kissed me. Didn't that mean she wanted to be with me?

Forget about Heidi, you idiot.

Everyone was still staring at me.

"I'll talk to Heidi," I said.

That seemed to satisfy my friends, and they went back to exchanging lovey-dovey gazes and enjoying their meal. I managed to eat my food, though I didn't enjoy it. I might as well have scarfed down a plateful of Styrofoam peanuts since I didn't taste the food at all.

Maybe I ought to go see Heidi.

No, that would be stupid. Only if we were dating would I feel the need to "work things out," as Eve put it. Since I wasn't involved with Heidi, I did not need to see her.

When I tried to volunteer for clearing the table and loading the dishwasher, four people told me emphatically "no" and all but shoved me out the door. "Talk to Heidi," they said, almost at the same time, like a chorus of meddling friends.

I should've gone to my room and forgotten about Heidi. I intended to do that. Honestly, I did.

But my feet had plans of their own.

That was how I wound up standing in front of the door to Heidi's room with my fist raised to knock. I froze then, staring at the metal numbers attached to the door. Heidi must've been inside. If I came here to see her, I ought to knock. Why was I hesitating?

Because I had become a brainless idiot.

I rapped on the door.

When it opened a few seconds later, Heidi gaped at me. "Damian?"

"Yeah, that's still my name. Glad you remember it." If I'd tried really hard maybe I could've come up with something even dumber to say. "How are you? Ruth said you grabbed some food and took off without talking to anyone."

"I wanted to eat alone. Is that a crime?"

"No, but—"

"Good night, Damian." She slammed the door in my face.

What the hell?

I banged on the door until she opened it again. "What is wrong with you? I came here to make sure you're okay, but you're acting like I'm a criminal trying to break into your room."

"Go away, please. I don't want to sleep with you."

"What part of anything I just said implied I want to sleep with you?"

She flattened her lips, one hand on the door, one foot tapping furiously. "Just leave, okay? I don't have to explain myself to you."

"No, but—"

Heidi slammed the door. Again.

To hell with this. She had clearly gone insane since the last time I saw her, and I didn't feel like trying to talk her down. If she wanted to behave like a lunatic, she could go for it.

But not with me. I was done. No more fantasizing about Heidi or trying to make Heidi feel better or massaging Heidi's palm. It was over.

Not that we'd ever had a thing in the first place.

I stalked out of the guest house, veering toward my wagon. Whenever I needed a little peace and quiet, I retreated into my little gypsy home. I got about halfway there when someone ran up behind me and seized my arm, forcing me to stop. I half-turned to face that person.

Heidi was breathing hard, her tits heaving. "I'm sorry, Damian."

"For which part? Slamming the door in my face twice, or announcing out of frigging nowhere that you don't want to sleep with me?"

"All of it." She still had her hand on my arm, but now she slid it down to my hand, slipping her fingers between mine. "I panicked when I saw you, which has kind of become my signature move lately."

"What did I do? A palm reading was supposed to be fun, but I must've screwed it up somehow."

"No, it's not you. I've made a lot of mistakes with men, and I'm terrified I'll screw up this time too."

This time? That almost sounded like she was saying… No, she couldn't have meant *that*.

"I like you, Damian," she said, "and it scares me. So I panicked."

"Because I knocked on your door."

She moved closer, clasping my hand more firmly. "Because I'd been thinking about you ever since the palm-reading thing. I've been, um…fantasizing about you."

"I fantasize about you too."

"When I opened the door, and you were there, I wanted you. I still want you." She inched even closer, her breasts grazing my chest. "I want you all the time. Maybe I should stop fighting it."

"Maybe we both should." I wrapped my free arm around her waist, tugging her closer. "Come with me to the wagon."

"Thought you never seduced anyone in there."

"I haven't, not until now." I touched my lips to hers, a soft, gentle kiss. "Assuming you come with me. I'd love to spend the night with you in my gypsy sanctuary."

She laid a hand on my cheek. "Yes, Damian, I will."

"We can just talk if that's what you want. Talk and sleep together, and I mean 'sleep' as in catching some Z's."

"I want more than that."

"Me too." I led her toward the wagon, holding her hand the whole time, letting go only so I could open the door. As she climbed up the steps, her ass was inches away from my face. "Already loving the view."

She smiled at me over her shoulder. "You'll get a much better view in a few minutes."

Naked Heidi. Sure, I'd seen her naked before, but this time would be different. No comparison, actually. I would have her nude body underneath mine.

I climbed into the wagon and shut the door, stopping just past the threshold.

Heidi stood by the table, gazing down at it. She traced her fingertips over the surface, then laid her palm on it. "Later, I'd love for you to finish that palm reading." She looked at me. "If you don't mind."

"Love to—later." I strode up to her, laying my palm over her hand on the table. "This is your night, Heidi. You set the pace, you decide what you want to do, and you tell me what you want me to do."

"That's sweet, but it's unnecessary. I trust you, Damian."

"You trust me so much that you ran away from a palm reading. I'm not being sarcastic or grumpy. I'm stating a fact."

"I know. But I didn't run away because of you. I did it because you make me feel so good that I want more than friendship with you." She fingered the lapel of my shirt. "I want you, period. And that scares me, but I refuse to keep being a coward who's too afraid to admit what I want. So if you still want me—"

"Hell yes, I want you."

"Good." She pointed at the bench. "Sit down, please."

"The bed is a lot more comfortable for having sex."

"You said you'd do what I want."

I had said that, and I never reneged on a promise. So I dropped onto the bench and spread my arms across its back. "I'm all yours."

"Got any music? The steamy kind, preferably."

"Absolutely." I dug my phone out of my pocket and found a good playlist, one of my favorites, then I started the music. It played through a Bluetooth speaker embedded in the wall, thanks to an app I'd installed on my phone. "Steamy enough for you?"

"Mm, I like this. Belly dancing music."

While the Middle Eastern style music played, Heidi began to sway her hips. She got her whole body into it, like a real belly dancer, moving her sexy body in ways that made the blood in my brain pour down into my dick. She pulled her shirt off over her head, then unzipped her pants and got rid of them too.

I stroked my hardening cock through my jeans, imagining all the things I wanted to do with her tonight.

Heidi undid her bra and let it fall away from her body. She kept shimmying and gyrating while she removed her panties, and I couldn't tear my gaze away from her, couldn't stop myself from following every movement. Her tits swayed, her eyes fluttered shut, and she skimmed her hands up and down her body the way I wanted to do to her.

She knelt in front of me, pushed my knees apart, and positioned herself between them. "I've wanted to do this for so long, maybe since the first time I saw you. Can't wait anymore."

I reached for my shirt, about to unbutton it, but she stopped me with her hand on mine.

"Let me do that," she purred, her voice so sultry the sound of it made my balls tighten.

"Well, it is your night." I lowered my hand.

She unhooked the buttons on my shirt one by one while seductive music played, her movements synced with the rhythm of the song. Her hips kept swaying, despite being wedged between my legs. Her fingers grazed my skin as she made her way down my chest until she'd undone every button and my shirt hung open. Humming with pleasure, she glided her palms up my chest and then dragged her nails back down it. When her fingers found the fly on my jeans, she undid that too and pulled the zipper down, down, down until she'd exposed my cock.

"I love that you don't wear anything under your pants," she said in that hot-as-hell purr. With one hand, she pulled my dick out and cupped it in her palm. "This is what I've wanted to do so badly I had to make myself come every time I fantasized about it. Like this morning. You heard me, didn't you?"

"Yeah. That's why I ran to the restroom. I needed to make myself come too."

She slid her hand up and down my length. "Yeah, I figured out what you were doing even before I heard you come."

"You heard me?" I sucked in a breath when she flicked her thumb over the head of my erection. "Fuck, Heidi, that's hot."

"Things are about to get even hotter."

She grasped the base of my erection and bent to take me into her mouth.

I set a hand on her shoulder to stop her. "Are you sure about this? Ten minutes ago, you told me to go away and you don't want to sleep with me."

"Yeah, I know. But I only said that because I do want you, so damn much, and that scares me. My history with men isn't the greatest." She peeled my hand away from her shoulder and massaged my palm with her thumb. "You're not like anyone else, though, and I suddenly realized I don't want to fight this anymore. Can't promise I'll want a candlelight dinner with you, but for tonight, all I know is that I need to be with you. Okay?"

"Sure. I want that too." I glanced down at my hard-on. "I'd love to have your mouth on me, but you shouldn't make me come. Takes me a while to get up and running again."

"That's okay. We have all night."

"Do you mean you're staying until morning?"

"Yes. Now shut up and let me taste you."

I relaxed against the bench.

Heidi lowered her mouth and licked my crown, then blew air across it. She'd hardly done anything to me, but already I had trouble catching my breath. When she swept her tongue up my cock and back down to the crown, I gripped the bench's edge hard enough to crush the cushioning. She did that again, slowly raking her tongue up my entire length and then down the other side, her damp tongue leaving a cool trail in its wake.

"Fuck, Heidi, that feels—"

My voice died when she took me into her mouth, one hand grasping the base of my erection while she massaged my inner thigh with her other hand. She pumped me while her tongue darted out to tease my skin, and she gently sucked, moving her mouth up and down, over and over, spurring me to clench the cushions harder and gasp for breath. Her mouth felt hot and wet, her tongue velvety soft, and God, the way she rubbed my thigh, inching her fingers closer and closer to my balls…

She skimmed her fingers past my balls and massaged the skin behind them.

I'd never experienced anything like this before. No one had ever touched me in that spot, but it felt incredible.

Heidi sped up her movements, pumping me faster, sucking me harder. I threw my head back and groaned, and I swore my eyes rolled back in my head for a second. Pressure built inside me as an electric current rushed down my spine, making every hair on my body stiffen, and I knew I'd lose it soon. I couldn't manage to groan, let alone speak, but I couldn't stop myself from grasping the back of her head and fisting one hand in her hair. She grunted out ravenous little noises like she loved having me in her mouth.

I came like a bomb going off. My back bowed, and the only sound I could make was a strangled gasp. She kept sucking, taking everything I had without flinching or even letting up, not until I'd spent everything inside her mouth.

She sat back on her heels and wiped her lips with one hand. "I loved doing that for you."

"Yeah," I said, still breathing hard, "I loved you doing that for me too."

Laughing, she leaned in to wrap her arms around my neck. "Mind if kiss you? Most guys don't want to kiss me when I've just given them head."

"I don't mind."

"Maybe I should drink something first."

"Don't worry about it."

I took hold of her face and tugged her closer, mashing my mouth to hers and plunging my tongue between her lips to get a deeper taste of her. Maybe I did taste myself a little, but it was only a hint of a salty tang, and I didn't care. I'd kiss her if she'd just eaten a big plateful of raw garlic and onions, or even sauerkraut. I hated that stuff.

When I finally relinquished her lips, I smiled and rubbed the corner of her mouth with my thumb. "About time I got to taste you."

Chapter Eleven

Heidi

Damian was nothing like any man I'd ever known before. Ollie was a great guy, but we just weren't right for each other, a fact I realized way too late to avoid humiliating myself. But here in this lushly decorated wagon, I knew I wouldn't make a mistake—not with Damian. Not tonight, anyway. If this didn't last beyond one night, I knew at least I'd walk away with an amazing memory.

I couldn't decide if I wanted it to last longer.

He needed a few minutes after the blow job to recover, but he let me undress him while he lay there watching me do that. I swore he enjoyed seeing me take his clothes off more than he enjoyed my little striptease. Maybe he loved it because I let my fingers graze his skin as often as possible, and I showered kisses over his chest and biceps before I moved on to getting rid of his pants. I kissed his thighs too, and his hips, and I tickled his belly button with my tongue.

"You're getting me going again in record time," he said. "Damn, Heidi, you are the sexiest, most passionate woman on earth."

"We haven't had sex yet. How do you know I'm passionate?"

"By the way you gave me head. No woman has ever done it like that."

I'd loved feasting on him, more than I'd ever loved giving a man oral sex before tonight. What was it about Damian that made me crave him with a hunger so deep and all-consuming that I couldn't stand the thought of not being with him? Maybe tomorrow I'd worry about that. Tonight, I wanted to be with him.

He led me to the curtain that concealed his mini-bedroom and held it open so I could climb onto the bed. The covers were already pulled back. The plush padding of the mattress cradled my body and made me feel like I was floating on the ocean. Maybe I felt that way because I knew Damian would touch me any second. Maybe I always felt weightless when I was with him, like the burden of all my worries had lifted off me.

Damian crawled onto the bed, straddling me. "Don't be shy. If there's something you want me to do that I'm not doing, tell me."

How many guys would say something like that during sex? I would've bet Ollie did, though I'd never slept with him. Nobody else would—except for Damian.

"You're so sweet," I told him. "And so damn hot."

He chuckled. "Thanks. You're smokin' hot too."

I moved my arms above my head on the pillow, linking my hands.

"Love these tits," he said, smirking right before he took my nipple into his mouth and suckled it.

"Oh yes, please keep doing that."

He curled his tongue around my stiff peak, then tugged it with his teeth.

I arched my back, loving the sensation of electricity zinging through me, from my breast down to my sex. He kept tormenting my nipple, licking, sucking, and scraping it while I writhed and moaned, sending more jolts of electric pleasure straight down to my core. When he pulled his mouth away, I made an impatient noise.

"Don't worry," he said, patting my hip. "I'm nowhere near done with you."

He slid his lips down my belly, swirled his tongue inside my navel, and kissed his way down to my hip. I moaned, or maybe I said "please," couldn't swear to anything right now. His mouth and the feel of his body sliding down mine destroyed my willpower and my ability to think. Screw thinking. What did I need a brain for right now? Only to deliver more of those delicious waves of electric pleasure.

Damian placed an open-mouth kiss on the hollow of my hip, his warm tongue dampening my skin. The coolness when he pulled his mouth away made me shiver the tiniest bit. With one hand, he exerted gentle pressure on my inner thigh, urging me to spread my legs for him. I couldn't resist anything he wanted me to do, so I opened for him. He shimmied backward until his face hovered over my mound, then he dropped onto his elbows. With his mouth almost touching the hairs down there, his breaths excited my skin.

He pushed his mouth between my folds.

I felt his breaths on my slick skin first, followed by the roughness of his evening stubble, and finally, his tongue scraping over my flesh as he dragged it up one side of my folds and then the other. He licked his way down to my opening, swirling his tongue around the rim. I needed him to touch my clit, needed it so intensely that I bucked my hips, silently pleading with him to devour me the way I wanted him to the most.

"Not yet," he said, lifting his head to peek up at me over my hips. "I want to keep you on the edge until you're a wild, thrashing animal. Only then will I let you come. Relax, I won't push you too far. I'll know when you really need it and give you exactly what you want."

I already burned for him, after the way he'd stroked his tongue over my flesh. Whatever he might do to me tonight, I knew it would leave me breathless and satisfied. How did I know that? No idea, but it didn't matter. For one night, I needed to experience sex with this man and know exactly how much satisfaction he could give me.

One night only. No spooning. No hand-holding tomorrow. One night of mind-blowing sex, nothing more.

Damian dipped his head between my thighs again, and I couldn't worry about anything anymore. He traced his tongue around my rigid nub without contacting it, teasing me with his agile tongue and his heated breaths. My skin came alive, starting at my clitoris and blossoming outward until my entire body felt more awake and alive than ever before. I couldn't catch my breath, and he'd barely done anything to me. He watched me over my mound, his gaze capturing mine and refusing to let me glance away for even half a second. I swore he looked straight into my soul with those searing brown eyes. My breathing grew heavier, like the most delicious weight had settled on top of me and now it bore down on my body. I wanted him on top of me like that, thrusting inside me while his weight pressed me into the mattress.

He flicked his tongue across my nub.

I jerked and gasped, stunned by the power of the sensations that raced down my nerves, sharp and electric. My clit pulsed, my sex too, and I prayed any second he would send me hurtling over the edge. I clenched my fingers in the silky sheets, panting while he slowly dragged his tongue around my taut bud, eliciting more little shocks, making me cry out.

"Oh God, Damian, please." I couldn't stop the whimper that burst out of me. "Please, I need—oh God."

He latched on to my clit and sucked it hard.

My body froze, every muscle taut and ready, and even my lungs couldn't function. My gaze stayed glued to his while he nipped and suckled my nub, and the pleasure escalated higher and higher, my ears ringing because I couldn't breathe.

Then I came. The climax detonated inside me, so intense that choked gasps were the only sounds I could make. It felt like a thousand tiny explosions under my skin, setting me on fire from head to toe with ricocheting waves of pleasure inside my body. My sex yearned for his cock inside me, clenching again and again but with nothing to fill the void.

He didn't stop tormenting my flesh until he'd wrung every last spasm from my body.

I was breathing so hard I almost hyperventilated. Ridiculous. But I couldn't deny the truth of it. Was it only the way he'd touched me that drove me wild? Or was it *him*?

His tongue, that was all. His tongue and his piercing gaze.

And his incredible body. And his sexy smile.

No, it was only his tongue, nothing more.

Damian rose onto hands and knees, straddling me with his face above mine. He bent his elbows a little, just enough to bring his face closer to mine. "Don't panic yet. Save that for tomorrow."

"You want me to panic in the morning?"

"No, but I realize you probably will. We're about to shatter that celibacy vow of yours."

"Think we already did."

He smirked, and even that expression was devastatingly erotic. "What we've done so far was only blowing off steam. Now, we're going to turn that steam engine up so high it'll shatter."

"Yes, please, I need super-hot sex."

"It will be super hot, but not the way you mean." He bent his head to nuzzle my nose. "There are many kinds of hot sex, and I'm about to give you the kind you need the most, even if you don't realize it yet."

What did that mean? The hormones flooding my body made it hard to concentrate on anything, especially his words. "Hot sex" were the only words I could understand.

He leaned over the bed's edge, stretching an arm down to reach under the bed. His face tightened while he struggled to get whatever it was he wanted down there. Then he grinned and held up a condom packet. "Ready to go."

"You keep condoms under your bed? Thought you never seduced women in this wagon."

"That's true. I bought some condoms today in the resort gift shop because I hoped you might want to do more than flirt with me, eventually." He ripped the condom packet open with his teeth. "Thought it would take longer. Damn, I'm even better than I thought, getting you to beg me for sex."

I couldn't deny I'd begged with my actions and my intentions, though I hadn't outright begged for it. The implications of my need for him might hit me later, but for now, I wouldn't think about anything except having Damian inside me.

He rolled the condom on and knelt over me again on all fours. "I won't hurt you, not ever."

Why was he saying that? If he meant physically, I never thought he'd hurt me like that. "What happened to 'I love to talk dirty'? We're having sex, not going to a couples therapy group."

"No talking, not tonight. Next time, I'll talk dirty to you for as long as you want."

But not tonight? Why? I was on fire for him, and he kept saying things that sounded…like things he shouldn't be saying.

He kissed me, soft and slow, his tongue slipping between my lips with such gentleness that it made my throat ache. But when he toyed with my tongue, all that delicious excitement I'd felt a few minutes ago came rushing back, enlivening every part of me. When he positioned his knees between my legs, I couldn't stop my knees from bending and my thighs from parting, like my body wanted him so badly it had to offer me up to him in the most blatant way.

Damian settled his body on top of mine.

My breaths quickened. My pulse accelerated. I wanted him so much, but I didn't know if I could handle the way he would make me feel. *I won't hurt you*, he'd said. I clutched his biceps, where he'd planted his elbows on the mattress at either side of me.

"Shh," he murmured, brushing his lips over mine. "Forget about everything else and be with me tonight."

He pushed inside me inch by inch, his cock gliding deeper with such exquisite slowness that my breaths became pants and my heartbeat pounded in my ears and my chest. I gripped his arms tighter while he thrust in and out, taking his time like he relished every second of making love to me. The easy pace made it impossible for me to block out all the things I didn't want to feel, like the sensation of his body on mine, warm and strong, or the scent of him that enveloped me. With his head alongside mine, his hair tickled my cheek, and every time he exhaled it sent a rush of warm air over my earlobe.

My body cradled his, inside and out.

Damian groaned softly like this was the best thing he'd ever felt. Every thrust aroused me more, little by little, until the feel of him sliding in and out, his body grazing my nub, had me gasping and lashing my arms around him. My stiff nipples scraped against his chest, the friction so delicious that I dug my nails into his back.

"Faster," I pleaded. "Please, faster, harder."

"Not this time," he whispered into my ear, his voice strained and rough.

"But I—"

He covered my mouth with his.

And still, he moved his hips in that easy rhythm. In slow, out slow, over and over, oh so patient that even while he kept his lips glued to mine, he didn't try for a deeper kiss. Lips on lips, nothing more. How could that be so intensely erotic? He took my body with a gentleness no man had ever shown me before, and my chest tightened from the knowledge of what that might mean, but my mind couldn't decipher anything more complex than the need to come that built inside me second by second.

I wrapped my legs around him, my ankles locked behind his ass.

The climax rippled through me like no orgasm I'd ever experienced before. It came over me as slowly as he'd taken my body, the intensity of it growing with every thrust of his cock until my gasps became throaty moans and the moans turned into strangled cries. I gripped him with every part of my body, from my arms and legs to the muscles deep inside me that milked him with spasms that grew stronger with each wave of pleasure.

My heart thrashed in my chest. Desperate noises erupted out of me.

He pulled his hips back and plowed into me, his cock throbbing as he let go, releasing everything he had inside me. After two gentler thrusts, he let his body go slack on top of me. He raised his head, gazing at me with a soft expression that conveyed things I didn't want to think about right now.

"Damian, I—"

With two fingers, he sealed my lips. "Hush. We don't need to talk. You can tell me to go to hell in the morning."

"I wasn't going to say that."

"Glad to hear it." He claimed my mouth in a kiss that was soft and slow and full of longing. Then he slid off my body to lie beside me, one arm draped over my belly. "Let's get some sleep."

"Okay."

I rolled onto my side facing away from him.

He tugged me into his body, one hand on my belly.

We were spooning. Oh no, we couldn't do that. It was too…intimate.

But I couldn't make myself tell him to move or make my muscles work so I could move away from him. I should've gotten up and left, but I didn't want to leave. For one night, I could let myself enjoy sleeping with Damian.

Tomorrow… I'd worry about that in the morning.

Chapter Twelve

Damian

I woke up in the best way imaginable, with Heidi Mackenzie snuggled up to me. We'd fallen asleep with my front to her back, but now we lay face to face. She had her arm hanging over me, her sweet body tucked against mine, and her silky hair brushing against my face. Her nose brushed me too. And her lips. Was that an unconscious invitation for me to wake her with a kiss? Sure looked like one to me.

Laying a hand on her hip, I pressed my lips to hers and let them linger there until she sighed delicately. Then I gave her ass a quick squeeze. "Good morning, Heidi."

Her lids fluttered open, and a lazy smile curved her lips. "Good morning, Damian."

She hadn't seemed this relaxed when we fell asleep last night. I'd kind of expected her to panic the instant she woke up and realized she'd spent the night with me. Instead, she was smiling in the sweetest sleepy-sexy way.

And of course, my dick decided now was the right time for some morning wood.

Heidi screwed up her mouth. "Is there a live snake between our bodies, or is that *your* snake stiffening up?"

"It's me. Sorry, it happens every morning." But I was sure I'd get much stiffer this morning than I ever had before. How could I not? Heidi's luscious body was touching mine and the scent of her, that indescribable feminine aroma, made my cock wake up even faster than usual.

She laughed. "I've slept with other men, so I know all about morning hard-ons."

"Good. Then you won't mind taking care of the problem for me like you did last night."

"Mm-mm, no can do." She sat up and stretched, making her gorgeous tits lift and jiggle. "One time only, Damian. Last night was amazing, but we will never do that again."

Oh damn. I'd hoped making love to her, really making love to her, would banish that stupid idea. She'd broken her celibacy vow, but only for one night. Yeah, right. I'd believe that on the day Bigfoot walked out of the woods and introduced himself. He'd have a southern accent. Why not? It was my stupid fantasy.

No, my fantasy had unfolded last night, with Heidi.

But she wanted my body and nothing else. Well, she thought she did. I knew it was bullshit. We'd talked and shared personal stuff before we had sex, before last night when she ran after me to ask me to fuck her. She liked me, but she was terrified of getting hurt again.

I had no idea how to convince her I wouldn't be like her douchebag ex.

"We like each other," I said. "It's not a crime, and you don't need to run away from me because of what happened last night."

She slid off the bed, standing on the top step. "Thank you for the mind-blowing orgasms, but we will never have sex again. We are not dating."

"But we're friends, right?" Friends with the best benefits ever. I wanted more than that, but I wouldn't push. Heidi needed gentle nudges in the right direction, though.

"No, we're not friends." She hopped off the steps, bending over to hunt around on the floor for her clothes. "I'm a guest, and you're the concierge. That's it."

Okay, last night had freaked her out even more than I thought.

I jumped off the bed and over the steps, landing a few feet from Heidi.

She startled and yelped.

"Didn't mean to scare you," I said. "But I don't want you to leave until we've talked about this. Please, Heidi, let's have a real conversation like we did before."

"I'm hungry, and the food is in the dining hall."

"Stay here. I'll go get some food for us."

"No, Damian," she said firmly, managing to look resolute and stubborn while she was naked and struggling to get her bra clasps hooked.

"At least let me help you with that." I moved closer and reached for the back of her bra.

She batted my hand away. "I can do it myself."

"Okay, fine." I raised my hands. "I surrender."

Heidi's gaze swept over me from head to toe. She licked her lips when her focus landed on my groin.

Yeah, the morning wood had arrived.

She cleared her throat and tore her gaze away from my dick. "Get dressed, please."

"I know nudity doesn't bother you in general. I mean, you used to be a naturist. So I'm assuming you want me to get dressed because *my* nudity bothers you—in a sexy way."

"Don't flatter yourself." She finally got her bra done up and started pulling on the rest of her clothes. "You aren't so hot that I can't keep my hands off you, or my eyes off you."

But she had watched me lately. A lot. Especially when I was naked.

I wouldn't point that out to her. Only an asshole did something like that.

"Get dressed," she said again, notably without the "please" this time.

"Yeah, okay, relax." While I found my clothes and put them on, Heidi hurried out of the wagon. I called out, "Your clothes are wrinkled, Heidi, and I think your shirt is on backwards."

She froze mid-step, threw me an annoyed look over her shoulder, then stomped off.

Maybe I shouldn't have told her that, but I figured she'd want to know if she looked like she just got back from a night of hot sex. I couldn't seem to do anything right with her. Not this morning, at least.

I headed for my room in the guest house and changed into casual clothes. Today was my day off, so I didn't need to wear either of my work uniforms—the resort version or the gypsy version. Jeans and a T-shirt would do fine today. Maybe I'd go nude later. Then again, maybe I shouldn't. Heidi was upset about last night, and seeing my nakedness might make her panic again.

Why did I care? She'd made it clear we weren't dating and never would be.

Maybe I wasn't a Casanova type, but I could get a date if I wanted one. No woman had ever turned me down, for a date or sex. Maybe that sounded a tad arrogant, but I didn't mean it that way. Could I help it if women lusted for me? Like I'd told Heidi, I gave awesome dating.

But Heidi wouldn't go on a date with me.

Had I ever actually asked her for a date? "Have dinner with me," I'd said when I approached Heidi minutes after she'd arrived at the resort. That wasn't a question. It was a statement, like I planned to throw her over my shoulder and take her back to my cave for a dinner of barbecued squirrel with pine nuts on the side. Was I being a dick today? No, I'd treated Heidi with kid gloves because I worried about freaking her out.

Maybe that was the problem. I was being too nice. She'd liked me yesterday when I'd told her "have dinner with me" and when I'd announced I loved whispering filthy things into a woman's ear. Last night, I held back and tried to show her my tender side. Maybe I was going about this the wrong way. Heidi might respond better to my rakish side since making sweet love to her had resulted in panic.

Couldn't hurt to try.

But I'd relished making love to her.

I went to Heidi's room, but she either wasn't there or refused to let on that she was. Knocking, even banging, on her door resulted in silence. Since I'd already changed into my off-duty clothes, I trotted downstairs to eat breakfast. Heidi wasn't there. I ate fast and split.

Outside the guest house, I bumped into Ollie. "Have you seen Heidi?"

He smirked. "Only when she was running out of your wagon with her clothes on backwards."

"You better not have said anything to her about that."

"I'm the good one, Damian, remember? You're the bad boy."

"Does that mean you haven't said anything to Heidi about how she, uh, was in my wagon with her clothes on the wrong way?"

My best friend snickered. "I kind of doubt she went into your little love nest with her clothes like that. But no, I didn't say a thing to Heidi."

I let out the breath I hadn't realized I was holding. "You don't know where she is now."

"No." He tipped his head to the side, studying me. "You like her a lot, don't you?"

"Mind your own business, Ollie."

I walked away—okay, stomped away—without giving Ollie a chance to say anything else that would make me irritable. Some guests were already on the lawn, including Ruth and Sylvester. I flopped onto a chaise beside them.

"Good morning, sunshine," Ruth said. She scrutinized me for a moment, then said, "I see storm clouds brewing around you. What's wrong? Did you and Heidi have a fight?"

"We're not dating, Ruth."

"You can have an argument even if you're not dating."

"I don't want to talk about Heidi."

Ruth clucked her tongue. "You two definitely had a fight."

Grumbling, I shoved myself up out of the chair. "I'm going for a walk."

"If we see Heidi, we'll let her know where you went."

I might've actually growled, like a wild animal.

Rather than heading for the nature trail, I veered across the lawn to take the almost-hidden path to my pilot project. Lenny and Georgie nickered when they saw me, but oddly, they were already standing at the fence near the gate.

Then I noticed why.

Heidi stood at the fence, half-hidden in the shadows of the surrounding trees. She kept a six-inch gap between her and the fence and bit her lip while she watched the horses. And she'd gotten her clothes on the right way.

"There you are," I said.

She swung her head around to stare at me. "Damian? I thought it was your day off."

"It is. How did you know that?"

"Well, I…" She hunched her shoulders. "I asked Ollie."

"Because you're dying to spend more time with me, alone. That's cool." I rested an arm on the top bar of the fence, facing Heidi. "Ever have sex in the woods?"

"No dating, Damian."

"I mentioned sex, not dating." Leaning toward her, I gave her my best suggestive smile. "Unless you're ready for that upgrade."

"What upgrade?"

"From sex to dating. I told you we could start with getting it on, then you can upgrade to having dinner with me."

She crossed her arms over those gorgeous tits. "I'm done with men."

"But you had your way with me last night. That was the best blow job in history."

"This was a bad idea."

Heidi started to walk away, but I snagged her arm. "What was a bad idea?"

"Coming here to see the horses. I should've guessed you'd show up. Are you stalking me?"

"I had no idea you would be here. You're terrified of horses."

"Thought I'd try a little more immersion therapy."

Georgie nudged my arm, so I scratched under his chin. "Did you even pet one of these guys?"

"No, I've only been here for a couple minutes."

"At least give Georgie some love before you go." I wanted her to give me some too, but I kind of doubted that would happen.

Heidi stretched out a hand to stroke Georgie's neck, then scratched under his chin.

She turned to walk away again.

"I'll see you later, Heidi, when you get desperate to kiss me." I said those words in a teasing tone, and I knew she got that because she threw me a grudging smile over her shoulder.

And I watched her ass while she walked away.

Chapter Thirteen

Heidi

I stalked back to the lawn and flumped onto an Adirondack chair. Nobody was playing miniten or any other game at the moment, though a handful of people sat in chairs or on the grass in small groups, talking and laughing. I didn't feel like laughing. Damian had me feeling…uncomfortable. Why had he felt the need to turn a night of mind-blowing sex into an intensely intimate encounter? Why couldn't he just give me amazing orgasms and leave it at that? No, he had to say sweet, sexy things and look at me like I was the most beautiful woman he'd ever seen. Instead of getting his rocks off and saying good night, he'd made love to me with a kind of tenderness no other man had ever shown me.

That bastard.

How was I supposed to keep pretending we weren't involved, that all I wanted was meaningless sex, if he wouldn't cooperate? Caring and sharing had never been a part of any relationship I'd ever had with a man. Even the nicest ones didn't want to cuddle after sex. None of them had ever been as patient with me or as concerned with my pleasure. I'd told Damian I trusted him, and I meant it. Even when I slammed a door in his face, he didn't get angry. He worried he'd done something wrong. And all the other things he'd said to me last night…

We can just talk if that's what you want. Talk and sleep together, and I mean 'sleep' as in catching some Z's.

Men never wanted that. Bang and run, that was the usual way things went. Either that or bang and fall asleep.

This is your night, Heidi. You set the pace, you decide what you want to do, and you tell me what you want me to do.

Damian had kept that promise. He never did anything I didn't want. If I had told him not to make love to me, I was sure he would've stopped. But I hadn't wanted him to. Even while part of me panicked, the rest of me reveled in the sweet, sensual glory of Damian loving my body.

"Don't be shy," he'd said last night. "If there's something you want me to do that I'm not doing, tell me."

Then he'd assured me he would never push me too far sexually, and he'd know exactly what I needed and when. I couldn't deny he had known, almost like he could read my mind. Maybe a palm reading genuinely did provide supernatural insight.

There are many kinds of hot sex, and I'm about to give you the kind you need the most, even if you don't realize it yet.

Had I needed sweet, sensual, loving sex? Since I'd never experienced that kind before, I couldn't say for sure whether I'd needed it. Oh, who was I kidding? I'd needed it, he gave it to me, and now I had to deal with the consequences of letting him make love to me.

One of the last things he'd said to me before we fell asleep replayed in my mind, as clearly as if he were whispering it into my ear right now. *I won't hurt you, not ever.*

God, I wished he hadn't been so…wonderful. Walking away from him had been way too hard, and it gave me a sharp pain in the back of my throat. I barely knew Damian, but I felt like he knew me, for sure. Should I give him a chance?

A chill shivered over my skin, but a luxurious warmth swept in behind it.

If that indicated something, I refused to think about what it was.

Damian sauntered out of the woods.

That man looked as steamy-hot in jeans and a gray T-shirt as he did in his gypsy-vampire outfit. The way he had his shirt untucked made me want to push my hands up under the fabric and run them over his smooth chest. God, I loved his body. Even seeing him with clothes on made me want to lick him from head to toe, especially that beautiful dick.

Okay, I wanted him. The slickness between my thighs would've contradicted me if I'd claimed I didn't want him anymore. Getting it on with Damian had only intensified my lust for him. Avoiding the man seemed like the only prudent choice.

But I didn't want to stay away. I wanted him naked, this time with me on top. The thought terrified me, but also got me even wetter. Maybe I could have sex with him again, just once, purely to satisfy my craving for his body.

Yeah, right, I'd screw him one more time and then I'd be over it. *What kind of idiot have you become, woman?*

Damian started to turn left, toward the far end of the lawn. But then he saw me, and his mouth slid into a sexy smile. He waved.

I waved back without thinking about it, spurred by a politeness reflex.

He took it as an invitation and jogged across the lawn toward where I sat.

Oh crap. I could not see or speak to Damian when I was still turned on by fantasies of him.

"What's up, Heidi?" Damian asked as he stopped beside my chair.

"Nothing. You waved, so I waved. It wasn't an invitation."

"But you wanted me to come over here." He bent to rest his hand on my chair's arm, his face way too close to mine. "Let's go for a walk. Just the two of us. I promise not to do anything you don't want me to do." He slanted in more, moving his lips to within millimeters of my ear. "I may not be awesome at everything, but I will give you the best dating you've ever had. My hand-holding will make you shiver with anticipation, and when I put my arm around your shoulders, you'll get so hot for me it'll make you weak in the knees."

"That's silly. Holding hands is not erotic."

"It is the way I do it. And I haven't even gotten to the kissing yet. One peck on the cheek will have you begging me to make you come."

My sarcastic laugh came out as a splutter. "Does this kind of thing work for you? Dirty hand-holding? Seriously? That's ridiculous."

"It's all in the delivery."

He picked up my hand, simply cradling it in his.

Warmth rushed through me.

But when he touched his lips to my cheek, I almost gasped. Which was idiotic. A chaste kiss on the cheek did not make me weak with lust. Except my legs did feel a touch wobbly like if I tried to stand up, I'd fall back onto the chair.

"Come with me," Damian murmured. "Please, Heidi, say yes."

"I… What are we going to do on this so-called walk?"

He chuckled. "Walk and talk, that's all."

"Well, in that case… all right."

Damian straightened and offered me his hands, helping me get up. He settled a palm on my lower back as we strolled toward the nature trail.

And damn, that gentle touch sent a delicate tingle chasing over my skin.

"What did you mean 'it's all in the delivery'?" I asked while we headed into the woods. "You barely kissed my cheek."

"But the things I said and the way I said them got you worked up. That's what I meant." He danced his fingertips over my spine, the touch light and teasing. "Sometimes the right words spoken the right way are more enticing than actions."

I couldn't deny that was true, but only with Damian had I ever experienced it.

"When I talk dirty to you," he said, "you'll feel it inside your body like I'm fucking you."

After the way he so easily turned me on with his words a minute ago, I couldn't deny he might do exactly what he suggested. My body awakened at the mere thought of Damian whispering dirty things in my ear.

We strolled down the main trail hand in hand like he'd suggested, and I found myself relaxing even though we didn't speak a word to each other. It felt nice to spend time with a guy without the pressure of expectations. Damian didn't expect anything, I knew that. But I kept assuming he'd turn into a dick like my ex—like all my exes. Why did I keep picking losers?

I hadn't picked Damian. He had chosen me, though he let me set the pace.

Maybe we were kind of—almost, but not quite—dating.

"Which trail do you want to take now?" he asked as we approached a fork in the path.

One fork led to the hot spring. The other path, the main trail, headed toward the lake but had some offshoots that led to areas that were great for seeing the wildlife and scenery. If I chose the hot spring trail, that might imply I wanted to get naked with Damian in the steamy blue water. Okay, I did want that. The second I thought of it, I needed to go there with him. But I shouldn't. Not yet.

"Straight ahead," I told him. "But you can choose after that."

"Okay."

We ambled down the trail a little further, then turned onto a side path that I knew led to a small meadow where wildflowers bloomed. Still, we didn't talk. Damian held my hand, that was all. He smiled at me too, whenever I glanced at him, but it was a soft, sweet smile. I'd never been a big fan of holding hands, but with Damian, I found I loved it. He kept rubbing the back of my hand with his thumb, gently, and while we wandered toward the meadow, he threaded his fingers through mine.

Once we got to the meadow, he suggested we lie in the grass, amid the wildflowers, and relax. I already felt super relaxed, thanks to his sweetness, but I didn't tell him so.

We stretched out on the grass with a blue sky above us.

His hand stayed linked with mine.

Damian shifted in place like he was getting more comfortable. "Can I ask you a personal question?"

"Since when do you need permission? I told you all kinds of personal stuff the other day."

"But you're still dealing with last night, so I figured I'd be a nice guy instead of an asshat and ask permission before grilling you."

"That's very considerate," I said with only part sarcasm. He was a genuinely nice guy. "Fine, grill away."

"Why did you dump Ollie to go back to your ex? Why did you break up with that other guy in the first place?"

A wave of cold swept through me, raising all the hairs on my arms and sinking deep under my skin. Nobody had asked me those questions before. I'd never wanted to talk about it except to tell Mara and Ollie that I kept going back to Grant because he always seemed sincere when he begged me to forgive him. Should I tell Damian everything? What if, after hearing about it, he didn't want to be with me anymore?

Not that it mattered. I couldn't get involved with him.

So, uh, why was I holding his hand?

My voice had a mind of its own and decided to tell him everything. "I have a habit of picking the wrong guys. I convinced myself I should be with Ollie because he's such a sweetie, and I knew he'd never hurt me the way other guys have. But I had no business getting involved with him when I'd just broken up with Grant."

"Ollie says things were good when he was with you."

"Yeah, it was good. So of course, I trashed it." I pulled my hand free of Damian's and hugged myself. "Grant can be very charming, especially when he's making me believe he loves me even when I know how many times he's cheated. Shelby told her boyfriend about me and Ollie, and her boyfriend told somebody else who happened to know Grant. When Grant found out I was with someone else, he called me and begged me to take him back."

"He used his charm to convince you."

"Like I said, Grant is good at that. It was the fifth time he'd cheated on me, that I know of, but I believed it when he said he loved me and he'd never do it again." I levered my body up into a sitting position but kept hugging myself. "Like an idiot, I fell for his lies again. For six months, I struggled to make it work with him, until I realized I'd made a huge mistake. I should never have broken up with Ollie, that's what I thought. So when the Kitten Brigade came back here for a vacation, I convinced myself I needed to win Ollie back. I think you know the rest of that story."

"Uh-huh." Damian sat up, braced with one hand on the ground. He studied me for a moment like he was considering how to tell me what a pathetic moron I was. He didn't say that, though. Instead, he laid a hand on my knee and said, "You don't have to tell me, but I'd like to know the real reason you dumped Ollie and kept going back to Grant. It's not only because of his charm, is it?"

Damn, sometimes I hated how perceptive Damian was. How could I hide from the truth when he kept gently guiding me toward it? Maybe I should've told him to buzz off, but instead, I did the last thing I should've wanted to do.

I told him the truth.

"Guess I've always felt like I don't deserve a good man," I said. "Whenever I find one, I shove him away. Ollie wasn't the first nice guy I dumped for no good reason. I have a bad habit of ditching the good ones and latching on to the assholes who have charm and sweet words on their side."

"Why do you think you don't deserve someone who appreciates you?"

"Because…" I dropped my face into my hands, feeling the sting of tears trying to form. I did not want to cry in front of Damian—or anyone, but especially not him.

He pried my hands away from my face and held them sandwiched between his palms. "You don't have to tell me. But if you want to, I'll listen. I'm your friend, if you want me to be."

Gazing into his earnest eyes, I couldn't remember why I kept pushing him away and telling him I didn't want more than friendship. Damian was so kind and patient and thoughtful. He was also drop-dead sexy and amazing in bed, not to mention a great kisser. The only other guy I'd known who had all those qualities was Ollie, though I'd never slept with him. And I'd never wanted him the way I wanted Damian.

"I don't want to blame my parents," I said, "but they have used me as a pawn in their arguments. It always feels like they want me to choose between them. I can't do that. Whatever their faults are, they're still my parents, and I won't get rid of one of them to make the other happy. So I've tried to please them both, which just winds up with both of them getting mad, at each other and me. Guess I made up for not being able to make my parents happy by trying to make men happy. Maybe that's why I pick jerks. Maybe that's all I deserve because I'm so damn screwed up."

"You are not screwed up, Heidi."

"Of course I am. I let you make love to me, then I ran away." I tore my hands free of his. "You're a nice guy. You should go find a girl who won't drive you insane with her neurotic behavior."

"If you're trying to dump me, you can't do that. We're not a couple, right? That's what you keep saying. And that means you can't give me the big heave-ho." He leaned in, his mouth a breath from mine. "You're stuck with me."

"So you're going to stalk me because I had sex with you."

"No." He brushed his thumb over my bottom lip. "I'm going to be the best friend you've ever had. I'll give you so much awesome friendship that you won't be able to live without me."

"Why do you bother with me? I'm a mess."

He sighed, regarding me in silence while keeping his lips within kissing distance. Then he picked me up and stood, cradling me in his arms. "Let's go to the lake and swim."

"I don't have my swimsuit."

"This is a nudist resort, Heidi. No swimsuit required." He set me down, settling his hands on my hips. "But we can walk on the beach if you'd rather."

"Okay."

While he led me away from the meadow, I tried to figure out what Damian was really after. He couldn't want to date me. I told him what a mess I was, and he responded by sighing and staring at me, right before he suggested a nude swim. Would I ever understand Damian Petrescu?

Not likely.

Chapter Fourteen

Damian

I took Heidi for a walk down the beach, but we didn't swim, with or without clothes. She seemed edgy after sharing her anxieties with me, so I didn't push for more than a walk. I couldn't remember the last time I'd done something like this, just walking and talking with a woman, no flirting or sex involved. It felt good. Heidi clearly thought she was a flake, but I never saw her that way, not even when we'd first met months ago. Nobody who worked as a pharmacy technician could be a flake.

Heidi was smart and together, but she didn't seem to realize it.

Though I hadn't thought she would want to hear more about my happy family, she asked me to tell her stories about them. So I did. She seemed to like that, which surprised me, though maybe it shouldn't have. Maybe hearing about my family made her feel better or…something. She got more relaxed and at ease the longer we strolled down the beach and talked. She did tell me more about her family too—good things this time. Her parents weren't total jerks, I learned. When she was a kid, Heidi's parents always gave her everything she wanted for Christmas, except for the year when she wanted a hot-air balloon.

Yeah, I could understand not wanting to give a kid that for a present.

But I would never understand why her parents made her the center of their marital problems and made her feel like their divorce was her fault. Maybe they hadn't meant to, but everything they'd done made her feel that way.

On the way back to the resort, I told her funny stories about my parents and my brother.

"Does your family like Halloween?" Heidi asked after I'd finished one of my stories. "Or is that not part of gypsy culture?"

"We love Halloween, but it's not a gypsy tradition. We're Americans as well as gypsies, and Americans love dressing up and trying to scare each other."

Heidi smiled. "Yeah, we do. Well, not me, but lots of other people."

"You don't dress up for Halloween?"

"Sure, I do. But my costumes are sexy, not scary." Her smile turned teasing, and she bumped her shoulder into me. "Do you wear your hot gypsy outfit for Halloween?"

"No, I didn't start dressing that way until I came here and decided to play up my Ludar heritage for the tourists. Honestly, I haven't done the Halloween-costume thing in years."

"Seriously? I would've thought you'd love that holiday."

"I used to, but I kind of grew out of it."

She arched her brows. "Damian the gypsy vampire doesn't like Halloween anymore? Maybe you need to loosen up a little too."

I let go of her hand to sling my arm around her shoulders. "Maybe I do. A little. I have spent years working at a prison, which isn't the most relaxing environment."

As we reached the edge of the woods, with the lawn in sight, she stopped and looked at me. "Want to finish that palm reading?"

"Maybe later. Why don't we go into the entertainment room and play a game?"

"Like what?"

"Anything you want. Poker, Monopoly, Go Fish, Twister."

She laughed. "Does anybody play Twister anymore? I'm not sure that's a safe game to play with you."

We wandered across the lawn and into the guest house, with my arm still around her, and we played silly games for two hours. Nobody bothered us because Eve and Val had taken a big group into town for shopping and sightseeing. The rest of the guests were either in their rooms or on the lawn enjoying the sunshine. Heidi and I had the entertainment room to ourselves. I could've taken advantage of that fact and turned it into an afternoon of naughty games, but I didn't. Spending time with Heidi felt even better than sex.

Yeah, I actually thought that. Playing board games with Heidi was better than making love to her. Nobody would believe I could feel that way.

I wanted to take Heidi into town and buy her dinner at a nice restaurant, but I figured that might trigger her anxiety again. So instead, we got our food from the dining hall and took it outside for a moonlight picnic. I got a battery-powered lantern from the supply closet so we wouldn't need to hunt around in the dark for our food. After we ate, we turned off the lantern and enjoyed lying on our blanket on the lawn with the stars and the moon above us.

After that, I escorted her back to her room.

Yeah, there was a good-night kiss. A chaste one.

How long could I last without tasting her again? The flavor of her mouth drove me crazy, but the taste I hungered for the most was her luscious cream.

In the morning, I brought her breakfast in bed. Turned out she slept in short-sleeve pajamas, not sexy lingerie. Still, seeing her in PJs got me just as turned on as lingerie might have. We sat on the bed, side by side, to enjoy our meal and tease each other.

After we'd finished our French toast and bacon, Heidi turned to me. "You don't have to hold back. I'm not as fragile as you think. I know I acted like I am, but honestly, that's not the real me. I'd kind of forgotten who I am until you helped me remember."

"I didn't do anything. You found your way again all on your own."

She feigned shock. "Damian Petrescu is refusing to take credit for giving awesome dating and awesome sex?"

"Very funny. I take full credit for the sex, but the rest was all you." I raised my brows. "Thought we weren't dating, anyway. Friends only, you said."

"Oh, forget about that. We're dating."

I stared at her. Probably with a blank expression. Or possibly with my mouth hanging open. Maybe both.

She gave my shoulder a little shove. "Why are you catatonic because I admitted we're dating? I thought you'd be happy."

"I am happy, but I feel rightfully shocked. Thought you'd need a lot more time to get over your anxieties." I couldn't help smiling with smug satisfaction, though it was the sarcastic kind. "Damn, I'm even better than I realized. One night of hot sex and two days of wooing, and you're begging me to be your boyfriend."

"There's been no begging. Don't turn back into arrogant Damian. I'm starting to like the sweet guy under the Dracula-knockoff exterior."

"Now you're back to calling me a knockoff?" I wrapped an arm around her, tugging her against my side, bringing our faces to within a hair's breadth of each other. "Maybe it's time I give you my awesome dirty talk. You'll never insult me again once you've heard me whisper filthy things into your ear."

"Go on. I'm ready for that."

"Maybe later. This is a workday for me, so I need to get into concierge mode."

"Okay. What about tonight?" She snuggled up to me, running her palm over my chest. "I need you to talk dirty and fuck me, Damian."

I coughed, like that would ever stop my dick from getting hard. Which it was. Right now. "Tonight, for sure. I swear a solemn Ludar oath to fuck you senseless tonight."

She grinned.

And I went to work.

I wanted to spend my lunch break with Heidi, but her friends commandeered her for a girlie shopping trip in town. Instead, I ate alone in the office.

My cell phone rang while I was wolfing down a big bite of my turkey club sandwich. I fished it out of my pocket and answered while still chewing.

"Damian, don't speak while eating. How many times have I told you that's uncouth?"

"Mom?" I swallowed and cleared my throat. "It's my lunch break, so yeah, I was eating. Pardon my rudeness for not wanting to starve."

She clucked her tongue. "My sweet boy is becoming a heathen out there in the woods."

"Did you call to give me a verbal spanking? Or was there a genuine reason?"

"Of course there's a reason." She paused, probably for dramatic effect. My mother had always loved doing that. "We're coming for a visit, to see what about the Oregon woods has lured our son into the nudist lifestyle."

"I work here, Mom. It's a legitimate job, not an excuse for getting naked and sleeping with hot girls. And for your information, I keep my clothes on during work hours."

"We need to check on you. Your father is booking our flight as we speak."

"No, Mom, you will not invade the resort. I'm a big boy, and I can take care of myself. I think we're all booked up, anyway." I had no idea if that was true, but I hoped so. I loved my family, but they—especially my mom—could be a bit much. Heidi would panic for sure if my mother showed up and started grilling her like a shish kebab.

"Ollie reserved rooms for us," Mom said. "And he told Mary you have a girlfriend, so she told me. I should have heard that from you, Damian, not from Ollie's mother."

Yeah, my mom and Ollie's mom were good friends, and sometimes Ollie inadvertently told his mom something I didn't want my parents to know, and then Mary would tell my mom. I couldn't blame Ollie, though. He'd always sucked at lying, and besides, it was my problem, not his.

"Who is she?" Mom asked.

"I, uh, well…" Was it wrong to tell my mother to go suck a lemon? "I only just started seeing this girl, and I don't need you guys getting in the middle of things. Please hold off on your visit until later."

Maybe I should've begged. Or shouted. Or begged in a shouty voice. But no, that wouldn't have worked. Once my mother made up her mind, there was no stopping the runaway train.

"We'll see you tomorrow," she said. "I can't wait to meet your girl."

Given the tone of her voice, I knew she meant "I can't wait to aim my evil stare at your girl while giving her a full physical including a pelvic exam." My mother was a good person, but she could do the evil-stare thing better than anyone. She also tended to get overprotective.

What was it about this resort that made our families decide to invade the place for surprise visits? Eve's family had done it. So had Mara's. Now my mom was planning a "visit" I was sure would match the Invasion of Normandy in scale and drama.

Since I seemed to have no choice in the matter, I told her, "Fine, I'll see you guys tomorrow."

"Your brother is coming too. With Emily and the kids."

A total family invasion? Somehow, some way, I had to prepare Heidi for this.

Yeah, no problem. She freaked when I made love to her, but she'd handle the invasion of the Ludar horde, no problem.

I said goodbye to my mother, then dropped my head onto the desktop, facedown, and groaned.

Chapter Fifteen

Heidi

Shopping had sounded like a good idea when my friends suggested it, but it turned into the longest retail torture session ever. I didn't care about push-up bras or novelty T-shirts. Even cute skirts couldn't drag my attention back to the present. No, I kept remembering the other night when Damian made love to me. Memories of our nature walk tormented me too—the way he'd held my hand, the feel of his lips on mine, our conversations, his patience and kindness. All of that affected me with almost as much strength as the lovemaking had.

I liked Damian. A lot. I told him we're dating.

My tummy fluttered, and my pulse accelerated. Was it fear or excitement? Maybe both. Being with Damian felt like a dangerous and thrilling adventure, one I didn't want to end, not yet. Being here at the resort gave us a chance to explore this whatever-it-was between us without the distraction of our families getting involved. Sure, we had lots of friends here, but I remembered the fiascoes that happened when Eve's family and Mara's family had turned up, on separate occasions, to push their noses into their budding relationships with Val and Ollie. Mara and Ollie had survived her parents' visit. Eve and Val got through it too when her parents, her brother, and her sister showed up.

But I didn't know if I'd survive something like that. My parents would never in a million billion years show up here, at a nudist resort. I barely talked to them anymore except on holidays and birthdays. Damian's parents wouldn't come here, would they? No, of course not. I was being paranoid, worrying about something that wouldn't happen.

Even lunch at a nice restaurant didn't rouse me from my Damian daydreams.

When my friends and I got back to the resort, I told them I was tired and wanted to go back to my room. They probably believed me since I'd been yawning a lot today. Staying awake half the night fantasizing about Damian had left me at less-than-optimal wakefulness.

I trudged into the guest house, shoulders hunched, hands jammed into the pockets of my cargo pants.

And I ran straight into Damian.

"Sorry," he said, grasping my shoulders when I teetered. "Are you okay? I wasn't looking where I was going."

"I'm fine. And I wasn't looking either."

"Did you not have a good time in town?"

Shrugging, I took a step backward. The feel of his hands on my body had set off a faint tingle on my skin. "It was okay. Guess I'm not in a shopping mood today."

His features tightened into a pained expression. "I need to tell you something, and it might make you anxious again. Please don't panic. It's not as big a deal as it sounds like."

I was getting anxious just listening to him say that. But I would not panic. No way. I was done with that. So I pulled my hands out of my pockets, rolled my shoulders back, and said like a mature, level-headed woman, "Whatever it is, you can tell me. I'll be fine, promise."

"Okay." He said that like he wasn't at all sure he believed me, not that I could blame him for being skeptical. "My mom called me earlier. Turns out Ollie mentioned to his mom that you and I are dating, and she told my mom, so now the whole family knows, and…" He winced. "My parents and my brother are coming for a visit."

"Here?" I was so proud of myself for not shrieking that word. It had come out sounding a touch surprised, but in a mature and level-headed way.

"Yeah, here."

"When? Like, next week or something?"

He winced again, harder. "Tomorrow."

I swore every ounce of blood in my body evaporated, leaving behind an icy chill. Damian's family? The gypsies who read palms and who-knew-what-else? What if his mother put a curse on me? *Get a grip, woman, you will not panic again, absolutely not.* I pulled in a slow, deep breath and exhaled it little by little.

Damian grasped my shoulders again, gazing into my eyes with the sweetest look of concern. "It'll be okay. My mom likes to put on a show of being a mystical gypsy, but she's actually a tax accountant, and she's a nice person deep down. Once she gets to know you, she'll love you."

"Are you lying through your teeth to make me feel better?"

He winced for a third time. "Yes. But only a little. My mother takes…getting used to."

"Uh-huh."

"I tried to talk her out of coming here, but she's determined. Mom can be pigheaded, especially when it comes to me and my brother."

"Really?" I said with a smirk. "That's a shocker. I mean, you're so not pigheaded."

His lips kicked up at one corner. "I prefer to call it sexy determination."

"I suppose that's a mostly accurate description." I kissed him. "I'll be okay, even if your mom curses me to be frigid just to stop you from dating me."

"Nothing will make me do that." He pulled me into his arms. "But I want to make sure you're okay with this. You are wearing cargo pants again, after all."

"I like them. They're comfortable."

He gave me a skeptical look. "Are you sure it's not because you're anxious again and trying to hide that gorgeous body?"

"Yes, I'm sure. Maybe I'm not quite ready to go nude again, but I'm telling the truth about cargo pants. I have decided I like them." I patted one of the many pockets on my pants. "Lots of places to stash lip gloss and mascara."

He squinted like he was scrutinizing me. "You don't look like you're wearing either of those."

"No, but I could keep them in these pockets if I wanted to wear them."

"Right." He stroked my back with his palms. "Are you absolutely sure you want to be here when my parents show up?"

"Yes. I'm positive." It was my turn to wince. "Though I can't promise I won't get a teeny bit anxious when I meet your mom. I will not panic, though. I've made a vow to myself."

"Is that like your celibacy vow? Because you kind of ditched that one."

"And it was your fault." I wriggled against him, loving the way he hissed in a breath. I was rubbing myself on the bulge in his pants, after all. "If you weren't so damn sexy, I would've kept that vow for six months."

"But you won't break your no-panicking vow."

"That's right. I understand if you don't believe me, though."

He kissed my forehead. "I believe you, Heidi. I have to get back to work, but we could have dinner tonight. In my wagon. The atmosphere will be sensual and seductive."

"Just like you. Please say you'll make love to me tonight."

"That's a certainty." He kissed me, taking his time, making me feel warm and liquid in all the best ways before he peeled his lips away from mine. "Meet me in the wagon at eight."

"Okay."

He walked out the guest-house door.

And I went upstairs to take a nap. Yeah, I actually slept. Despite knowing Damian's parents were coming tomorrow, I felt more relaxed and at ease after talking to him. When he held me in his arms, all my anxieties melted away. Maybe that meant something, and maybe I'd panic if I let myself examine it more closely, but I'd worry about that later. Tonight, I planned to revel in the pleasure of making love with Damian.

Tomorrow... Well, I hoped his mom didn't lay that frigidity curse on me because I needed to have sex with Damian. Lots of sex. And talking too.

If his mom cursed me to silence, that might be even worse than no sex.

Wow. I loved talking more than screwing. Who knew that could happen?

Chapter Sixteen

Damian

I would've loved to say I cooked dinner for Heidi, but I didn't have that kind of skill. Making mac and cheese from a box was about all I'd ever done in the kitchen. I lived on frozen dinners and takeout, so I couldn't impress Heidi with my culinary prowess. Maybe I didn't cook for her, but I did go to the guest house and grab two trays full of food for us, then hauled it all back to the wagon. I had our meal set out on the little table by the time Heidi knocked on the door. The interior always had subdued lighting, produced by a single lamp, so the atmosphere was ready to go.

When I opened the door, Heidi smiled.

"Come on in," I said. "Your romantic dinner is hot and ready."

"Are you talking about the food?" she asked as she ducked inside. "Or are you describing yourself?"

"Both, in whichever order you prefer."

Heidi wore a short, tight dress that accentuated her breasts and hips. The sapphire color of the fabric brought out her eyes, even in this light. She looked good enough to fuck, but then, she always looked like that, even in cargo pants.

"Would you like to eat right away or do the palm reading first?" I asked. "Or if you can't wait to get me naked, we could have sex first."

"Let's eat." She glanced down at my groin, then peeked up at me through her lashes. "Food, I mean. I'll have you for dessert."

"You stole my line. I was about to say the same thing to you."

"I'm sure you can come up with something even better. When you talk dirty to me."

We sat down on the cushions at the table, side by side, and talked while we enjoyed our dinner. The food wasn't fancy, but that didn't matter. It smelled good, tasted good, and filled our bellies. What more did we need?

The longer we sat here in this cozy little wagon, the more I needed to get her naked. Dinner and conversation were awesome, but I knew what it felt like to be inside her, watching her expressions and listening to her noises while she edged toward climax. And when she came… Christ, I loved that. As much as I'd enjoyed making love to her, I wanted something else tonight.

She had implied she wanted me to talk dirty to her. I wanted that too.

Once we'd finished eating, I took hold of her hand. "Time to finish your reading."

"I'd love that."

Cradling the bottom of her hand in my palm, I traced the lines on her skin, avoiding the thumb, letting my fingertips graze her flesh as I explored her palm. "Last time, we never got to Mars or the lines."

"Go all the way, Damian. Read me good and hard."

Yeah, I was hard now for sure. Heidi could do that to me so easily.

I swirled my finger over the skin just above her thumb. "This is Inner Mars. I can see you have tenacity and boldness, but in moderation." I slid my finger across her palm to the outer edge, below her pinky. "Outer Mars shows me your perseverance and emotional strength." I moved my finger to the lower center of her palm. "The Plain of Mars is trickier to interpret. This is where the lines come into it. I'll need to explore them to lay bare your inner truths."

"Do it, Damian. Lay me bare."

"Are you starting the dirty talk without me?"

"Sorry." She made a zipper motion across her mouth. "I'll just listen. Your voice makes me so hot."

"I need to examine the length, depth, and curvature of every line. Where they cross mounts. The intersections of the creases. Everything matters when I'm delving inside you." I traced the lines with my fingertips like I had earlier, but this time I did it slowly and kept my touch light to tease her skin. I loved the way she ran her tongue over her lips and caught the bottom one between her teeth. Her reactions had my dick getting even harder every second. "These lines tell me a lot about you. I know you're smarter than you want everyone to think, you have a big heart, and you relish every minute of your life. You're independent, but your restlessness has left you unsatisfied."

Pink speckled her cheeks, and I swore I could smell her desire.

With one finger, I followed the line at the center of her palm. "I sense changes coming in your life. Embrace them, don't hide from your fate."

"And what do you think my fate is?"

"To scream my name all night long."

She turned her palm over, so it lay flush with mine. "I'm ready, Damian. Talk to me."

I set her hand on her lap. "No touching, not yet. First, I need to tell you everything I plan on doing to your body tonight."

"You don't want me to touch you?"

"Of course I want that, but not yet." I turned sideways to the table and stretched my legs out. "Sit on my lap, Heidi, facing me. Wrap those sexy thighs around me but keep your hands and your lips to yourself. For now."

She straddled me, her ass resting on my thighs, and hugged my hips with her legs. She set her hands on her thighs.

"Perfect," I said. Leaning back, I set my hands on the floor behind me to hold myself up. "I love your body, Heidi, every inch of it. Tonight, I'm going to explore your skin from head to toe, with my tongue and my lips and hands, until you're moaning and gasping. I've been fantasizing about you all day, about all the things I want to do to you and with you. Take that dress off, Heidi. I want to look at you."

She peeled the dress off, revealing…her, completely naked.

"No underwear this time?" I said. "You must want me bad, like you're desperate for me to make you come."

"I do, and I am."

With her on my lap, I had trouble focusing on all the naughty things I wanted to say to her. So I let myself drink in the vision of her, nude and straddling my thighs, and the words tumbled out of me. "I love your tits. They're the perfect size for my hands, and I know your nipples taste so damn good. I love sucking on them and making you squirm."

"Oh yes, please do that to me."

I surged forward, latching my hands behind her back, just above that sweet ass, but I kept my mouth several inches away from hers. "Not yet, baby. I haven't finished telling you my plans for your luscious body."

She bit her lip, letting it go little by little. "Tell me, please, Damian. Tell me all of it in your panty-melting voice."

"You don't have any panties for me to melt, which is too bad. I would've loved to shred your underwear." I tipped my head closer, but not too close, enough that I could exhale a soft, teasing breath onto her lips. "Have you ever worn silk lingerie?"

"No."

"I've got a silk scarf, one I bought for you."

"When did you buy that? You haven't left the resort."

I let my lips spread into a slow, sensual smile as I tugged her closer. "I ordered it overnight delivery, just for you, so I could drag it across your soft skin and make you wild for me. You'll shiver and moan and beg me to fuck you."

"But I'm ready to do that right now."

"Patience, baby. There's no rush." I traced my tongue over her bottom lip, loving the way she sucked in a breath. "I need to touch you, tease you, taste you for so long that you'll feel like you're losing your mind, but in the best way. I want to hear you beg me to make you come, but I won't, not until you're so wet it's dribbling down your inner thighs and you can barely breathe because you're so damn excited."

"I already feel that way." She spread her palms on my chest, swirling them in circles. "As for being outrageously wet for you... Well, feel it for yourself."

My cock throbbed, letting me know it couldn't wait much longer to be inside her. I couldn't wait either. Something about this woman made me harder than ever before and hot enough to melt steel. I slid my fingers down between her ass cheeks, feeling her slick heat.

She grabbed my hand, shoving it between her thighs. "Feel how much I want you."

"Fuck," I growled, like an animal. I felt like a wild beast right now, with her cream coating my fingers and the heat of her body penetrating my jeans. "We're skipping the rest of the dirty talk. I need to have you right now."

I stripped off my shirt and unzipped my jeans.

"Condom?" Heidi said.

"Shit." I leaned over to grab one from the box I'd left on the steps that led to the bed. Screw the bed. This time, I needed her right here on the floor.

Heidi started to move off my lap.

I grasped her hips to hold her in place. "Don't move. I want you here."

"Oh God, yes."

"This will be fast and hard." I pulled her snug against me and got to my knees, then dropped us onto the cushions on the floor with her underneath me. In seconds, I had the condom on. "Scream for me, baby."

I braced my hands at either side of her head and thrust into her, hard and fast like I'd promised I would. Couldn't go slow. Couldn't be the gentle lover, not tonight.

She wrapped her legs around me.

And I couldn't have held back even if I'd wanted to. Every pounding thrust made her tits jiggle, and when I pumped faster, the wagon started to shake. The heat of her surrounded my cock while the scent of her cream drowned my senses, and I couldn't stop myself from pummeling her like a mad man. She clutched my arms, her nails piercing my skin and scraping down my biceps. I lunged my head to seize her nipple and suck on it. She threw her head back and let out a sharp cry.

Words burst out of me, but I had no idea what I was saying.

Her body tensed, and she stopped breathing, her mouth gaping open and her eyes squeezed shut.

"Come for me, baby," I snarled.

She came like she was following my command. Her body clenched my cock over and over, making me growl like a beast again and grit my teeth. A bolt of white-hot lightning shot down my spine, and I couldn't hold it back anymore. I came so hard I couldn't see or do anything other than punch into her twice more until I had nothing left to give.

I collapsed on top of her, gasping for breath.

Heidi folded her arms around me, breathing as hard as I was. After a few minutes, she whispered in my ear, "Holy shit, Damian. That was… Oh God, you're amazing."

"Thanks." I lifted my head to look at her. "You were totally amazing too. I thought I was the master of dirty talk, but you outmatched me."

"Let's call it even. We both rocked."

"Definitely." I rolled off her, though all I could manage to do was lie sprawled on my back. "Good thing we ate first. I needed all those calories. Think I burned at least ninety percent of them in the last few minutes."

"Me too." She turned onto her side and kissed my shoulder. "Sorry I scratched you up. Does it hurt?"

I lifted my arms to examine them. I had red slashes on my biceps. "A few scratches, that's all. I'll survive, and it was totally worth the pain."

"Maybe I should kiss it better."

"After what just happened, I think I need sleep more than tender loving care."

"Yeah, I'm wiped out too. Let's go to bed and snuggle up."

I kissed the tip of her nose. "Sounds like a plan."

Chapter Seventeen

Heidi

I woke up but couldn't convince myself to open my eyes, much less get out of bed. Damian had his arm draped over my belly, his body cradling mine from behind, and his gentle breaths fluttered my hair. I loved lying here like this. It was peaceful and sensual at the same time. How could I love being with Damian, the last man on earth I ever wanted to get involved with? He was strange and cocky, sweet and sexy, dirty and funny. Okay, maybe I did see why I enjoyed spending time with him and making love with him.

So yeah, my celibacy vow lasted less than two days after I arrived at the resort. Months of no sex, and all it took to shatter my willpower was a palm reading. Why had I thought celibacy would cure me of my insecurities? That had to be the dumbest idea I'd ever come up with. Here with Damian, in this cozy little bed inside a cozy little wagon, I felt freer and stronger and more alive than ever before.

Damian stirred behind me, his cock stiffening.

I couldn't resist wriggling my bottom to rub it against his dick.

He pulled me tighter against his body and chuckled softly. "Good morning, sex kitten."

"Are you calling me that because we had awesome sex or because I'm part of the Kitten Brigade?"

"Both." He nuzzled my throat while his dick got even stiffer. "How about a quickie before breakfast?"

"Uh-uh." I turned my head to look at him, which put our faces an inch apart. "This morning, I need it long and slow and hot as hell."

"I can do that." He glided his hand down my belly to tease the hairs on my mound with his fingertips. "Should I let your screams echo through the resort, or do you want me to swallow them for you with a deep, thrusting kiss?"

My sex pulsed at his suggestion, and I no longer had any reason to pretend I didn't want him like crazy. "Deep and thrusting, please. Drive me crazy with your mouth and your dick."

"Anything for you, baby."

He'd started calling me baby last night, and I loved it. When other men had called me that, I didn't like it so much. But Damian knew how to shape those two syllables into the sweetest, sexiest pet name I'd ever heard. I even liked it when he called me sex kitten.

"It's weird," I said while he kept teasing me with his fingers, "but I don't feel anxious anymore. I'm not worried I'll make a fool of myself again, and I don't care if everyone finds out we're sleeping together. I want to be your girlfriend, but that's not terrifying anymore. I love it when you call me baby and sex kitten." I settled my hand over his on my mound and bent one knee, my foot planted on the bed, so I could push his hand between my folds. "Touch me everywhere, Damian. Touch me with your hands, your mouth, your tongue, every part of you. I'm done fighting how much I want you."

He chuckled again. "I figured that out last night."

"Good, then I don't need to explain it to you."

"No, I understand everything." He stroked me with his longest finger, making me suck in a sharp breath. "And I know how much you love dirty talk."

"Oh God, yes. Whisper filthy things to me, please."

"Every time you beg, it makes me want to fuck you until you can't walk anymore."

"Keep going. Touch me, talk to me, anything you want."

He slid his hand out from under my palm, laying it on top of mine. "I'm going to make you come with your own hand, but you won't move a muscle. I'll do everything."

I moaned because it was all I could manage to do. He'd hardly said anything, and already I was throbbing for him, in my clitoris and deep inside my body. With his erection plastered to my backside, he moved my fingers like I was an instrument and he was the virtuoso plucking my strings, drawing pleasure out of me like a song. I thrust my hips in time with his movements, feeling my own slickness on my fingers and the heat of his palm on the back of my hand.

"Damian," I whispered while he used my fingers to toy with my clit. "Damian, yes."

"Kiss me, Heidi."

I twisted my head around, seized his nape, and pulled him in for a deep kiss. Our tongues thrust in time with the movements of our joined hands, and when he pushed our fingers inside me, I cried out. Just like he'd promised, he swallowed my cry while plunging his tongue in time with the thrusts of our fingers.

Someone knocked on the door. "Damian? Are you in there?"

Damian tore his mouth away from mine and shouted, "Go away, Ollie. We're busy."

He never stopped pumping into me with our fingers, even while he shouted those words. The man had skills, for sure. Awesome skills, like he'd told me.

I moaned, then he sealed his mouth over mine again.

"Sorry to interrupt," Ollie called out, "but I thought you'd want to know your parents and your brother are here. Your mom seems awfully determined to barge into wherever you are. I told her to check in your room first, but she'll be back any minute."

Damian froze with his tongue in my mouth and our fingers inside me.

We both opened our eyes, our gazes locked.

He groaned so deeply I felt the vibrations in his chest. He sat up and rubbed his eyes with the heels of his hands. "Okay, we'll be out in a minute. Keep Mom away from the wagon for as long as possible."

"I'll try. But you know how she is."

"Sorry, Heidi," Damian said. "Looks like my family showed up early. I wasn't expecting them until this afternoon."

"That's okay. Maybe I should be gone before she storms the wagon."

"Why?"

His look of genuine confusion made me want to hug him, but I didn't understand why he seemed baffled.

"Your family is here," I said. "Your mom is here. I shouldn't be lying naked in your bed when she shows up, should I? Don't want to make this any more awkward for you than it has to be."

"My mother can be overprotective, but she isn't a monster. She's not about to throw a hex on you or something." He leaned over me, held up by one bent arm, his face so close I felt his breaths whispering over my lips. "You might want to get dressed, but not until after I finish what I started."

"We can't have sex now."

His lips kinked into a devilish smirk. "But I can finish you off."

"There's no time. Your family—"

My voice died the instant he shoved his hand between my folds and plunged three fingers inside me, pumping hard and fast. He stretched his thumb up to rub my hard nub.

And I came. Just like that. My back arched, my mouth fell open, and my entire body went rigid for a split second before the climax pulsated deep inside me and stole my breath. I clenched the sheets.

Damian covered my open mouth with his, silencing the single sharp cry that burst out of me.

"There," he said, "you're all done."

He jumped off the bed, grabbed my dress, and tossed it at me.

"Are you kidding me?" I asked. "You can't give me an orgasm, then take me out there to meet your mother."

"Get dressed, Heidi. She'll be here any second."

He didn't sound or look panicked. The idea of his mom finding us in flagrante didn't seem to bother him at all. I felt a little shaky, but that might've been from the climax I'd experienced seconds ago. It had been like a bomb exploding inside my body.

I got dressed.

So did Damian, and he found a hairbrush for me too. At least my hair wouldn't flash like a neon sign announcing, "Just got fucked by a hot gypsy." My dress was a little rumpled, that was all.

He gave me a quick kiss. "You look beautiful, baby."

"You're full of it, but your bullshit is sweet."

The door burst inward.

A dark-haired woman stood on the second step, her mouth tight. Her gaze locked onto Damian, then swerved to me. She lifted one perfectly plucked brow, staring at me for a second or two before zeroing her attention in on Damian again. "*Bună ziua, fiu.* Are you going to introduce us?"

"*Mamă,*" Damian said, "you can't barge in like you own the place. It's my wagon, not yours."

"If my boy has taken up with a sallow blonde, it's my responsibility to make sure he's not in over his head."

"You're being rude, *Mamă*. Heidi is my girlfriend, and she's not sallow."

The woman stepped into the wagon and marched straight to me. "*Scuze*, child, but I need to speak with my son alone."

Damian slung an arm around my shoulders. "No, you don't. Since you haven't bothered to ask, this is Heidi Mackenzie. We're dating. I like her, a lot, and you are not chasing her away."

The woman scanned me up and down, then offered her hand to me. While she shook it, she said, "I am Monica Petrescu, royal seer of the Ludar and divine conduit to the spirit world."

"Cut the crap, Mom," Damian said, though he didn't sound angry.

I leaned in close to him and whispered, "I thought your mother's name was Ileana."

"No, that's her stage name when she's doing her shtick for the neighbors."

His mother shouted over her shoulder, "Adrian, what in heaven's name are you doing out there? Come meet the foreigner our son has taken up with."

A man with salt-and-pepper hair mounted the steps, halting at the threshold. He smiled when he saw Damian. "Hey, kiddo, what's up? Is this your new girl? She's a looker, for sure."

Monica Petrescu shook her head, her lips ticking up into a faint smile. "Introduce yourself, dear."

The man climbed into the wagon and offered me his hand. "Adrian Petrescu. I'm not a royal anything or a conduit, and neither is my wife."

"It's nice to meet you," I said as we shook hands.

Adrian glanced at his wife. "She doesn't sound foreign to me."

Monica huffed. "She is clearly not Ludar. Her skin is so pale."

"Stefan's wife isn't Ludar either. We love her anyway."

Damian tightened his arm around my shoulders, and I let him tug me closer.

This was going to be one doozy of a day.

Chapter Eighteen

Damian

I could've wasted hours on trying to convince my mother that Heidi was not a foreigner just because she didn't have Ludar ancestry. Mom loved to trot out the Romanian phrases whenever I introduced her to a girl. How many Ludar women were there in the world? Probably not that many these days, at least not many who knew they were Ludar. There weren't exactly hordes of Rom of any ilk these days.

Heidi took it all in stride despite Mom's attempts to unsettle her. She might've looked a touch anxious now and then, but I stayed close to offer silent support. I also provided vocal support when my mother got too involved in her gypsy royalty routine.

Like when she waved a hand in a grand gesture and said, "Give me your hand, child. I need to read the lines and determine whether you are the right woman for my boy."

"Stop that, Mom," I said. "It's up to me to decide if Heidi is the right woman. Besides, I've already given her a palm reading, and it told me she has a beautiful heart. That's all I need to know."

Mom squinted at Heidi, roving her gaze over my girlfriend like she was checking for signs of demonic possession. "All right. If you read her, then I accept your assessment. Provisionally."

"Gee, thanks, Mom." Yeah, there was sarcasm in that statement. I loved my mother, but she seriously needed an editor to review every word she wanted to speak before she spoke it.

We all climbed out of the wagon.

My brother and his wife were waiting nearby, and they hurried over to us.

Before my mom could speak again, I barged in. "Heidi, this is my brother, Stefan, and his wife, Emily. Where are the kids, Stef?"

"We left them with Emily's parents. This sounded like an adults-only reunion, and I'm not talking about the nudist thing."

He threw a meaningful glance toward our mother.

Yeah, we both knew she was going to keep harassing Heidi, all in the name of protecting her full-grown son who knew how to take care of himself.

Stefan shook Heidi's hand, then looked at me. "Wow, you hit it outta the park this time, didn't you? This girl's wicked hot."

"And also a very nice person and very smart," I said pointedly.

My brother grinned. "You must have it bad. Should we start thinking about wedding dates?"

"No," our mother said. "I have not fully approved her yet."

I sighed. "Mom, you don't get to pick my girlfriends anymore. I haven't let you do that since I was fifteen, and we both know why."

Stefan chuckled. "Yeah, Mom only wanted us to date Ludar girls, but the only ones she could find had buck teeth and hairy moles on their faces, or they dressed like vampires." He glanced at my clothes, his brows lifting. "Guess you're into that now, though, huh? Does Heidi bite your neck, or do you bite hers?"

I rolled my eyes.

"Damian looks good in black," Heidi said. "But he dresses that way strictly for the tourists. The rest of the time, he wears a uniform."

"Uniform?" Stefan said, looking way too pleased about that. "Thought you quit the prison-guard thing so you could get away from that stuff."

"No, I quit to get away from the prison."

Heidi, who was standing next to me, slipped her arm around mine and leaned in to whisper, "Sorry. I didn't know the uniform thing was a secret."

"It's not, but I hadn't mentioned it to my family yet."

"Maybe we should show them your pilot project."

Would that appease my mother? Probably not, but it might distract her for a while. My mom wasn't an evil queen, but I knew she'd keep up the act for as long as possible to see how Heidi reacted.

"Okay," I said, "let's do it."

Heidi kissed my cheek.

Mom raked her assessing gaze over Heidi from head to toe. "Is her dress on backwards?"

I probably growled. "Mom, cut it out."

Heidi's dress was wrinkled and not exactly on straight, but it wasn't backwards.

My mother harrumphed, but then something past my shoulder caught her attention. Her expression brightened. "There's my darling Ollie. I have to say hello to that dear boy. *Scuze*."

She marched toward Ollie with Dad trailing after her.

"Don't worry about Mom," Stefan said to Heidi. "She's testing you, that's all. As long as you don't run away screaming or whack her with a baseball bat, you'll do fine."

"Thanks," Heidi said, sounding less than convinced.

"Ignore my brother," I said. "He's on strong meds to keep him from seeing leprechauns under every tree."

"Not leprechauns," Stefan said. "Vampires. I have erotic hallucinations about a sexy female vamp sucking on my…" He glanced down at his groin. "Neck."

"I don't think your 'neck' is big enough for anybody to suck on it."

Stefan threw an arm around his wife and hugged her close. "Oh wait, it wasn't a vampire. It's Emily who likes to sink her teeth into me."

Heidi smiled and laughed. "Guess naughtiness runs in the family, huh?"

I glanced at Mom and Ollie to see her holding his head with both hands and kissing his cheeks. Dad slapped Ollie's arm. Mom dragged Mara into a bear hug, then performed some kind of made-up gypsy blessing by waving her hands and tipping her head up.

Yeah, Mom loved to do that. It was part of her "Ileana the Gypsy Queen" act. Why she needed a stage name, I had no idea. When I was ten, I asked her. She told me she was "building the fantasy" for the neighbors and other people who asked her to entertain them at parties.

And people thought I was a show-off.

Well, I must have inherited it from Mom.

My parents came back over to us, and I led them all into the guest house to show them their rooms. Heidi rushed off to change clothes, but when she rejoined us, she stayed right by my side and didn't seem disquieted at all by my mom's antics.

Since her change of heart happened after we had sex, I could've convinced myself I was just that good in bed. Sure, I was good. But sex with me had never cured a woman of her insecurities. The first time I'd met Heidi, she had been a vivacious, carefree girl who loved to go nude and play miniten. Then she'd embarrassed herself with Ollie and, combined with all the times she'd forgiven her cheating ass of an ex, she'd lost her self-confidence.

Maybe screwing me hadn't cured her, but the time we'd spent getting to know each other must have played a part in her ongoing transformation. It was more like a return to her true self. She didn't need to change, just to get back to that carefree, fun girl she'd once been.

After my family got settled in, Heidi and I took them out to the pilot project. While we petted the horses and talked about my plans for horseback nature tours, Mom gradually let go of her haughty act and turned back into a semi-normal person. Like me, she could never quite be normal—and like me, she didn't want to be. But Mom started smiling and joking with the rest of us, so I knew she wouldn't harass Heidi too much more.

My family might have surprised me with their visit and their early arrival, but nobody surprised me more than Heidi. When Georgie nuzzled her cheek, she not only didn't freak, but she kissed his nose too and scratched under his chin. She also started a conversation with my mother, and they talked about everything from horses to palm reading to embarrassing stories from my childhood. Heidi told her own childhood stories, but she left out the stuff about her parents being such dicks.

I didn't blame her for omitting that.

Not once did Heidi seem anxious. I hadn't seen her this relaxed and outgoing since that day months ago when I'd first seen her.

Watching Heidi with my family, I got a strange pain in my chest. Her eyes sparkled in the sun, and whenever she smiled, I swore the entire world got brighter. I wanted to pull her into my arms and just hold her.

Was I falling for Heidi Mackenzie? I didn't know, but the idea that I might have been didn't bother me at all.

Chapter Nineteen

Heidi

At first, Damian's mom had seemed like a tough cookie who would rather spit at me and curse me to become a toad than call me "sweetie" and hug me. She hadn't done the latter yet, but she hadn't done the former either. That seemed like a good sign.

Monica Petrescu was a performer, like her son, though she played up the magic aspect while Damian relied more on sex appeal. They shared the same charisma and charm, though. I liked seeing him through the lens of his family. It showed me different sides to him that I might not have noticed otherwise and proved to me that he wasn't patient and sweet with only me. He treated his family the same way, even when he was a touch frustrated with his mom's antics.

I liked Monica, but I wasn't sure if she liked me until she cornered me in the hallway of the guest house. Since it was lunchtime, Damian had escorted us to the dining hall, but his mom waylaid me. Damian saw it and raised his eyebrows at me, like he was asking if I needed help. I smiled, and he seemed to get the picture that I could handle his mom.

Compared to my parents, the Petrescus were the perfect mom and dad.

Once the others had disappeared into the dining hall, Monica faced me. "You are not Ludar."

"No, I'm an average American girl."

She squinted at me. "My son doesn't know it yet, but he's in love with you."

Damian in love with me? I kind of doubted that. Sure, we liked each other—a lot—but love seemed like a giant leap. Being with Damian made me feel more like myself than I had in years, since before I hooked up with a cheating loser. Damian would never cheat on me. I had no facts to back up that belief, but I trusted him so much more than I'd trusted any other man in my entire life. I loved being with him, and I loved the way he made me feel, but I had no idea if I might fall for him.

Even if I did, I shouldn't let Damian feel that way about me. After meeting his family, I realized exactly how screwed up mine was. I couldn't drag him into my mess of a life. He deserved happiness and love, but I didn't know if I could give him that, or if my family would drain it out of him.

What if I was too screwed up to save? Damned by my parents' toxic relationship?

"I like Damian a lot," I said to Monica. "He's a great guy. But I think it's too early to start talking about love, especially with his mother. That's something he and I need to talk about, alone. No offense."

"I'm not offended, dear." She took my hand, turning it over so the palm faced up. Head down, she ran her fingers over the lines on my palm. "I like you, Heidi, but I can't give your relationship with Damian my blessing until I've spent more time with you."

"My relationship with him is something Damian and I should discuss without anyone else involved. I hope you and I can be friends, but honestly, the only person whose opinion matters to me is Damian."

She peered up at me, her head still bowed. "Your lines tell me a lot about you, but what you've said tells me even more."

My mouth had gotten dry, and I couldn't think of any response. What had I said? I wasn't sure which words that came out of my mouth had told her what she needed to know.

She clasped my hand in both of hers and met my gaze. "Your loyalty and spirit are a comfort to me."

Monica released my hand, then walked into the dining hall.

What on earth had she been talking about? I had no idea what our conversation had proved to her. Maybe she'd been reading my palm, and that had comforted her. Whatever.

I wandered into the dining hall, to the table where the Petrescus had gathered. The only empty seat was right next to Damian, so I sat down there.

Damian laid his hand on my thigh and murmured, "Mom saved that seat for you."

"What?"

"Stefan wanted to sit there, but she told him to move his ass. Well, she told him to 'relocate your derriere,' but it's the same thing. She wanted you to sit beside me." He squeezed my thigh, aiming his sweet smile at me. "Mom likes you."

"Oh. I'm glad."

"But not as much as I like you."

Warmth blossomed in my chest, blooming outward until it suffused my entire body. It wasn't lust, though. This feeling stemmed from something softer and sweeter, something that touched a part of me no one had ever managed to touch before. How did Damian always know the right thing to say? How did he pull off being arrogant and dirty but tender and caring too? The contradictions somehow made sense because he was…Damian.

I didn't get a chance to respond to what he'd said. His brother started talking to him, and I enjoyed listening to their banter. They loved to tease each other, but underneath the sarcasm, I could tell they loved each other. They loved their parents too, and Monica and Adrian adored their sons.

My parents had worried more about whose fault this or that was than about whether I had a happy childhood.

A lump hardened in my throat.

But then Damian squeezed my thigh again, flashing me his heart-melting smile, and I forgot to worry about the past.

Everyone chatted during lunch, with lots of good-natured teasing and laughter thrown in too, but I couldn't make myself get as involved in the conversation as I used to do. Maybe the old me would come back eventually, or maybe that version of me had been an illusion. Recent events had made me gun shy about pretty much everything, so I probably shouldn't condemn myself as a lost cause until I'd recovered from my own mistakes and come to terms with my opposite-of-perfect family.

Damian kept squeezing my thigh occasionally and giving me supportive smiles. Tender smiles. The kind that made my tummy flutter.

I couldn't help smiling at him too. Whenever our eyes met, our lips curved up. I wondered if he felt the same chest tightness and tummy flutters every time we looked at each other. I hadn't spent much time around Damian until this week, yet I'd started to feel like I'd known him forever. Which was crazy. But it felt too good to fight it.

After lunch, as we exited the dining hall, Damian pulled me aside and waited for everyone else to file out of the building. They were headed for the lawn where Eve and Val had arranged to hold a soccer match. Once they had all departed, Damian grasped my hands and tugged me closer, our bodies almost touching.

"I need to have you all to myself," he said, "at least for a while. Family time is great, but we're still figuring out this thing between us, and having everybody else hanging around makes that more difficult."

"Yeah, it kind of does." I inhaled a deep breath just so I could enjoy the enticing scent of him. Why did he always smell so damn good? It wasn't cologne. He had a naturally delicious scent. "What did you have in mind?"

"Let's go to the hot spring."

"You mean the place where couples like to go to get it on?"

His lips twitched upward the tiniest bit, and he tugged me even closer, wrapping his arms around me. "No, I mean the hot spring where people who aren't total horndogs go to relax. The getting-it-on part is optional."

"I'd love to go there with you, with or without sex."

"Good. I haven't gone there much since I started working here. Too busy."

Hand in hand, we left the guest house and ambled past the lawn toward the nature trail. The soccer game was in full swing, with Val and the younger guests competing against the Silver Foxes. Val had been a professional soccer star—though in the rest of the world they called it football—and his team even won the Olympics. Still, the Silver Foxes always made him work for every goal.

Damian accelerated his pace as we entered the woods.

"In a hurry?" I asked.

"Of course I am. You won't strip naked for me until we get to the hot spring." He eyed me sideways. "Unless you aren't going to do that at all."

"You didn't give me a chance to grab my swimsuit, so I won't have much choice, will I?" Smiling, I bumped my shoulder into his. "Planned it that way, didn't you?"

"No, I would never do that. I'm not, like, an exhibitionist or anything." He wrapped an arm around my shoulders, strapping me to his side. "Okay, yeah, I am an exhibitionist."

"Uh-uh. You're a sexy Ludar prince with magic palm-reading skills, but I haven't seen you do anything that might qualify as exhibitionism."

He grinned. "Not yet. Maybe I've been holding back for professional reasons."

I spotted the sign that announced the hot spring was to the right, and I broke into a dead run, sprinting down the offshoot path. Over my shoulder, I shouted, "Catch me if you can."

Damian grinned again and took off after me. "The chase is the best part."

Our laughter echoed through the woods as we raced down the trail. I kept glancing back to see how close Damian was getting, but I decided he must've been holding back because he never got closer than fifteen feet or so behind me. The second I burst into the little clearing around the hot spring, I tore my clothes off and flung them away, not caring where they landed. I was breathing hard, but smiling too, and I hadn't felt this exhilarated…ever. How could letting Damian chase me become the best time I'd ever had? It was a silly, frivolous thing to do.

Maybe that was why I loved it. Silly and frivolous used to be my forte.

Damian dashed into the clearing, stopped a few feet from me, and got rid of his clothes. He was still grinning, like he had during our entire chase, and he breathed even harder than I did. He bent over, hands on his thighs. "Gimme a minute. I'm too old for high-speed pursuit."

He turned his head to the side to smirk at me.

"Yeah, sure," I said, "you're totally wiped out. Guess you aren't as manly and athletic as I thought. Oh well, we can put off swimming in the hot spring until you're feeling better. I'll get dressed."

I leaned over like I was about to pick up my shirt.

Damian straightened and pulled me into his arms. "No clothes. Once you take them off, they stay off until we go back to the resort."

"Is that the Ludar prince's royal decree?"

"You're damn straight it is." He shuffled toward the hot spring, forcing me to back up to it until my heels reached the rocky edge. "Dive in, Heidi. The water's warm, but not as hot as you."

He pulled his arms away.
And I dived backward into the blue water.

Chapter Twenty

Damian

Heidi and I did not have sex in the hot spring. She was game, but I suggested we should wait awhile before we got it on again. Yeah, I said that. Me. I'd never taken a celibacy vow, and I wasn't exactly known for my restraint when it came to sex, but I'd never pestered a woman to sleep with me either. Still, not doing it when the girl wanted to wasn't my style either. What about Heidi made me want to do anything, even go without sex, just to be with her?

When Heidi dived backward into the hot spring, her face had lit up with the most beautiful, joyful smile I'd ever seen. I got a weird tightness in my chest, like I was having a high blood-pressure attack or something. For a minute, maybe longer, I stood there and watched her paddling around in the blue waters with steam curling up from the surface. Her joy softened into a look of blissful satisfaction, but that didn't make sense. How could she feel blissfully happy from swimming?

The more important question was, why did I feel blissfully happy watching her?

When she dunked her head under the water, I jumped in feet first. Water sprayed up around me.

Heidi surfaced, drenched and grinning. "Took you long enough. I thought you'd gone catatonic the way you were staring at me. Or maybe you think I'm crazy."

"You're crazy-hot, that's for sure." I swam to her and hugged her body to mine. "I like watching you have fun. Nobody does fun better than Heidi Mackenzie."

"I kind of forgot how to enjoy myself." She swept wet hair away from her face, then clasped her hands at my nape. "You helped me remember. Thank you, Damian."

"Nah. All I did was seduce you. The 'fun' part you did all by yourself."

Her lips curled into a sexily teasing smile. "Seduction is the fun part."

That was when I made my insane announcement. "Let's not have sex for a while."

Her brows shot up. "Are you serious?"

"Yeah. I'd like us to get to know each other and spend sex-free time together." Yeah, I must've gone stark-raving bonkers. I had a gorgeous, incredible woman in my arms, and I told her we shouldn't sleep together.

Heidi snuggled up to me, her slick, naked body mashed to mine and those beautiful tits mounded against my chest. "But I want you, Damian. Right now."

"We kind of rushed into the whole naked-and-grunting phase of our relationship. Let's hold off for a little while, okay?"

She blinked slowly, twice. "You're serious, aren't you?"

"Yes."

"Okay." She wriggled away from me, paddling backward. "Wanna chase me in the water?"

"That wouldn't be a fair race. I mean, I've got muscles." I raised my arms, elbows bent, and flexed my biceps. "See? I'll catch you in five seconds at most."

"I'm in great shape, so you'll lose that bet."

"Bet? Guess we should have stakes, then. Five bucks?"

She shook her head, giving me that teasing smile again. "If I win, you take me—the dirty way. Right here, right now."

Those sounded like dangerous stakes, but I could swim faster than a girl. Couldn't I? "Okay. And if I win, you play miniten in the nude, but we don't have sex."

"You're on."

Heidi spun around and started swimming.

I hoisted myself out of the water onto the ledge and leaped into the pool. Even without a springboard, I could propel myself pretty far.

Heidi glanced back and shrieked—with joy, not terror.

Splashing down a foot behind Heidi, I lashed an arm around her waist and tugged her into me. "I win."

She splashed me. "Cheater."

"I said I could catch you in less than five seconds. Never claimed I'd do it by swimming."

"Yeah, I should've written a contract that spelled out the rules of our wager." She wriggled around until she was facing me. "You're way too smart. I'll have to be more careful in the future when we make bets."

I cleared my throat. "You do realize that now you have to play miniten, clothes-free."

"Yep. I never welch on a promise."

We swam in the spring for a little while longer, but we didn't make any more bets. Instead, we did goofy things like diving in cannonball style, splashing each other mercilessly, and chasing each other just for the hell of it. I let Heidi catch me twice. Gotta give a girl a chance, right? It wasn't her fault I had masculine prowess on my side.

Heidi rolled her eyes and splashed me when I said that out loud. "Are all Ludar princes arrogant and sexist?"

"No, only the ones you beg to fuck you."

She splashed me again.

When we finally left the hot spring, Heidi didn't put her clothes back on.

I raised one brow. "Does this mean Heidi the hot naturism enthusiast is back?"

"Maybe. I did promise I'd play miniten in the nude if you caught me."

Had I expected her to renege on our bet? Maybe I had, but not because I thought she was a coward. Overcoming fears usually took longer than a couple of days. Didn't it? I couldn't say for sure since I'd never had any anxieties as strong as hers. I would've loved to believe I'd been the reason she came out of her khaki-clad shell, but even I wasn't a big enough dick to do that.

I threw our clothes over my shoulder, and we walked back to the resort while holding hands. When we emerged from the woods, both naked, and sauntered over to the lawn, everyone stopped to stare at us. Ollie grinned. Mara clapped and grinned. Eve waved and grinned. Val folded his arms over his chest and nodded appreciatively.

Sylvester Norris hollered, "Way to go, Damian! You got our girl out of her funk."

"Watch it, Sly," I hollered back. "Might use my mystical gypsy powers to curse you if you don't stop harassing Heidi."

"Harassing her?" Sly waggled his eyebrows. "Our boy Damian's in love, eh?"

I had no idea how not wanting Sylvester to make Heidi feel weird about going nude equated to me being in love with her. A screw must've popped loose in the old fart's head.

Heidi and I played against Sly and his wife, Ruth, and beat them in two miniten games. Then we whupped Heidi's friends Shelby and Taylor, and after that, we creamed Val and Eve. Heidi grinned and laughed and shouted cheerfully sarcastic comments at our opponents, like I'd heard she used to do. I'd met her during the peak of her get-Ollie-back craziness, so I never got to see her in full-on Heidi mode—happy, carefree, and enjoying life with zeal. Did I have zeal? I wasn't sure, but nobody had ever described me that way. "Zeal" seemed like the appropriate way to describe Heidi, though. I couldn't wait until she climbed out of her funk all the way and became the girl everyone had described to me, the girl who lived every moment to the fullest and burned with the brightest candle on earth.

After miniten, we got dressed and headed out to the horse pasture. Heidi had suggested it. She wanted to spend more time with Lenny and Georgie, not only to keep her immersion therapy going but also because she loved the boys and they loved her. Maybe Heidi wasn't ready for a trail ride, but she got more and more comfortable with the horses every day.

"Wanna brush them?" I asked about ten minutes after we got to the pasture. We were outside the fence, but Heidi had spent the entire time petting and talking to the boys. "It'll mean going through the gate, but I'll be right beside you the whole time. What do you say?"

She stopped blinking for a few seconds, her gaze trained on me, then she blew out a breath that relaxed her tensed shoulders. She smiled. "Yeah, I'd love to brush them."

"Awesome." I got a brush out of the shed and brought it to Heidi. "Here. You hold on to this while I open the gate."

I swung the gate open just enough to accommodate us and sidled through it first, then waved for Heidi to come in.

Georgie walked right past me and ambled over to Heidi to nuzzle her cheek.

She giggled. "His whiskers tickle."

"He's definitely in love." I scratched Lenny behind his ears. "At least this guy still likes me. I was starting to feel rejected."

Lenny walked over to Heidi and nuzzled her hand, the one holding the brush.

I shook my head. "Damn, I *have* been rejected. How can I compete with two big strapping males who could trample me?"

Georgie wiggled his lips over hers.

"Jeez," I said, pretending to be offended, "no way can I compete with a Georgie kiss. He's never done that to me."

She grinned, the brilliant expression aimed at me. "You're the only big strapping male I let kiss me with tongue."

"Well, at least I've got one thing on them." I laid a hand on Lenny's chest and pushed. "Back, Lenny. Come on, back up." When the horse walked backward a few paces, I patted his neck. "Good boy. Now, let Georgie have his turn first. I know Heidi's irresistible, but she can only brush one of you at a time."

"I'm irresistible?" Heidi said.

"Absolutely." I rubbed Georgie's forehead. "Males of any species are putty in your hands."

"Maybe I'll test that hypothesis later and knead you like putty."

Oh yeah, that sounded wonderful. My dick definitely loved the idea since it jerked the second I pictured Heidi kneading my body with those sexy hands.

"Start brushing," I told her. "To these guys, it's like a day at the spa. I'll be right beside you the entire time."

Heidi began brushing Georgie's neck, tentatively at first, then she relaxed into the task. She looked at ease, like skimming a brush over a horse's coat was the most soothing thing she'd ever done. I loved brushing animals. It always made me feel the way Heidi looked right now. Once Heidi had brushed Georgie all over, even his rump, she walked over to Lenny and gave him the same treatment.

I stayed with Georgie, to keep him out of the way.

Once Heidi finished with Lenny, we walked back out the gate.

"You brushed a horse all by yourself," I said. "That's a big step."

She shrugged one shoulder. "You were right next to me the whole time."

"Not when you brushed Lenny. I stayed with Georgie then."

"I know. But you were close by." She kissed my cheek. "Thank you, Damian. It's good to get over at least one fear, but I know I still have more of them to deal with."

"One step at a time, that's the best way to do it."

She wrapped her arms around my waist, pressing her body to mine. "Let's go play chess."

I pulled my head back, gazing at her with a new appreciation. "You really aren't an airhead bimbo, are you?"

She gave my ankle a gentle kick. "Hey, that's not a very nice thing to say. Did you ever think I was an airhead bimbo?"

"No, but I'm sure that's what a lot of the dickwads you dated thought. From what you've said, they sure didn't treat you like a mature, intelligent, sexy-as-hell woman."

"What does 'sexy as hell' have to do with being smart?"

"Nothing. I threw that in there because you've got your hot body glued to mine." I linked my hands at the small of her back. "Not that I'm complaining."

"Have you changed your mind about sex?"

"No. So we'd better play chess. Anything sexier than that will give me a hard-on for sure."

"Okay." She kissed me on the mouth this time. "Prepare to be annihilated on the chessboard."

She took off down the trail.

And I raced after her with Heidi's laughter echoing through the woods.

Chapter Twenty-One

Heidi

I slept with Damian that night, in my room, naked, though we didn't do anything remotely sexual. I loved lying in his arms, listening to his shallow, even breaths and feeling them whispering against my neck. Ever since the first night we had sex in his wagon, I'd been sleeping better than I had in years. The more time I spent with him, the less I worried about making a fool of myself or doing something dumb like going back to my ex. No, Grant could never convince me to do that. Never again.

Damian had to go back to work in the morning, so after breakfast, we kissed goodbye. I spent the morning hanging out with my friends. I had kind of ignored the Kitten Brigade a lot of the time, caught up in pretending I didn't want Damian, then sleeping with Damian, and now wishing I were with him instead of with my friends. I loved these girls, but I felt like my best self when I was with him.

A morning full of Kitten Brigade craziness kept me occupied, and I did have fun. But my thoughts always gravitated back to Damian. Sweet, sexy, naughty, tender Damian. I'd only been half teasing when I told him I'd love to knead him like putty.

I ate lunch in the dining hall with Damian and the Kittens. They made lots of suggestive, teasing comments about the two of us, but Damian took it all in stride. He never got annoyed with anybody, not even when Sylvester stopped by our table to give Damian a box of glow-in-the-dark condoms so he wouldn't, as Sly put it, "get confused in the dark and forget where you put that saber."

That had to be the dumbest joke ever, but Damian laughed and said, "When was the last time you even pulled your saber out of its sheath, Sly?"

"More often than you might think." Sylvester winked. "I'm old, not dead."

I'd gotten used to senior citizens making sex jokes. But I tried not to visualize the Silver Foxes doing the bump-and-grind.

Damian handed the condom box back to Sly. "In that case, maybe you better hold on to these."

The senior citizen winked again. "You can get your own box in the gift shop."

Sylvester opened the package to bring out a handful of packets, which he gave to Damian. Then he walked away with the box of rubbers.

Damian stuffed the glow-in-the-dark condoms in his pocket.

I leaned in to whisper in his ear, "Those could be fun."

"Mm-hm." He glanced at me sideways. "Maybe we'll try them out tonight."

Oh God, I hoped he meant that.

Damian studied me the way he often did when he wanted to ask me something. "Do you like working as a pharmacy technician?"

"Huh?" I snapped back to reality, shattering the fabulous fantasy I'd been enjoying that involved him naked on his stomach while I licked my way up his backside. "No, I don't love my job. It's okay, and the pay is decent, but I only became a pharmacy technician to try to appease my parents. They wanted me to be a doctor. I wanted to be an event planner. So we compromised, and I became a pharmacy technician."

"How is that a compromise? Event planning has nothing to do with medicine."

I shrugged. "At least I didn't have to go to medical school."

"Event planner makes a lot more sense for you. I bet you'd rock that job."

His statement made me feel glowy inside, but I also got a tightness in my throat. "Your food is getting cold."

Neither of us mentioned my job again.

When lunch was over, Damian went back to work, and I played rummy with the Kittens in the entertainment room. Yesterday, Damian and I had played chess in here by ourselves, and I'd beaten him twice. He beat me once. Though I'd always liked chess, the game had never been so much fun before. Damian would occasionally hold a chess piece to his forehead, shut his eyes, and make ghost-like moaning noises for a few seconds. Then he'd slap the piece down on the board and declare, "I have seen the future. I'm going to win, so you might as well surrender now."

"You don't surrender in chess. You resign."

"I never give up."

"No kidding." I made my move, taking his pawn. "It's one of the sexiest things about you."

"Let's make this a little more interesting and play strip chess."

"Maybe next time."

Playing rummy with my girlfriends wasn't as much fun as doing anything with Damian, but I enjoyed it anyway. I lost every game, though. Thinking about the Ludar prince who had pursued me with tenderness and sensuality kept me distracted. I hoped he'd meant it when he said we could have sex tonight. Making love with Damian felt so good, and not just because of the orgasms involved. It felt right. The intimacy we shared meant more than lust.

After the card games, my friends wanted to go on a nature hike, but I wanted to stick closer to the resort. Yeah, okay, I was hoping to catch a glimpse of Damian while he performed his concierge duties. All morning, I'd kept seeing him walking from the guest house to the caretaker's house, or from the guest house to one of the other buildings. He always noticed me and waved, flashing me a sexy grin. All his smiles were hot, from the subdued ones to the I-want-your-body-now variety.

Every time he smiled at me, I smiled back, overcome by a giddy sensation.

While my friends marched down the nature trail, I hung out on the lawn, relaxing in an Adirondack chair. I didn't see Damian for an hour. Then he walked out of the guest house wearing his Ludar prince garb, looking so damn lickable. Maybe I'd told him on the day I arrived that his Dracula-chic outfit didn't do anything for me, but I had lied. We both knew it, even then. Now that I was done fighting my attraction to him, I could say it out loud.

I wanted to do more than simply say it, though. I wanted to shout it to the rooftops, through the sky, and straight into outer space.

I cupped my hands like a megaphone and hollered, "Woo-hoo, Damian, strut that gypsy-vampire sex appeal."

He grinned and blew me a kiss.

So I blew him one too.

Everyone else on the lawn gave me knowing smiles. Ruth Norris clapped and said, "You go, girl. About time you found the right man, and a hot one too. Bet he's a god in bed."

"He sure is," I shouted loud enough everyone, including Damian, could hear it.

Damian blew me another kiss, smiling with so much sizzling sweetness that my heart stuttered. Only he could be sweet and naughty at the same time.

I watched Damian unlock his wagon and bring out the sandwich board that advertised "a genuine Rom experience" and listed his specialties—palm reading and tarot reading. He set the sign up a few yards in front of the wagon's door, which he left open.

As soon as he disappeared inside, I wandered toward the guest house.

I ran into Mara just coming out of it. She almost collided with me since she had her head down, focused on the clipboard she held.

"Oh!" Mara said, her head jerking up. "Sorry. I wasn't looking, was I?"

"No problem. What's got you so distracted? Must be some heavy marketing stuff." Though Mara was the marketing director at Au Naturel, I didn't think she'd be pondering pay-per-click advertising while walking out of the guest house.

Mara shook her head. "Wedding stuff. Ollie and I are getting married in three weeks, and I still haven't nailed down all the details. Ollie offered to help, but I know he's super busy with work. Besides, men don't get all the wedding stuff."

"Yeah, I guess not. Maybe I can help."

"Oh no, I couldn't ask you to do that. You're a guest."

"I'm a friend too, right? So I absolutely can volunteer to assist the bride."

Mara gave me a grateful smile. "That would be wonderful, but honestly, you don't have to."

"Once upon a time, I wanted to be an event planner. Even interned with a real expert. And I would be honored to take some of the wedding load off your shoulders, Mara. It's the least I can do after how sweet you've been to me, even when I was trying to steal Ollie from you."

She stared at me for several seconds. "That would be amazing, Heidi. Thank you."

I took the clipboard from her. "Let's go sit on the lawn and see what we can work out for you."

Mara and I spent two hours hashing out the details, first while sitting on the lawn, then in my room in the guest house. We didn't have the entire wedding mapped out, but we had a plan. I insisted we split the duties, not only to keep Mara from sinking under the weight of it all, but also to get things done faster. We had a lot of calls to make, but the most important task required a trip into town.

"We have to get you a gorgeous dress," I said while Mara and I walked down the stairs, heading for the main doors of the guest house. "Isn't there a dress shop in town? I think I remember seeing one."

"Yeah, there is a shop." At the bottom of the stairs, Mara stopped and bit her lip. "Um, would you mind going with me to find a dress? Eve is so busy, and I don't want to bother her."

"Sure, I'll go with you."

Mara smiled. "Thank you, Heidi. You are such a wonderful friend."

Her compliment made me feel a little weird, but I knew she meant it. Mara Severins was the kindest person on earth, and I was lucky to have her as a friend. I told her that out loud too, which made her blush. Yeah, I completely understood why Ollie fell for Mara. They were so perfect for each other.

Were Damian and I right for each other? I tried not to think about that too much. Not yet.

He found me at dinnertime and suggested we should take our meal to go and "dine in Ludar splendor inside the mystical gypsy wagon where pleasure is always on hand." Then he'd winked and added, "Or by mouth, whichever you prefer."

"Maybe I prefer the cock method of receiving gypsy pleasure."

"I was hoping you'd say that."

"Does this mean you'll make love to me tonight?"

He molded his lips to mine, holding them there for a moment that felt like a blissful eternity. Then he held my hand to his forehead, shut his eyes, and made those ghost-moan noises again. When he looked straight into my eyes, he murmured, "I foresee nudity, sweat, the scent and flavor of your cream, and multiple orgasms."

If anyone else had told me that, I would've laughed and walked away. But whenever Damian talked that way, I got wet and tingly between my thighs. And whenever he smiled at me in that sweetly understanding way, I got an ache in a different place altogether—in my heart. It was the best kind of pain. Maybe I was falling for him. Here, tonight, in his gypsy wagon, I suddenly realized I wouldn't mind if I did tumble head over heels for him.

No, I wouldn't mind at all.

Chapter Twenty-Two

Damian

Okay, so I lasted less than forty-eight hours before I crumbled and made love to Heidi again. I never claimed to be a bastion of willpower, did I? Besides, she seemed to be better and better every minute, dealing with her anxieties faster than I could've ever dreamed she might. Was it temporary? No, I didn't believe that. Heidi had suppressed her natural tendencies for months out of shame and fear, but now she was unleashing them one by one. It was real and permanent. I believed that.

My prediction for last night came true. And the wagon might've been rocking and rolling, which I hadn't foreseen with my bogus hand-on-the-forehead prediction. That might've been only a ploy to get her to touch me, not that I needed an excuse.

This morning, I woke up with Heidi sprawled on top of me, her cheek on my chest and her hair spilling over my skin. Gently, I brushed enough hair away so that I could see her face.

She was smiling in her sleep.

Yeah, my heart melted when I saw that. She looked so…at peace.

I lay there covered in Heidi for ten minutes before she finally roused, fluttering her lids and sighing. Her body writhed on top of mine as she tried to stretch, though she couldn't quite do it from that position.

She lifted her head to gaze at me with a dreamily satisfied smile. "Good morning."

"Any morning when I wake up with you is the best morning ever."

"For me too." She wriggled, and my already stiff dick twitched. "Ready for wake-up sex?"

"I'm always ready for you." I rolled us over onto our sides and skimmed my hand over her hip to her thigh. "Wish I could spend the day with you, but I'm on duty again."

"That's okay. I can entertain myself." She rolled onto her back to stretch her entire body, her arms above her head, and moaned. "You really do work hard, don't you? I watched you running here, there, and everywhere for hours yesterday."

"You watched me for hours? Sounds like stalking. Maybe I should lock you up in my private jail cell so I can interrogate you the Ludar way."

"Only if the Ludar way means lots and lots of sex. I wouldn't mind handcuffs."

"Sorry, I don't have any of those." But maybe I could order some online, the kind with padded cuffs designed for sexy playtime.

Heidi stared into space for a few seconds, then she pushed up onto her elbows. "Where was your family yesterday? I didn't see them at all."

"They went sightseeing. I gave them a map of all the best attractions in the area, including restaurants, so they could have the full tourist experience."

"Aren't they disappointed you didn't go with them?"

"Nah, they understand I have a job to do. Besides, they came for a surprise visit, which means I didn't have a chance to beg for time off. They get it." I sat up, allowing myself five seconds to admire her breasts before I got back to business. "My family will be hanging around the resort today, so you might have to submit to more of my mom's well-meaning, if misplaced, protective harassment."

"I like Monica. She's a tough cookie but with a soft center, like a caramel-filled sugar cookie."

"Sugar cookie?" I chuckled. "Let's not tell Mom you described her that way. She likes to think she's a force to be reckoned with."

"Oh, she is. But considering what my parents are like, Monica is a breath of fresh, cool air."

"Well, I hope you still feel that way after today."

She sat up and tickled my chin. "Relax, Damian. I'm not a basket case anymore."

"You never were one."

I grabbed my phone off the top step and checked the time. "Afraid we'll have to skip wake-up sex. I need to be at work in twenty minutes. Didn't realize I'd slept so late."

She kissed me. "You go on. I might relax in your bed for a while if that's okay."

"You can rub yourself all over my bed for as long as you want. I love having your scent all over me and my sheets."

"I'll make sure to cover this bed with me." She pulled the sheet up and rubbed it over her belly, then up to her breasts, massaging them with the soft fabric. "Have fun at work."

The last thing I wanted to do right now was to walk away from the beautiful, naked, horny woman in my bed, but I had to go. I'd never missed a day of work at any of my jobs. So I kissed Heidi and said, "Call me if you're still tangled up in my sheets at lunchtime. We can eat in bed."

"Even if I'm not still in your bed at lunch, we can eat here."

"It's a date. Now, I need to get dressed and go."

Heidi watched me while I climbed off the bed, found my clothes, and pulled them on. She kept rubbing the sheet over her belly and chest while licking her lips. Damn, she was the sexiest woman in the universe. So what if I'd never visited another planet? I knew without any doubt that not even the naughtiest alien sex kitten could've been hotter than Heidi Mackenzie.

I left her in the wagon, on my bed, naked and willing. And I went to work.

Yesterday had seemed like a blur, with one guest after another asking for my help. I must've run back and forth between the guest house and the caretaker's house two dozen times, not to mention all the trips to the daycare center on the opposite side of the guest house. Kids made so many messes, but that wasn't my job. I had to ferry stuff over there because the parents forgot their diaper bags, or they left the kid's medication in their room, or Mommy needed her Xanax. I only got one call like that. Mostly, I brought aspirin to those moms and dads. Considering how loud their kids loved to scream, for no reason I could see, I understood why their parents needed headache medicine.

Today turned out to be no less exhausting. Ollie and Mara were supposed to take a group of guests on a guided nature hike, but I got a call from Ollie not five minutes before the hike was scheduled to begin. The second I picked up the call, before I even said hello, Ollie started talking.

"Help," he moaned, doing a totally fake anguished voice. He added a sarcastic whimper at the end of his moan. "Mara just told me she can't co-lead the hike because Heidi's helping her with the wedding plans. You can't leave me alone with these old farts. They're crazy."

I'd forgotten the hike was a special event for seniors. And why was Heidi playing wedding planner for Mara?

"You love the fogies," I said. Since he'd used his sarcastic fake moan to make me feel sorry for him, I decided to use my sarcastic baby-talk voice to irritate him. "And they think you're the cutest wittle thing in the whole wide world. Sing a song for them, wittle Awee."

"Awee? What in the world is that supposed to mean?"

"It's your name in baby talk. Better get used to that kind of thing. I'm sure you'll have Mara knocked up any day now, if you haven't already."

"We're waiting until after the wedding and the honeymoon."

"Uh-huh. You know what they say about best-laid plans."

He snorted. "You are so not funny, man. Get out here and help me before the gray-hair brigade jumps on me like a horde of zombies."

"Why don't you get Val or Eve to help?"

"Val went into town to buy bathroom supplies. Man, these people use a lot of toilet paper. Anyway, Eve is busy teaching an arts-and-crafts class. I think it's how to make shit out of duct tape or something."

"Hey, don't knock duct-tape shit. I had a girlfriend who made me a wallet out of that stuff, and not only was it waterproof, but it lasted forever."

"I remember that wallet. The duct tape was rainbow-colored." Ollie sighed, sounding genuinely miserable. "Please lead this hike with me. I hate doing it alone, and we haven't had a chance to hang lately."

Yeah, we were both too busy with work and women.

"Okay, fine," I said. "I'll be your bodyguard."

I tucked my phone into my pocket and hurried to my room to swap my uniform sneakers for a pair of hiking boots and to grab my favorite baseball cap, then I headed out to the lawn. Ollie and the fogies were waiting there. My best friend was laughing at something one of the older guests had said. He slapped the guy on the arm and started talking while making big hand gestures.

Yeah, he looked stressed-out and desperate for help.

When Ollie saw me approaching, he grinned. "The D-Man is here! Let's get this party started."

"Party?" I said when I reached him. "I thought it was a nature hike and you were about to drop dead from stress if I didn't show up to lend a hand."

Ruth and Sylvester Norris pushed past the other guests to get to me and Ollie. Ruth patted Ollie's cheek. "This dear sweet boy needs all the help he can get."

"Hey, I'm not helpless," Ollie said. "Damian needs fresh air. That's the only reason I conned him into doing this. Excuse me, I talked him into it, not conned."

My best friend was smirking. Oh yeah, he had totally conned me into this.

"You didn't need me at all, did you?" I asked, pretending to be offended. I raised my hands, fingers spread, and tipped my head back like I was communing with the sky. "I call upon the ancient gods of the Ludar to lay a horrendous curse on Oliver Jackson. May he lose his sense of smell forever."

"Awesome," Ollie said, grinning. "I'll never again get nauseous when I smell liverwurst."

One of the older guests, who I didn't recognize, raised his hand. "Can you curse my ex-wife? She got the Boca Raton house in the divorce, but she only wanted it because I loved that place. She hates Florida."

I stifled a laugh. "Sorry, man, I only curse people who annoy *me.*"

Ollie gave the introductory speech about the rules of the hike and the things we might see along the way. We both strapped on hefty backpacks stuffed full of snacks and water bottles, plus a few outdoor essentials like bug spray and calamine lotion. For the next half hour, we explained nature to a dozen senior citizens. Well, Ollie did the explaining. I wasn't anywhere near as well-versed in the wildlife and plant life as he was.

We had lunch at the lake, on the beach. While the guests broke off into three groups and entertained each other, Ollie and I set up our picnic blanket a short distance away from everybody else.

A hummingbird buzzed past us, and Ollie smiled like he was reminiscing about something.

I elbowed him in the side. "Are you ever going to tell me why you get sentimental about hummingbirds?"

"Sorry, I've been sworn to secrecy. It's a private thing between me and Mara."

"Whatever." I ate a bite of my sandwich before I asked the question I'd wanted to ask him since he tricked me into going on this hike. "Why did Mara bail on you at the last minute? That's not like her at all."

"She bailed on me last night. I couldn't say no. She's super stressed about all that wedding junk."

"You do realize you can never speak the phrase wedding junk when you're within earshot of Mara. Practice saying 'yes, dear, I'd love to pick out place settings with you.' Then ooh and ah over that crap when you're shopping with her."

Ollie threw a potato chip at me, which bounced off my nose. "What do you know about weddings? You're a confirmed bachelor."

I wasn't feeling confirmed anymore. The more time I spent with Heidi, the more I wanted to do lots of things that didn't involve sex. Cuddling sounded awesome. Maybe some adoring gazes too. Hand-holding would be perfect. I could recite a poem or something like that too. Maybe I'd love to just hold her in my arms for a long, long time.

"Whoa-ho," Ollie said, looking genuinely surprised. "Were you just daydreaming lovey-dovey thoughts about Heidi? Never seen that look on your face before. Is Damian Petrescu, the Ludar play-boy, finally ready to settle down?"

"What if I am? It's not a crime."

"No, it's awesome. We could have a double wedding."

"Double what? Whoa, slow down there, Ollie. I've been with Heidi for a few days, and you're getting married in less than three weeks."

He shrugged. "Okay. We can plan your wedding later."

"Aren't the girls supposed to do the planning?"

Ollie snorted. "You really don't understand women, do you? They expect us guys to act like we enjoy talking about stuff like who sits at which table at the reception and whether to have a buffet or a formal dinner."

"Which did you decide on?"

"Haven't decided anything. That's why Mara is panicking." He swigged some water, wiping his mouth with his hand. "Thank goodness Heidi offered to help her with all that. Mara's a lot more relaxed now that she has an unofficial wedding planner."

"I'm sure Heidi will love taking care of the details."

We went back to eating and enjoying the sunshine, and Ollie didn't harass me anymore about Heidi and whether I wanted to settle down. The rest of the nature hike seemed to drag by, though, probably because I kept thinking about Heidi and wondering what she was doing, if she was having fun, whether she would be happy to see me when I got back from the hike. Would she wonder where I'd been? Would she miss me?

Those thoughts made me feel anxious and a little giddy.

I stifled a groan, realizing exactly what that meant. Oh yeah, Ollie would love this.

The Ludar playboy was falling in love.

When we walked out of the woods, our group of seniors wandered off in various directions. Ollie spotted Mara on a chaise and jogged across the lawn to kiss her and sit on the grass beside her chair. Those two were perfect for each other, and they had something I never used to think I wanted—real, soul-deep, forever love. The idea of that kind of connection had always sounded like baloney to me, but the more time I spent with Heidi, the less dumb it all sounded. I guessed that was because I was falling for her.

And I liked it.

I saw Heidi at the instant she saw me. She was with her girl-friends, whose names I couldn't remember offhand, laughing and making hand gestures, probably to go along with whatever jokes they were telling each other. When Heidi noticed me, her face went blank for a second, then her expression lit up with the most brilliant smile I'd ever seen.

A pang stabbed into my chest, and my throat went thick.

Heidi sprinted across the lawn to me, flung her arms around my neck with her feet off the ground, and kissed me. When she unglued her lips from mine, she slid down my body until her feet touched the ground, but she kept her arms wrapped around my neck. "I missed you, Damian."

She felt so damn good crushed against me that I couldn't stop myself from admitting, "I missed you too."

And I grinned as wide as she was still doing.

No doubt about it. I was in love.

Chapter Twenty-Three

Heidi

For the rest of the week, I hung out with Damian as much as possible. Whenever he needed to work, I spent time with the Kittens or with Mara. The wedding plans came together quickly, and we got all the right venues booked and ordered all the right flowers and other accoutrements. Mara and I had been friends for a while now but working with her on the wedding stuff made us even closer. I couldn't have been happier for her and Ollie. Better still, I'd stopped feeling guilty over my half-assed attempt to steal Ollie from Mara all those months ago.

The past was the past. No point in dwelling on it.

Wow, was that me thinking those words? Guess I'd changed more than I realized.

No, not changed. I got back to being myself, and a large part of the reason for that was Damian.

The Petrescus went home after four days, but before they left, Monica took me aside for a little chat. I'd realized a few days ago that she wasn't trying to scare me off. She simply wanted to make sure her son ended up with the right woman. I'd kind of assumed since she'd announced she accepted me provisionally that she would hold off on welcoming me to the family until I had a proven track record with her son.

But on day four, Monica and I stood under the bows of a big pine tree on the far side of the lawn, alone.

She eyed me up and down, her expression indecipherable. "Do you love Damian?"

"What?" The question surprised me, but I collected myself and gave her the most honest answer I could. "I don't know yet. We haven't been together for very long. I like Damian so much, and I want to get to know him better. He means a lot to me."

Monica nodded slowly. "That's good. My son is in love with you, but I'm sure you've realized that on your own since the first time I told you that. If you break his heart, I will lay a hex on you."

"Do whatever you feel you need to do. But I have no intention of hurting him." When I was with Damian, I felt more like myself than I ever had in my entire life, but I couldn't tell Monica that, not unless I told Damian first. "He's the sweetest, kindest, smartest man I've ever known. Whatever happens between us, I'll always care about him."

"I'm glad to hear it." She picked up my hand, sandwiching it between her palms. "I sense you're a good, strong woman, but I'd feel better knowing more about your soul. With your permission, I'd like to do a tarot reading for you."

"Sure, I'm cool with that." I doubted Monica's tarot reading would be as much fun as Damian's palm reading, but I would do whatever it took to win over his mom. If she wanted to hypnotize me and make me grunt like a monkey, I'd go along with that too.

Monica pulled a boxed deck of cards out of her pocket. "We can do it right here. Let's sit cross-legged on the ground."

We sat down facing each other, and she slid the deck out of its box and onto her palm. "This is the old-style Rider-Waite deck. I've tried newer, fancier ones, but the old-school version works best for me."

"Tradition is good."

"I'm glad you feel that way because tradition is extremely important to my family."

"Yeah, I figured it was based on the things Damian has said. It's nice that you guys all get along so well."

While she shuffled the deck, Monica studied me again, though this time her lips curled at the corners the tiniest bit. "You are a clever girl, Heidi. I'm sure that's part of the reason Damian adores you. But what you just said makes me think you and your family don't get along well. Is that true?"

"Yeah." Would that be a black mark against me in Monica's book? Even if it were, even if she rejected me, I would stay with Damian for as long as he'd have me.

"That's a shame." Monica cradled the shuffled deck in her palm, her free hand hovering over it. "But there are different kinds of family, you know. The one you're born with might not always be the best one for you. I'm not insulting your parents, that's not my intent. I'm sure they mean well deep in their souls, and all I'm saying is that you shouldn't feel limited by your past."

I couldn't think of anything to say in response. Monica was a wise woman, but I'd need time to digest her comments. Another kind of family? I didn't know about that.

Monica patted my hand. "Relax, dear, there's nothing to worry about. I'll do a three-card spread."

She dealt three cards, laying them on the grass one by one from left to right, pausing between each card to explain it. The first card showed a woman seated on a throne, wearing flowing robes and a big crown.

"The High Priestess," Monica said. "She symbolizes the mystery of a future that hasn't yet been revealed as well as the wisdom, tenacity, and passion of the querent." With her head bowed, she moved only her eyes to glance up at me. "The querent is you, dear."

"I have wisdom?" A nervous laugh bubbled out of me. "Think you picked the wrong card."

She shook her head. "No, dear, the tarot never lies."

Monica dealt the second card, which featured a naked man and woman with a sun-being hovering above them. She studied it for a moment, then gave me that head-bowed look again, this time with a faint smile on her lips. "The Lovers. This card suggests attraction and obstacles overcome, but it also indicates choices must be made in a relationship and sacrifice may be required."

Was she trying to scare me away after all? I would not sacrifice Damian because of what a few dumb cards claimed to know.

She dealt the third and final card, which showed a compass and a strange humanoid creature plus a winged angel-like being and a bird. "The Wheel of Fortune. This means your destiny awaits if you choose to accept it."

"Does it happen to say what my destiny is?" Not that I believed in this crap, but I appreciated the beauty of the cards and Monica's interpretation of them.

"The tarot does not give specifics. All will be revealed at the appropriate moment."

"What if I don't notice when that happens?"

She smiled gently and touched my hand. "Trust yourself, dear. Be open to the possibilities, and when the time comes, you will understand."

I couldn't help smiling a little. "You really are good at this stuff. I can see where Damian gets it from. He's amazing at palm reading."

"Yes, he's always had a flair for it. Damian sometimes does tarot readings, but it's not his first choice." She held the Wheel of Fortune card out to me. "Keep this. Maybe it will remind you of the potential for happiness and keep you open to the possibilities."

I accepted the card, cradling it in my palm. "Thank you, Monica. I'm glad I got to meet you, and Adrian and Stefan too. I hope we'll see more of each other in the future."

"We will." She rose, offering a hand to help me up. She winked and smiled. "I foresee many future meetings for the two of us, dear."

"Looking forward to that." And I meant it. In the space of a few minutes, Monica Petrescu had made me feel better in ways I couldn't describe. Damian made me feel the best, but his mom had done something for me I couldn't even explain, not yet.

We headed for the driveway where the rest of the Petrescus, and Ollie and Mara, waited alongside a station wagon that served as a taxicab. The driver was shutting the rear door where I could see he'd stashed the family's luggage. It was time to say goodbye.

Damian's dad and brother hugged him, then they shook my hand to say goodbye. My honey hugged his sister-in-law too. But while Ollie and Mara wished the rest of the Petrescus a safe trip home, Damian's mom pulled him into a bear hug and whispered something to him. He looked slightly surprised by whatever she'd told him. She kissed his cheek and came over to me.

Monica hugged me.

I tried not to seem stunned. After the conversation we'd had earlier, I shouldn't have been surprised, I guessed. But I was.

She shocked me even more when she whispered, "You will make a fine addition to the Petrescu family."

Monica kissed my cheek and got into the taxi with her husband. Stefan and his wife climbed in too.

Damian slipped his hand into mine while we waved and watched the vehicle drive away.

Ollie slapped Damian's arm. "What did Mommy say, D-Man? Is she planning the wedding?"

"Shut up," Damian said with a smile. "Don't you need to go assistant-manage something?"

"Uh-huh. We'll leave you and Heidi to talk about…whatever."

Ollie and Mara left us.

Damian slung an arm around my waist, settling his hand on my hip. "Mom whispered to me that she gave you a tarot reading, and it showed good things ahead for us."

"Yeah, but she also said I might need to make a sacrifice."

"In tarot, that can mean a lot of things. Besides, that stuff's a bunch of bunk, right?"

"Sure, yeah, a bunch of bunk."

He tugged me more snugly to him. "Let me give you a palm reading. That'll make you feel so good you won't worry about anything for at least three days."

"That will only work if it's a naughty palm reading."

"For you, there's no other kind." He kissed my forehead. "Let's grab lunch and sequester ourselves in the wagon for a good, long reading."

"Can't be too long. Your lunch break is only an hour."

"I'll make up any overrun by working late. Come on, say yes."

"Okay. Yes."

He grinned.

I grinned.

Damn, we were a pair of lovestruck fools, but I didn't care. It felt beautiful and hot and sweet and sexy, all the things that made me forget about everything else in the world.

We stole some food from the lunch buffet in the dining hall, then hid out in the gypsy wagon to eat and…do other things. Multiple orgasms were on the menu for sure. Damian didn't get halfway through the palm reading before I dragged him down onto the pillows and rode him like a wild gypsy cowgirl.

He was half an hour late getting back to work, but nobody cared.

That night, after another round of palm-reading steaminess, I lay sprawled over Damian on the bed inside the wagon, satisfied in more ways than I could count. I'd never felt so at ease or so happy in my entire life, and I wanted to explain to him how much it meant to me, how much he meant to me. But I couldn't make the words come out, not yet.

In my mind, I told him. *I love you, Damian.*

Chapter Twenty-Four

Damian

A week after my family went home, it was time for the Kitten Brigade to leave too. Heidi had been a member of that group since the first time they came to Au Naturel, and I assumed she would go home with them. I didn't want her to leave. Heidi and I had grown so close lately that just the thought of watching her ride away in that pink RV got me choked up. Real manly, right? At least nobody saw me doing that.

We hadn't talked about where we would go from here, so I had no reason to expect her to stay with me. She had a job back home, after all, even if she didn't love it. Mara raved about everything Heidi had done to help her prepare for the wedding, but the prep work wasn't done yet. I supposed Heidi could still help out from home, with video calls or whatever.

I wanted to beg her to stay. Seriously. Me. I wanted to beg on my hands and knees.

Heidi came out of the guest house with her friends, and they piled into the RV, each giving Heidi a hug. She had her purse over her shoulder, but she didn't climb in with them.

I stood at the front of the vehicle, in the gravel driveway, staring at her like a desperate moron and praying she wouldn't get on that RV.

The door closed. Heidi stayed on the ground.

She was about to bang on the door so they'd let her in. Right?

Heidi backed up to get out of the way as the RV's engine revved up.

I lingered there paralyzed until Shelby, who was driving the bus, honked the horn and waved for me to get out of the way. Shouting "sorry," I hustled over to where Heidi stood. She gave me a strange look while the RV turned around and rolled off down the driveway, out of sight.

"Are you okay?" she asked. "You almost got mowed down by a giant, lumbering RV."

"I'm fine." I scratched the back of my neck, head down. "You must be, uh, taking a cab to somewhere to meet up with your friends later, right?"

That did not sound at all pathetic. What in the world was wrong with me?

Heidi stared at me for a minute, then she laughed. Holding my face in her hands, she urged me to raise my head and look at her. "You were worried I was leaving you. That's so cute, Damian. You're always confident and smooth, but it's nice to know you have an anxious side too."

"You like my anxiety? That's crazy."

"I like that you care enough to worry about losing me. You're not, by the way. I'm staying."

"But you have your purse, like you're going somewhere."

She rubbed her thumbs over my lips. "Relax. I'm taking Mara into town so she can buy a wedding dress."

"Oh." How dumb did I feel? Thumb-sucking, babbling, drooling-lunatic dumb. "You're sticking around until the wedding, then."

"I'm sticking around, period."

"What about your job?"

She shrugged one shoulder. "I quit."

"What? When?"

"This morning. Didn't get a chance to tell you yet because I was helping my friends get ready to leave." She draped her arms around my neck, brushing her fingertips through my hair. "I've got enough money in the bank to get by for a couple months, which gives me time to figure out what my next step is. Val and Eve offered me a job here—a nonspecific, whatever-I-want job—but I need to think about it."

"The resort needs an event planner."

"Let's talk about that later. Right now, I need to go with Mara."

"Was her mom upset that you're taking over the wedding planning?"

Heidi leaned her body against me, her fingers still toying with my hair. "No, Sheryl understood. She wants Mara to be happy, and she only became the wedding dictator because Mara didn't want to make her mom feel bad. She was afraid to say what she wanted. Naturally, Sheryl assumed her daughter needed the most expensive, designer everything."

"But she doesn't. Mara wants something cozier and more relaxed."

"That's right. How did you know?"

"I've been working with Mara for months now."

"Right. I almost forgot." She danced her fingertips down my neck, spreading her hand over my shoulder, then she dragged her palm down to my chest. "What should we do this evening, after you get off work?"

I cupped her ass with both hands. "How about we go into town and have dinner at a real restaurant? No buffet, no senior citizens poking their noses into our business, just the two of us."

"Are you asking me out on a date?"

"Yeah, I guess I am."

She smiled. "I'd love to go on a date with you, Damian."

The urge to fist-pump was strong, but I ignored it. "I'll pick you up at eight, at your room. Okay?"

"I'll be ready." She eyed my work uniform. "Are you going to, like, wear a suit or something? Should I dress up?"

I hadn't even considered how we might dress, but nudity was pretty much off the table. The authorities frowned on naked people strolling into a restaurant. I did own a suit, for special occasions. For years, I'd worn a prison-guard uniform, and now I wore the resort uniform. To wear a nice suit again might feel weird, but I looked forward to it. And I couldn't wait to see Heidi in whatever fancy dress she decided to wear.

"Yes, we're dressing up," I said. "The only restaurant in town is the steak house, but I hear it's nice."

"It is. And they usually have live music. A string quartet or something like that."

"Sounds perfect. Have you been to the steak house before?"

Heidi bit her lip again and swerved her gaze away from mine. "Um, once. Back when I was trying to steal Ollie away from Mara. Her ex-husband showed up, and he took me on a date strictly to make Mara jealous. It didn't work. I thought it was a real date, though. Stupid, right?"

"No, that's not stupid. Ollie told me about Nico the Numbskull, and I'm sure he did a bang-up job of sweet-talking you into going out with him."

"He did that all right."

I moved my hands up to her back and tugged her closer. "You're a smart cookie, but everybody gets duped once in a while. Now, let's stop talking about other people and focus on tonight." I bent my head to murmur in her ear, "No underwear, please."

"Not even a bra?"

"Wear one if you'll feel more comfortable that way, but definitely no panties."

"Yes, sir." She caught my earlobe between her teeth, tickling it with her tongue. "No underwear for you either."

"I never bother with those, you know that."

"Just making double sure."

Since I still had my mouth almost touching her ear, I flicked my tongue out to tease the skin under the lobe, loving the way she sucked in a breath. "I never got to use that silk scarf I bought for you. Tonight, I'm going to strip you naked and drag that silk over you so slowly, skimming it across your skin over and over until you beg me to fuck you."

"Oh God, I can't wait for that. I want to go down on you in the restaurant."

I froze as the meaning of what she'd said filtered through my lust-drunk brain. "Are you just saying that, or would you actually do that sometime? Have you done something like it before?"

"No, never. But yes, I want to do that to you." She skated her tongue up my throat. "Tonight."

Damn, and I thought I was the master of dirty talk. My dick jerked the second she spoke the word "tonight" in her sultry voice.

"I, uh, better get back to work," I said, taking a step backward. "But we're on for tonight, and I'm game for anything you want to try."

Mara emerged from the guest house, heading this way. She waved to Heidi.

"See you tonight," I said.

Heidi lunged forward to kiss me. "I'll put my mouth on a different part of you at dinner."

She grinned and trotted toward Mara.

I watched the two girls get into Mara's car, then I waved as they drove off. I went back to work, but it took all my willpower to focus on my job instead of fantasizing about tonight with Heidi. Still, I behaved like a diligent employee and got things done. Sure, I might've locked the office door for five minutes while I jerked off to a fantasy of Heidi going down on me in the restaurant, but that happened during my lunch break. No shirking of duties involved.

At precisely eight o'clock, I approached the door to Heidi's room and knocked.

The door swung open half a second later.

She started to smile, froze, and then went slack-jawed. "Holy cow, Damian, you look like James Bond. You own that color, like the universe invented black just for you."

I'd worn a black suit with a pale-blue shirt and a black tie. I even had shiny black shoes. But I couldn't have guessed she would love my outfit this much. I loved hers too. Like, jaw-droppingly loved it. "You look absolutely incredible, Heidi."

Fuckable, actually, but I was trying to be a gentleman.

Heidi wore a cherry-red dress that clung to her body like a second skin. It featured a halter top that tied behind her neck and a peekaboo cutout that let me glimpse the slopes of her gorgeous breasts. When she twirled so I could see all of her, I discovered the dress was backless. Her red stilettos gave her ankles a sexy curve and made me want to fall to my knees at her feet so I could unhook the slender straps with my teeth and lick my way up her calf.

"Glad you like it," she said. "I bought this dress today for our date. Didn't want to wear something any of those jerks I used to date had seen."

She bought a dress for me. A hot dress.

"I didn't buy this suit for you," I said, "but none of the girls I've dated ever saw it."

Heidi fingered the lapels of my suit jacket. "I like being the first one to see you looking like James Bond."

I offered her my hand. "Shall we go? I made a reservation, so we'd get the perfect table."

"You think of everything." She slipped her hand into mine. "Sweep me off my feet, Damian."

"Anything for you." I swept her into my arms. "I'll carry you to the car like those guys in movies do."

And I did exactly that.

She giggled the entire time.

We walked into the restaurant arm in arm, and every man in the place stopped to stare at Heidi, even the ones who looked like they were ninety. I couldn't blame them. She was stunning.

A waiter took us to our table. The booth nestled in the corner farthest from the entrance, in a shadowy area, behind a brick planter full of small palm trees. That seemed like a weird choice for a steak house in Oregon, but whatever. When I'd made the reservation, I'd asked for a secluded table. This was it, for sure.

Once we ordered, I turned halfway toward Heidi and draped an arm across the back of the booth behind her. "Time for an appetizer."

"The waiter said it would take ten minutes."

"Not talking about that kind of appetizer." I slid closer to her, laying my hand on her thigh. "I need to taste you."

"A gentleman lets the lady go first."

I pushed my fingers under the hem of her dress, gliding them up her skin. "A real gentleman knows the lady always *comes* first."

"Oh, I see."

"Pull your dress up for me, please, and spread your legs."

Elsewhere in the restaurant, people laughed and chattered. Through the branches of those baby palm trees, I could see the movements of people at another table.

Heidi shimmied her hips, hiking up her dress until she'd exposed herself from the waist down. She parted her legs.

I caressed her inner thigh. "When you come, I'll swallow your scream with my mouth over yours."

Her breathing had grown heavier, making her breasts rise and fall. She gripped my thigh with one hand, curling her fingers over the seat's edge with the other.

"Watch what I'm doing to you," I said. "Watch me fuck you with my fingers."

She lowered her head, her gaze trained on my hand.

I slid my hand higher up her thigh and stretched out one finger to tease her mound. When she gasped, I covered those curly hairs with my hand.

Heidi spread her legs even more.

The scent of her cream inundated my senses, and my dick jumped like it couldn't wait to get inside her. *Not yet, bro, not yet.* I sucked in a deep breath through my nostrils, reveling in the aroma of her lust. Fuck, I wanted to shove my head down there and devour her. But I reined in the impulse and kept to the plan, thrusting one finger between her slick lips to massage her clit. She gripped my thigh harder while I skated my finger down one side of her folds and back up the other, coating my finger with her cream.

I lifted that finger to my mouth and licked it clean.

She choked back a moan.

God, I loved the way her cheeks had turned slightly pink and her eyes had gone hooded. There was nothing more beautiful in the world than Heidi Mackenzie at full arousal. I shoved two fingers between her folds, pushing them down until the heel of my hand rested on her taut nub. I rubbed it with my hand while I brushed my fingers up and down, up and down, slowly at first but speeding up little by little as she got more turned on. Her breaths became rhythmic gasps as her nails dug into my thigh.

"How badly do you need to come?" I whispered.

"So damn bad," she said between panting breaths.

I drove my middle finger into her channel as far as it would go, still massaging her clit with my palm and stroking her with my other fingers.

"Oh—God," she hissed under her breath, her gaze riveted to my hand.

Blood was rushing to my cock, but I couldn't focus on anything except the look on her face, a cross between intense pleasure and pain. I ground my hand into her nub, moving my fingers faster and faster and faster. Her body tensed, and her mouth fell open. The second I felt the first hint of a spasm inside her, I sealed my mouth over hers and thrust my tongue deep, swallowing the cry that erupted from her throat. Her body gripped my finger again and again while I kept working her flesh until she was done.

I broke the kiss, breathing almost as hard as she was.

"Wow," she said, her voice breathy. "That was...wow."

"I love it when a woman comes so hard she can't manage a complete sentence." I pulled my hand away from her body and raised my fingers to my mouth, licking them one by one with deliberate slowness, groaning at the flavor of her. "Not sure I need food. The taste of you could sustain me for days."

"But you promised me dinner." She didn't sound breathless anymore, though her cheeks were still pink. "And for the record, I spoke a whole sentence. I said, 'that was wow.' I wasn't incapable of speech."

"I don't think 'wow' counts as part of a sentence, but I'll be a gentleman and give you that one."

"Thank you." She laid a hand on my cheek. "And I mean thank you for the orgasm too."

"My pleasure."

"No, that's what comes next." She cupped my dick through my pants. "I did promise."

"Better fix your dress first."

She wriggled until she had her dress back in position, then she took hold of the zipper on my pants.

The waiter marched up to our table carrying the actual appetizers we had ordered. While he set the food down, another waiter ushered a party of four to the table beside ours. Though a partial wall separated the booths, the two guys sitting right behind me were tall enough to see us if they looked this way.

I leaned close to Heidi and murmured, "Think we better hold off on that thing you wanted to do."

She feigned a pout.

The waiter left, and we stuck to talking and eating.

Chapter Twenty-Five

Heidi

Rats. I had so wanted to give Damian head in the restaurant, especially after what he did to me. But fate intervened in the form of four obnoxious men who got seated right beside our booth and who kept laughing too loudly and glancing in our direction. Well, glancing at me. At my breasts.

Damian and I ignored them as much as possible. He even gave me his jacket so I could cover up my breasts in hopes that would make those twerps give up on leering at me. The tactic worked, thank goodness. We enjoyed our steak dinners and talked, then ordered a yummy, gooey dessert that we fed to each other. I'd never had a more perfect date in my life, despite the loud twerps in the next booth.

Between dinner and dessert, we danced. A jazz quartet played a lazy, sensual song while we shuffled around like two people who had no idea how to dance and didn't care. Damian held me in his arms while I rested my cheek on his shoulder. It was so romantic, and I wanted to commit this entire night to memory so I could relive it in my mind.

I kept Damian's jacket on until we walked out of the restaurant, not because I worried about men leering at me, No, I'd only thought about that for a few minutes, when those jerks were at their most obnoxious. I kept his jacket because I loved having the scent of him around me and the fabric that had touched him touching me. Once we walked out the doors, I gave it back to him.

"You can keep it," he said. "Looks better on you."

"But I want the whole Ludar James Bond experience on the drive home."

"How can I say no to that?" He took the jacket and slipped it on. "Sorry I don't have an Aston Martin to take you home in style."

"Your Ford Explorer is sexy enough for me."

As we headed into the parking lot, he pushed the button on his key fob to unlock the SUV. "If I'd known all I needed to get you in bed was a Ford Explorer and a suit, I would've given you that the first time we met."

"I wasn't ready for you yet. Now I am."

He opened the passenger door for me. "You were worth the wait."

I settled onto the seat, gazing up at him. "It wasn't the car or the suit that made me want you. It was the palm reading."

"Ludar seduction at its finest."

He shut the door and hustled around to the driver's side, climbing in. When he shoved the key into the ignition, I leaned over to place my hand over his, stopping him from turning the key.

"Not yet," I said. "Got a promise to keep."

"You don't have to—"

I sealed his lips with two fingers. "I want you, Damian. Right now. So I'm adjusting the plan. Got a condom?"

"When I'm with you, always." He dug a packet out of his pants.

"You're the best." I crawled onto his lap, straddling him. "And I do mean that in every way."

Smirking, he reached for the lever under the seat and pulled it. The seat back tipped down at a forty-five-degree angle. "Now we're ready."

I undid his belt and unzipped his pants, freeing his stiff cock.

He lunged forward, wrapped his arms around me, and dragged me down onto the seat with him. Grasping the back of my head, he pulled me in for a deep kiss. While our tongues tangled, he ran his hands up and down my back, and I shoved a hand between our bodies to fondle his cock. Oh wow, he was so hard. When he closed a hand over my breast and kneaded it, I moaned and writhed on top of him, desperate for more of everything—more kissing, more fondling, more of him.

A bright light flared on. Knuckles rapped on the window.

I sprang upright, bashing my head on the ceiling, and cursed under my breath. Squinting at the bright light, I struggled to understand what I was seeing. "Oh shit, Damian, it's a cop."

He sprang upright too, one arm around me, and fumbled with the button that lowered the window. "Hey, officer, what's up?"

The young cop eyed us with narrowed eyes, his flashlight aimed at us, but his mouth twitched into a faint smirk. He nodded toward Damian's lap where his dick was still visible. "You got a permit for that loaded weapon?"

Damian stared at the cop, his mouth open.

I suddenly realized Damian had pulled my tit out of my dress. Tucking it back inside the halter, I cleared my throat. "Are we breaking some kind of law, officer?"

"Yeah, you are. It's called public indecency."

Damian laughed nervously. "Sorry, man, we didn't think. Won't happen again."

"Uh-huh. I'll let you two off with a warning this time." The cop gave us a hard look. "Behave yourselves, kids."

"Will do," Damian said.

The cop ambled away.

I scrambled off Damian's lap. "Guess we better wait till we get home."

"Home?" Damian was just zipping up his pants. "I thought you were a guest."

Why had I called the resort home? The truth hit me, and I had to tell him. "Not anymore. The resort is my home, and I want to work there with you, Ollie, Mara, Eve, and Val. This is where I belong, with the kind of family that loves me no matter what."

"Everybody loves you, Heidi. Your parents are the only dicks in the room."

I leaned over the center console to kiss him. "You're so sweet. Thank you for tonight, and for everything else."

"You're welcome." He turned the key in the ignition, and the vehicle grumbled to life. "Now let's get home so I can make love to you the right way, without any risk of us getting arrested."

"Guess you better obey the speed limit in case that cop keeps tabs on us. We are degenerate criminals, after all."

"We haven't been arrested, so we're not criminals. Unless there's something you haven't told me."

I buckled up my seatbelt. "Nope. What you see is what you get."

Maybe that hadn't been true for the past few months, but it was now. I'd stopped hiding my natural tendencies and gotten back to being my truest self, the woman who took work seriously but loved life and knew how to cut loose. Damian had helped me get there. On the ride home, I couldn't think about anything else except how much this man I'd known for only a short time had changed my life. He meant more to me than any of the other guys I'd dated. Suddenly, I needed to tell him that.

But we had just pulled up in front of the guest house, and he was just getting out of the car, coming around to my side. When he opened the door for me, Damian offered me his hand to help me out. He was such a wonderful man and a gentleman to the core.

I clasped both his hands before he could even close the car door.

His brows crinkled. "Is something wrong?"

"No, everything is just right." I gazed into his eyes, my throat thickening. "I love you, Damian."

For a few seconds, his expression stayed frozen in that crinkled-brows look of worried confusion. Then the corners of his mouth kicked up, and his lips eased into a smile that gradually broadened into a grin. "I love you too, Heidi."

I grinned too.

He pulled me into his arms and kissed me. It was a long, slow, deliciously hot kiss, but it was also more than that. We imbued into it everything we felt for each other and so much more.

Once we finally forced ourselves to stop making out in the driveway, we headed into the gypsy wagon and made love for a long, long time. I fell asleep in Damian's arms.

In the morning, I woke up first and lay there luxuriating in the bliss of having his body entangled with mine. I listened to him breathing in a shallow, steady rhythm and combed my fingers through his hair while I reminisced about all the incredible times I'd had with him. Our relationship had barely begun. We had a lifetime to enjoy even better times. Life would bring bad days too, but for the first time in my life, I knew the good times would outweigh the bad ones from here on.

Damian had just started to rouse when my phone rang.

I tried to wriggle out from under him, but he was too sleepy to help much. So I resorted to gently smacking his cheek a few times until he woke up all the way.

"What?" he asked drowsily, pushing up onto one elbow. "Why are you hitting me? Spousal abuse can't start until we're married."

"Ha-ha. My phone is ringing." I clambered off the bed and snagged my phone from where I'd left it on the top step, near the head of the bed. I swiped right to take the call an instant before it would've gone to voice mail. "Hello?"

"Help!" Mara said, not actually screaming it but fake screaming instead, drawing the word out in one long exhalation.

"What's wrong, sweetie? Did something happen to Ollie?"

"No," she moaned, almost whimpering. "The wedding is in six days, and I suddenly realized I don't have any bridesmaids because I don't have any friends."

Oh boy, the wedding jitters had started early, and in true Mara fashion, she was freaking out. As her wedding planner, I supposed it was my job to calm her down. She was my friend too, despite what she'd just said, so it absolutely was my job to be there for her.

"Relax, Mara," I said. "Everything's okay. Why don't I come to your room? We can talk it all through, and you'll see there's nothing to panic about. How's that sound?"

"Yeah, okay. Thank you, Heidi."

I hung up and started hunting for my clothes. Damian had kind of ripped them off me and flung them wherever. And yeah, I'd done the same thing with his clothes. That suit lay here, there, and everywhere.

"What's up with Mara?" Damian asked.

"Oh, it's wedding anxiety, that's all. I need to take care of her this morning, so I won't be able to have breakfast with you."

"That's okay. The bride takes precedence." He sat up and stretched, yawning. "I'll check on Ollie. See if he's panicking on the inside. You know, the manly way men do."

"Uh-huh, sure. You boys go bang drums or measure your dicks or whatever."

We both got dressed—me in my dress from last night, since it was all I had, and him in his work uniform—and climbed out of the wagon. We both headed into the guest house, but we kissed goodbye on the first landing. Damian strode off toward the office while I continued up to the third floor where Mara and Ollie had taken up residence in one of the rooms ever since they got engaged. Yesterday, Mara had told me she and Ollie wanted to buy a little house near town, but they'd hadn't started looking yet.

After stopping off at my room to change clothes, I knocked on the door to Ollie and Mara's room.

Ollie swung the door open, looking harried. "Oh thank God. Maybe another woman can calm her down. Please, Heidi, she won't listen to me."

Poor Ollie. I wanted to hug him, in a friend way, but he pushed past me and hustled toward the stairs.

Mara sat on the bed hugging her knees and biting her lip. Her eyes were red and puffy.

I shut the door and walked over to sit on the bed next to her. "Did you guys have a fight?"

"No, it's nothing like that. I told him I don't have any friends, and I'll have to stand at the altar all by myself." She grabbed a tissue from a box on the bedside table and blew her nose. "Ollie said I won't be alone because he and Damian and Val will be standing there too, and so will the minister. That's when I started crying. And you know how guys are about tears. He told me to call my mom, but I called you instead."

"I'm glad you did."

"Ugh. I'm such a lunatic." She wadded up the tissue and tossed it into the wastebasket. "Ollie suggested it's hormones. What did I do? I managed to weep uncontrollably and shout at him at the same time."

"Ollie understands, I'm sure. Getting married is a big deal and comes with all kinds of stressful stuff that needs to be done."

She stretched her legs out, leaned back, and laid a hand over her lower belly. "It's more than that. Ollie doesn't mind if I tell you, so, um…" Mara sucked in a big breath and blew it out. "I'm pregnant."

"What? Mara, that's wonderful."

"I know, it really is. We found out yesterday, and at first, we were both over the moon." She shut her eyes and sighed. "But all this wedding craziness is getting to me. The hormonal mood swings aren't helping."

"Don't worry about any of that." I sat up straighter and pointed at myself. "You've got a crack wedding coordinator who's going to handle absolutely everything so the bride can take it easy."

"I can't make you do everything. I'm not even paying you."

"Forget about money. You are my best friend and seeing you and Ollie tie the knot is all the payment I need."

She half-smiled. "Thank you so much, Heidi. You're my best friend too."

I patted her knee. "And as for you not having bridesmaids, that's taken care of too. Eve and I will stand at the altar with you." I glanced at her red, puffy eyes, and realized I needed to do my best-friend job. "Let me get you a cool, damp cloth for your eyes and some chamomile tea to soothe your nerves."

Mara smiled a little more than she had a minute ago. "You're the best, Heidi. I love you."

"Love you too, Mara."

I hustled into the bathroom and got a cool cloth for her, then I insisted she lie down to rest. I settled the cloth over her forehead and partially over her face, so it covered her eyes. After that, I jogged downstairs to get the tea. Maybe I didn't have a paying job at the moment, but helping Mara made me feel useful in a way I hadn't experienced before. I couldn't regret quitting my job.

As I brewed the tea in the kitchen, I wondered if I might have found my new career path after all.

Chapter Twenty-Six

Damian

"Do women always go insane right before the wedding?" Ollie asked, though he didn't give me a chance to respond. "I mean, it's just a wedding, not a presidential inauguration. How could Mara think she doesn't have friends? Of course she does. I tried to calm her down, but no, she had to cry and sniffle and get all puffy-eyed and miserable. She wouldn't even let me hug her, and every time I tried to say something, she'd burst out crying again. She's gone totally nuts."

Ollie had stormed into the office a few minutes ago in a state of half panic, half misery, and flumped onto the chair beside the desk. I sat here in the big chair listening to him vent.

Now, my best friend threw his head back and moaned.

He wasn't angry with Mara. No, he had a much worse problem than that. He was so completely in love with her that he did the worst possible thing any man could do when a woman was upset for what, to us guys, seemed like absolutely nothing. He'd told her it was nothing.

Yeah, Ollie was freaking out too, but in a different way from how Mara had done it.

I was positive Ollie had told her it was nothing in a calm, patient, loving tone. But in my experience, that was also a bad thing to do when a woman started crying. When I'd told Ollie my opinion a minute ago, he had huffed and thrown his hands up, then said, "Then what *is* the right thing to do?"

"No idea, man," I told him. "Women are a mystery."

Ollie genuinely wanted to make his fiancée feel better, but being a guy, he didn't have a frigging clue how to do that.

Since he'd just finished his second diatribe and seemed to be taking a breather, I tried again to settle him down with a bad joke. "Maybe it's PMS. Girls go bananas when it's that time of the month. They can be like that chick in *The Exorcist*, so watch out if Mara's head starts to spin."

Ollie looked at me, suddenly calm and serious. "It's not PMS. Mara is pregnant."

"Are you serious?"

He nodded slowly.

I leaned across the distance between us and slapped his arm. "Congratulations, man. You're gonna be a dad. That's awesome."

"Yeah, awesome," Ollie said in a tone that suggested the news was the opposite of awesome.

"What's wrong? You're head-over-heels in love with Mara, and you've both been talking about having kids practically since the day you met."

"I know, but..." He squirmed in his chair. "What if I screw up?"

"Come on, Ollie, that's nerves talking. Wedding jitters, isn't that what they call it?"

He shrugged. "I guess."

We both needed some booze. Yeah, that would help. Okay, maybe booze wasn't the smartest plan to help my best friend, but I couldn't think of anything better. Desperate times called for desperate measures, right?

That was probably one of the worst excuses for a bender ever invented.

I stood up and slapped his arm again. "Get your butt outta that chair, Ollie. We're going to the pantry."

"What?" Ollie compressed his lips and glared at me. "How is a visit to the food pantry going to make me feel better?"

"You'll see when we get there."

He grumbled, rolling his eyes.

I kicked his foot. "Up. Now."

Ollie grumbled again but pushed out of the chair.

And we trundled downstairs, through the kitchen, to the locked door at the back. I had a key, naturally, being the concierge, so I unlocked the door and swung it open.

"Computer nerds first," I said, hoping a friendly jibe might get a smile from Ollie. It didn't, so I walked into the pantry first. "What are you in the mood for this morning? Bourbon? Beer? Vodka?"

"Isn't it kind of early for drinking?"

"Not when the groom is having a panic attack."

Ollie scowled at me. "I am not having a panic attack."

"When sweet little Ollie gives me a dirty look, I know he's freaking out."

"I'm as tall as you are, which means I'm not little."

"Sensitive this morning, aren't you?" I started browsing the bottles on the shelves. "I noticed you didn't dispute the 'sweet' comment."

"Women like nice guys."

"Mara says you're a snuggly-wuggly wittle cuddle bear." If I couldn't tempt him to drink, maybe some ribbing would work.

Ollie came up beside me, arms locked over his chest. "When did Mara ever tell you that?"

"She didn't. I read between the lines." I threw him a sideways glance and couldn't resist smirking. "When she calls you a stud muffin, I translate that as 'soft and squishy snuggly-wuggly Awee the cuddle bear.' My Ludar lidar confirmed it."

"Maybe you shouldn't harass me when I'm panicking."

"Oh-ho," I said, pointing a finger at him, "you admitted you're freaking out."

"No, I—Well, it's—" He flung his hands up and snarled. "You are such an asshole, Damian."

"That's my job. To piss off the groom so he stops worrying about every little thing." I grabbed a bottle off the shelf. "Well, that and get booze for you."

Ollie eyed the bottle with a hint of suspicion. "You can't seriously think booze is the answer."

"Couldn't hurt."

"It's not even nine a.m. I haven't had breakfast yet."

"Okay, let's get some food to go with our gigantic stash of liquor." I spread an arm to indicate our surroundings. "While we eat, we get hammered. Deal?"

He studied me for a moment, an exceptionally long one. Then Ollie smacked my arm and grinned. "Let's do it. I mean, Mara might dump me for doing this, but so what? I'll crawl back and beg forgiveness like a true cuddly-wuddly computer nerd."

"Sounds like a plan."

We walked back into the kitchen and started rummaging around for the manliest foods available. That's what Ollie said, not me.

"We need manly macho man food," he'd announced as we exited the pantry, aka the Big Closet of Booze.

I didn't even try to figure out what "manly macho man food" was and let Ollie scrounge up whatever he wanted. This was his panic-attack binge, so I decided to stand back and watch while he tore open cupboards and practically climbed inside them in search of the elusive "manly macho man food."

My best friend had probably lost his mind, but it was kind of fun to witness it firsthand.

Our breakfast wound up looking like the fridge had barfed up the contents of a buffet restaurant. Four kinds of sausage. Bacon. Hamburgers. Oh wait, that was bacon cheese hamburgers, so kind of all one thing. What else? Steak fajitas, guacamole, queso, several kinds of chips, baked beans, ham sandwiches, French fries, sweet potato fries, hash browns... I kind of lost track of things after that, partly because we'd raided every cupboard and the fridge but also because we had started drinking somewhere between frying up burgers and scarfing down deviled eggs.

We did not eat all of everything. No, we kind of...sampled everything.

Except for the booze. We might've guzzled that. One shot every time we found something else to eat. First bite of guacamole? *Have a shot of tequila, man.* First taste of sweet potato fries? Time for some Jack Daniels. *Hey, bro, is that some cheesecake in the fridge? Grab it while I steal a bottle of vodka from the pantry.*

Maybe the rest of the morning would've gone better if we'd eaten too much and thrown up the food and the booze. Unfortunately, we sampled but did not gorge ourselves. Not on the food. The liquor... Well, that was a different story.

Ollie glanced at the food littering the island. He blinked in slow motion. "Whoa, dude. Who's gonna clean piss—I mean clean this up."

Every time he spoke the letter S, it sounded kind of like a snake hissing.

I slapped my palm down on the island and burped loudly. "We're, like, you know, in charge or something. Aren't we? Con-sssseee-erge and... What the hell are you?"

"Uhhhh... Assistant manger?" He busted out in guffaws, covering his mouth with one hand. When he pulled his hand away, it had spittle on it. "Did you ever notice assistant manger starts with 'ass'?"

"Dude, you're not a manger. You're a manager." I snorted out a laugh. "Unless you plan on having Mara pop out that kid on your tummy. Get it? Like a manger or…whatevers."

Ollie thrust a bottle at me. "You need more of piss. This. What was I saying?"

I held up a hard-boiled egg. "Ever notice how these look like tits?"

"No, they don't," Ollie said with a laugh that came out like a pig snort. "They've got eggs inside 'em, not on the ousside. Outside. Ugh, I can't talk anymore."

"Do too look like tits. These, I mean." I picked up two eggs and held them to my chest. "See? Hard-boiled titties."

He started guffawing again. "You need a bra, man."

Thinking about tits made me think about Heidi. Yeah, she had the awesomest, fabulosiest boobs on earth. I glanced down at the eggs I was still holding to my chest, and the most awesomest idea ever hit me.

I punched Ollie's arm. "Got a wicked-amazing idea."

"Ow," Ollie said, clutching his arm. "That hurt, dude."

"Don't be a wuss-face." I slid off my stool and snagged a half-empty bottle of Jack Daniels. "Let's go find our woman-girls and, like, kiss them."

"Yeah, we should. Smack some love on 'em." Ollie sort of oozed off his stool and stumbled into me. "Let's do it."

We started for the door, but Ollie froze on the threshold. "Don't we, ya know, have to work or something today?"

"Nah."

"Awesome."

Yeah, two drunk morons thought it was a fantastic idea to find their girlfriends and show off how drunk they were.

At the time, it sounded like the best plan ever.

I grabbed Ollie's arm to stop him halfway down the hall. "We should change clothes first."

"Yeah," he said with a stupid grin. "And I know exactly what we should wear. The girls'll go nutso for it."

Chapter Twenty-Seven

Heidi

Mara and I were sitting on chaises watching Val and Sylvester playing kickball. They weren't concerned with who won but only with having a good time ribbing each other. Val wore his work uniform, but Sly went nude. Well, he was here to enjoy the naturist lifestyle.

Suddenly, Val froze with his foot on the ball. Something past our chairs had captured his attention and made his brows furrow.

"What's wrong?" Sly asked, then he tracked Val's gaze past us, and his face took on a similar expression. "Is that… No, it can't be."

"It is," Val said.

Mara sat forward. "What are you two talking about?"

"Look." Val pointed toward the guest house behind us.

Both Mara and I twisted around on our chaises to see what had caught the men's attention.

Damian and Ollie were walking toward us. Well, staggering toward us. They would move in a straight line for a couple of seconds, then list one way or the other while laughing and slapping each other's arms. Ollie tripped—over grass, it seemed like—and Damian seized his friend's arm to keep him from tumbling over. Just when Ollie regained his balance, sort of, Damian stumbled and staggered sideways.

Oh no. It couldn't be. They wouldn't. Not this early.

They each wore some type of skirt that seemed to be made of hand towels held together by a band of purple duct tape around the waist. No shirts, no shoes, no socks, nothing but those skirts.

Mara leaped off her chaise. "Ollie! What's wrong with you?"

I knew she hadn't figured out what her fiancé's problem was because she looked panicky and worried. If she'd recognized the truth, she'd probably be yelling at him instead of racing toward him.

Damian and Ollie aimed lopsided grins at…no one in particular.

Oh yeah, no doubt about. They were wasted.

I jumped up and hurried after Mara.

The boys halted, waiting for Mara to reach them. I got there two seconds after her.

Ollie swayed, grinning like the drunken fool he was. "Mara, babycakes, you're so friggin' hot."

He slurred those words.

"Pshaw," Damian slurred. "She's nothin' next to Hi-dee-ho-ho-ho."

Ollie rolled his eyes at Damian.

Mara's gaze flicked back and forth between the two men. "What's going on? Ollie, why are you acting this way?"

Jeez, had Mara never seen a drunk person before? Considering the snobby circles her family socialized in, maybe she really hadn't.

Damian tried to put an arm around me but missed and almost fell over.

I slapped a hand on his shoulder to steady him. "What are you doing? You two are wasted. At ten o'clock in the morning."

"Knew you were smart," he said, slapping his hand on top of mine on his shoulder. "You're so perty. Can we have sex now?"

Maybe I should've been more annoyed about their current state, but there wasn't any point in getting upset. Not until they sobered up. "Yeah, sure, let's go into your wagon of love and get it on. If you can crawl up the steps without vomiting."

He thrust out his free hand to me, turning it upside down. "Read my palm, hey? Tell me the foocher."

I assumed he meant "future," but it was hard to tell for sure. I patted his cheek. "That's easy. Your future involves a good long nap, lots of aspirin, and at least three days of groveling for forgiveness." I threw a sharp look at Ollie. "For both of you."

Mara was standing perfectly still, her gaze nailed to Ollie, her expression blank.

"You okay, Mara?" I asked.

She nodded. "I've never seen him like this. Why did you get drunk, Ollie? Don't you want to marry me?"

"Like crazy I do," he said, then he dropped to his knees and hugged hers. "I'm sorry, Mary—Mara. That's your name, right? I'm Awee. Sweet wittle pudgy-wudgy Awee."

Mara covered her face with her hands.

I thought she might be crying—until she lowered her hands.

Her lips were puckered, clearly because she was trying not to laugh.

"No, no, no," Damian said. "It's sweet wittle cuddly wuddly Awee, fuddly muddly...something."

I looked at Mara. "Why don't you take Ollie to your room so he can sleep it off?"

"Good idea." She peeled Ollie's hands away from her knees and convinced him to stand up. "Time for bed, honey."

He let her lead him away, leaning against her the whole time.

Damian latched his arms around my waist. "Is it my bedtime too?"

"Yes, it is." I half dragged him toward the guest house but changed my mind partway there and took him to the wagon. "Naughty little Damian needs some beddy-bye time."

"Oh yeah," he said, "lots and lots of that. Will you tuck me in, Heidi-hi-ho?"

"Uh-huh." After that, he'd have some serious explaining to do.

I managed to get him up the steps and into the wagon, but he careened toward the bench and fell onto it face-first—and promptly passed out. I pushed him onto his side, then grabbed a blanket and draped it over him. By then, he was snoring. What else could I do? I stretched out on the pillows on the floor and waited for him to wake up. Luckily, he had a laptop computer that was hooked into the resort's wi-fi, so I streamed movies while he snored.

Three hours later, he woke up.

Damian yawned loudly, stretched without moving much at all, and groaned. He squinted at me. "On a scale of one to ten, how mad are you?"

"Zero."

His brows rose, but then he winced as if that little action hurt. "Guess I should explain."

I shut the laptop and sat up, holding the computer on my lap. "Yeah, that might be a good idea."

"You see, Ollie was stressed out. And I couldn't think of a way to help him relax and stop worrying so much." He wriggled around until he was lying on his back and rubbed his forehead. "Admittedly, this wasn't my best idea ever."

"No kidding? Huh." I splayed my palms on the computer, tapping my fingertips on it. "So tell me, Your Ludar Highness, what exactly did you hope to accomplish by getting the two of you hammered? I'm assuming that was the plan."

"Yeah, it was." He shrugged. "I wasn't doing much thinking at the time. My best friend needed help, so I, uh…helped." Damian glanced at me sideways, looking almost sheepish. "Ollie was a lot happier after we pigged out and got smashed."

"Of course he was happier. Ollie was high as a kite." I leaned forward, my face a foot from his. "You were too."

"I'm sorry. Trust me, I'm regretting it now. And by the way, I knew it was a bad idea, but I did it anyway. For my friend."

"Mara was stressed too, but I didn't hand her a keg of beer."

"It's different for women. Guys don't do the whole heart-to-heart, let's-share-our-innermost-feelings bullshit."

"Well, at least you didn't hire a hooker." I shimmied closer. "What was Ollie so stressed about? I know why Mara's anxious, but what has Ollie got to be worried about?"

"He's scared he won't be a good father or husband. And he feels guilty for not knowing how to make Mara feel better."

"Do you know about her, um, condition?"

He stared at me for a moment. "Do you know?"

"Yes."

"So do I, if we're talking about the same thing."

We were both trying not to divulge a secret that we each thought the other knew, but we didn't want to betray a confidence from a friend. Mara told me, so Ollie must have told Damian. They'd been best friends since childhood.

"Mara's pregnant," I said. "That's what Ollie told you, right?"

Damian nodded.

I sighed. "She's got her hormones going crazy, but what's Ollie's excuse? He can't honestly believe he'll be a bad father. He'll be great at it."

"They'll both be great parents. We know that, but they're too anxious to realize it. They are getting married in five days."

"And they just found out they're having a baby. That is a lot of stress piled on them. Wish I could do more to help."

Damian raised a hand to cup my cheek. "You've done more than anybody to help Mara. Taking care of all the wedding details must've been a huge weight off her shoulders. You've done way more to help them than I have."

"Getting Ollie drunk might not have been the smartest idea ever, but you did it because you love your best friend."

"Ollie might be my best friend, but you're the best everything to me."

I wasn't sure that statement made sense, but I understood what he meant. If we hadn't said we loved each other last night, maybe I wouldn't have gotten it. But we had, and I did.

"You're my best everything too," I said, turning my face into his palm to kiss it.

He pulled his hand away and grimaced. "Need some water."

"Let's get you into bed first."

I helped him sit up, then hooked an arm around his waist while he laid his arm across my shoulders. We got him into bed without too much trouble, and I tucked him in.

"Be back in a few minutes," I said, kissing his forehead. "You rest. I'll bring water and some saltines."

"Thanks, baby. You're the best."

When I came back ten minutes later, he was still awake and sitting up. I'd brought him water but also a sports drink, for the electrolytes. He sipped that while I opened the box of saltines. I'd brought aspirin too, which he swallowed with the sports drink.

"Nibble on this," I said as I offered him a cracker.

After a few minutes of sipping and nibbling, he waved away any more. "My head's pounding. Think I need another nap."

"Lie on your back. I'll give you my patented headache relief massage."

"You patented it?"

"Not literally. I mean it's guaranteed to work."

He stretched out on his back, his head on the pillow.

I sat beside him, near his head, and began to massage his scalp with my fingertips.

"Mm," he moaned, "that feels so good."

For a few minutes, I massaged his scalp and his temples while humming softly. Then he drifted off, his lips curled up in the sweetest little smile. While he slept, I wandered outside to check on Mara and Ollie, but I ran into Eve first while she was exiting the guest house.

"Ollie's fine," she said when I reached her. "Mara is taking care of him, and she's not even upset about it."

"Mara's a lot stronger than even she knows."

"That's for sure. How's Damian?"

I couldn't help laughing a little. "Wishing he'd come up with a better plan to help Ollie relax."

Eve laughed a bit too. "Val thought it was a great idea. Men. They all think the answer to any problem is booze or sex."

"Good thing they have us to straighten them out, or they'd kill every brain cell they've got."

"So true." Eve tipped her head to the side like she was considering me. "Mara told me how you stepped up to take care of the wedding stuff. Sounds like you've done an amazing job in a short time."

"I owed Mara. After my stupid behavior when we first met."

"You aren't still feeling guilty about that, are you? We all understand what you were going through back then."

"No, I'm not feeling guilty." I shoved my hands into the pockets of my shorts. "But Mara has been such a good friend to me, and I want her to have the wedding of her dreams."

"She told me what you've done. The wedding will be perfect." Eve gave me that head-tipped look again. "Have you ever considered doing that sort of thing for a living?"

"I wanted to be an event coordinator, but my parents thought I should be a doctor. So I became a pharmacy technician instead. Thought that might make them happy, but it didn't."

"You're happy here, aren't you? We certainly love you."

"And I love all you guys too. I love this resort. It feels like home to me."

Damian felt like home too. Even when he got wasted.

Eve set her hands on her hips. "How would you like to become the event coordinator for Au Naturel Naturist Resort? You could do freelance jobs on the side too, like Mara does with the apartment complexes she owns."

For a moment, I could do nothing except stare at her. Had Eve just offered me my dream job? Yeah, she had.

"Are you serious?" I asked. "Because if you are, my answer is yes, yes, yes."

"The job is yours."

I shrieked and leaped up and down, grinning like an idiot. I even clapped my hands and did a little celebration dance.

All the naturists on the lawn turned to look this way, and every one of them smiled and cheered, though they had no idea why I was so happy. I recognized every face. These people were like family to me.

Maybe that's what Damian and Monica had both been trying to tell me. Family was what you made it, and my family was here—with a bunch of naked people.

I hugged Eve. "Thank you so much. This is my dream come true, and I won't let you down."

"Never for a second thought you might."

"Damian will be so happy." I wrinkled my nose. "Unless his hangover is still in high gear."

"Go tell him, sweetie. And welcome to the family."

I raced back into the wagon and leaped onto the bed.

Damian opened his eyes. "What's going on? Is the room actually spinning?"

"No, it's not. Sorry I woke you up, but I have amazing news and I couldn't wait to share it with you."

He yawned and scrubbed his face with both hands, then sat up. "What's the news?"

"I'm the new event coordinator at Au Naturel Naturist Resort."

Damian grinned and kissed me.

Chapter Twenty-Eight

Damian

Heidi must've loved me a lot if she could forgive me for getting drunk with Ollie. She understood why I did it, even if she disagreed with my methods. Once she found out she had a job here at the resort, she didn't care about my dumb idea anymore. Val and Eve did not fire me, though the next morning, they gave me and Ollie a speech about priorities and duties. We nodded at every point they made and promised never again to get drunk on a day when we were supposed to be working.

They weren't angry. But they ran a business, not a home for idiots who thought getting hammered was a reasonable solution for stress relief. Of course they had to give us both a talking-to. We deserved it.

Heidi and I spent the rest of that day lounging in bed while I nursed my hangover. Even after I recovered from my bender, we didn't feel like leaving the wagon except to get food. I wasn't up for sex, literally, so we watched movies and talked.

The next day, we teamed up to finish the wedding prep and keep the bride and groom from going nuts again. Val and Eve decided that was part of our jobs this week, so we didn't get in trouble for not doing our usual jobs. Well, my usual job. Heidi didn't officially start hers until after the wedding.

Two days before the big event, Ollie's family arrived, and an hour later, Mara's parents arrived. My family showed up too. The rest of the guests would be here in the afternoon, but we had lots to do today to get the three families settled in and prepared for the big day. Tonight would be the rehearsal dinner, but the bride and groom had decided against having a bachelor party or a bachelorette party. Instead, we would have one big celebration on the lawn.

Somehow, we survived those two days without any hitches. Mom and I offered free palm and tarot readings to everyone, and we put on a good show for the guests. I'd learned my flair for drama from my mother, so when the two of us collaborated on a show, it was the most fun anyone could have. Heidi was our sexy assistant. Though this wasn't a magic show, we included Heidi just because we wanted to. Mom had suggested it, and I loved having my girl with me while I did my Ludar prince shtick.

Afterward, she called me "the hottest gypsy on earth" and declared I was not a Dracula knockoff after all. I bit her neck just to prove her wrong, but it was only a love bite.

The party Friday night included music, both recorded songs and a live performance by Ollie. He played guitar and sang. Mara even joined him for one song, helping him croon "Bridge Over Troubled Water," which had become their song ever since the day Ollie had sung it to her when they had a private picnic not long after they met.

Heidi and I led a round of charades that resulted in plenty of raucous laughter.

Ollie spent the night in my room to keep up the tradition of the bride and groom not seeing each other until the ceremony.

I slept in the wagon with Heidi. Yeah, we did more than just sleep. When I made love to Heidi that night, I realized I'd fallen even deeper in love with her. Watching this woman wrangle the families and wedding guests, not to mention making sure every last detail got taken care of so Mara and Ollie would have their dream wedding, proved to me what I'd known all along. Heidi Mackenzie was one hell of a woman.

Saturday came so fast. The big day was here.

I didn't see Heidi until we got to the church. Ollie and Mara had considered holding their wedding at the resort, but they decided to go the traditional route instead and have it at the same church where Eve and Val had tied the knot. It was a beautiful building, with stained-glass windows and classic architecture.

Heidi came running up to me in the vestibule. "Can I talk to you alone for a minute?"

"Sure. Is something wrong?"

"No. Just come with me."

I excused myself, telling my parents I'd see them after the ceremony, and followed Heidi into what turned out to be a supply closet.

"What are we doing here?" I asked. "Please don't tell me Mara's getting cold feet."

"No, she's fine. Feeling cold isn't the problem." She backed me up to the wall, pressing her body against me. "I'm having a weird reaction to being the maid of honor."

"Are you getting hives?"

"No, I'm getting hot." She hooked a finger inside my waistband and tugged. "Fuck me, Damian."

"We're in a church. Isn't it a sin or something?"

"Do you care?"

I thought about the question for a few seconds, then wondered why the hell I was thinking about it. Heidi wanted sex. I was a guy, so of course, I wanted that too. My dick was firming up, so it wanted that for sure. But I still had this weird feeling that I shouldn't desecrate a sacred place or something like that.

Maybe falling in love had softened my naughty side, because I found myself easing Heidi away from my body. "I'll fuck you at the reception, okay? Not here in the church. It's Mara and Ollie's big day, after all."

"You'll do it at the reception? Promise?"

I couldn't help laughing. "You have my solemn word. I will drag you into the nearest closet and make you scream—at the reception."

Heidi took a big breath and let it out slowly. "Wow. Who knew a wedding could make me so horny?"

"Everybody reacts differently to big life events." I cradled her face in my hands and kissed the tip of her nose. "Let's go do our wedding jobs. Can't leave Ollie without a best man or Mara without a maid of honor."

"I love you so much, Damian."

Smirking, I slapped her ass. "I kinda like you too, Heidi."

We left the closet hand in hand but said goodbye in the vestibule so we could attend to our duties as maid of honor and best man. Since Ollie and Mara didn't have a flower girl or ring bearer, just the bridesmaids and groomsmen, Ollie led us guys into the chapel and straight to the altar where we would wait for the ladies to do their thing. First, the guests had to file in and take their seats, with Sylvester Norris as the usher. Yeah, he seemed kind of old for the job, but Sly was like family to all of us. He had a great time executing his duties, though he did more than show people to their seats. He told jokes and made a grand, sweeping gesture with his arm to let the guests know where to sit. He also said, in a booming voice, "Please be seated here. It has the best view in the house."

Yeah, every guest got the best view. Amazing, right?

Sly was full of it, but at least he was enjoying himself.

I let my gaze wander over the decorations that had transformed this simple chapel into a dream venue for a wedding. Heidi was responsible for all of it. Garlands of fresh greenery and daisies draped over the backs of the pews and around the edges of the altar, not to mention the doorways and the vestibule. The garlands didn't just have flowers and leafy stuff, though. I also saw sprays of baby's breath and sprigs of fern leaves. Heidi had gone all out. It was the perfect backdrop for the wedding of two naturists who worked at a rural nudist resort.

Once everyone had taken their seats, a violin began to play. The bridesmaids ambled down the aisle toward us with Heidi in front, all of them wearing pale-green dresses that had small daisies sewn onto the neckline. Heidi wore her hair up in a loose style that let tendrils hang down to kiss her cheeks. Eve followed Heidi to the altar. She looked pretty too, but not as beautiful as the maid of honor.

They took their places opposite us guys. I stood beside Ollie with Val Silva on my other side.

Any second, Mara would enter the chapel.

The violin music stopped, and for two seconds, we all waited in silence.

An organ began to play the wedding march.

Mara walked through the doors holding a bouquet of daisies and baby's breath, guided down the aisle by her dad. Peter Severins looked like he was fighting back tears, and when I glanced at where Sheryl Severins sat in the first pew, she was doing more than fighting back tears. They streamed down her cheeks. Ollie's mom sat right next to Sheryl, and she was crying too while the moms clasped each other's hands.

Mara looked like an angel in her flowing white dress and lacy veil that draped down her back and covered most of her hair, though it didn't cover her face. She smiled at Ollie with the most beautiful look of pure love on her face as she slowly approached the altar.

Would Heidi ever look at me that way? I glanced at her, and as if fate had inspired us both, she looked at me at the same time. Maybe I was gazing at her the way Mara had gazed at Ollie. I couldn't say for sure, but I felt a strangely good pressure in my chest and a gentle warmth that spread through me from head to toe.

Heidi blinked away tears, or tried to, and sniffled. She kept smiling at me almost the same way Mara had gazed at Ollie.

I hardly noticed the rest of the ceremony. Ollie and Mara said their vows, both of them crying, and promised to love and respect each other from this day forward. I watched them exchange rings. Why did I get choked up when they did that? I'd never been the sentimental type, but to see my best friend marrying the only woman he'd ever really loved, who loved him too… Okay, I got sentimental. I turned my head to the side and wiped my eyes so no one else would see.

Finally, the big moment came—the kiss.

Ollie cradled Mara's face in his hands and pressed his mouth to hers.

Cheers and clapping erupted inside the chapel, echoing off the high ceiling.

Ollie pulled Mara into his arms, still kissing her. They kept kissing for so long that somebody shouted, "Come on, Ollie, we want to eat. You can make out with Mara later."

Who shouted that? Sylvester, of course.

The newly minted husband and wife trotted down the aisle and out the doors, with the rest of us close behind. They raced across the vestibule and out the main doors, then climbed into a waiting limousine.

Another, bigger limo waited to ferry the bridesmaids and groomsmen to the reception venue.

Heidi and I sat beside each other during the ride, holding hands.

Like a real gentleman, Val had offered to be Bailey Jackson's "date" for the reception since the teenager was the only kid in attendance. Eve was his "secondary date," but she didn't mind coming in number two. Bailey was thrilled to be included in the wedding party and to see her brother get hitched. We arrived seconds after the bride and groom, but the party was already in full swing.

Music. Laughter. Dancing. And yeah, food. Sylvester wouldn't starve today.

Everyone was having a great time. Val danced with Bailey and showed her some classy moves, then he danced with Eve. I danced with lots of women but kept missing out on taking Heidi for a whirl since every other guy here wanted to hold the blonde bombshell in his arms. We glimpsed each other on the dance floor, but I'd have to wait awhile longer for my chance.

But it was my turn to dance with Mara.

"You're the most beautiful bride ever," I told her as I took her hand and we assumed the appropriate pose, moving slowly to the music.

"Thank you, Damian. But I'm sure you'll change your mind about that when you and Heidi get married."

Though I kept dancing, her statement stunned me. Maybe it shouldn't have, but then, Heidi and I hadn't been a couple for long.

"Married?" I said. "We're nowhere near that point yet."

"But you're moving toward it faster every day. Aren't you?"

"I don't know. Not thinking about that stuff."

Mara's lips curved upward in a knowing smile. "Oh yes, you are."

"No, I—"

She nodded past my shoulder and stepped back. "Heidi's ready for you."

I glanced over my shoulder and saw Heidi, standing alone at the edge of the dance floor and smiling at me.

"Go," Mara said. "And think about what I said. There's no such thing as too soon when you're with the right person."

Mara kissed my cheek and trotted off to find her husband.

I walked over to Heidi and held out my hand. "May I have this dance?"

"Yes, please." She settled her hand in mine. "I've been waiting for this dance forever."

And I'd been waiting for her forever. I just hadn't realized that until today.

Chapter Twenty-Nine

Heidi

Damian guided us around the dance floor, one hand on the small of my back and the other clasping mine. He looked gorgeous in his tuxedo, even better than when he'd worn his black suit. The expression on his face made me feel warm in the sweetest way and made my throat tighten. Was I giving him that same adoring look? I did adore him, so yeah, I must've been gazing at him that way.

The wedding had been beautiful, emotional, perfect. I loved watching Ollie and Mara speak their vows, but I loved dancing with Damian even more. Somehow, I could feel blissfully at peace and so damn horny all at the same time.

He bent his head to whisper in my ear, "Still want to get it on? I saw a closet in the hallway."

"Can you read my mind? I was just thinking about how horny I am." I slid my hand up to his neck and tickled his nape. "You make me feel every kind of good there is. And yes, I'd love to get it on with you in a closet or anywhere."

"Glad to hear it." He led me off the dance floor and toward the double doors that opened into the main hallway of the community center, which tonight served as a wedding reception hall. He glanced around as we exited the room, and the doors swung shut behind us. "You did such an amazing job with the decorations, and it's even more impressive considering how little time you had."

My cheeks warmed up. No one had ever complimented a job I'd done, certainly not the way he just did. "Thank you, but Mara and her mom had already done some of the work."

"They say you did ninety-nine percent of it."

"No, I just—"

He pulled us to a stop in the middle of the vestibule and turned toward me, grasping both my hands. "Don't do that, Heidi."

"What?"

"Don't downplay how much work you put into this. You did it. You." He tugged me closer. "You are an amazing woman. That's why I love you. That's why everyone loves you, but me most of all."

Gazing into his eyes, I knew he meant every word. "Thank you, Damian."

He took hold of a lock of my hair, twining it around his finger. "Marry me, Heidi."

"Huh?" Yeah, that was my response. One grunted syllable. I couldn't make any other sounds, not with him looking at me with so much love and sincerity on his face and in his eyes. My pulse pounded in my ears, my heart thudded in my chest, and the sweetest warmth I'd ever experienced glowed inside me. I loved him. I wanted to marry him. Now, if I could only get those words to come out of my mouth. But again, I could speak only one syllable. "Yes."

He cradled my face in his hands. "Are you sure? 'Huh, yes' isn't the most definitive answer."

"Sorry. I was surprised, that's all." I laid my hands over his, where he still held them on my cheeks. "Yes, Damian, my answer is yes. I love you, and I can't wait to marry you."

He smiled, and though it wasn't a big grin, it conveyed all the emotions he felt for me better than the most exuberant grin could. When he kissed me, he did it with the same heartfelt emotion, pressing his lips to mine but not deepening the kiss. He held his mouth to mine for a moment that seemed to last forever, but only in the best way.

Then he pulled away, his lips curving into another heartfelt smile. "Didn't mean to blurt out the question like that, but I suddenly couldn't wait."

"I'm glad you blurted it out."

"Maybe we shouldn't tell everyone until later. This is Mara and Ollie's big night."

"Yeah, we should wait." I looped my arms around his neck. "We'll have the best wedding planner ever, huh?"

"Definitely." He linked his hands at the small of my back. "And I'll have the best partner for the rest of my life."

"Me too."

He hugged me tight and kissed me.

The doors to the reception room swung open.

We turned our heads in that direction.

Val and Eve locked the doors in the open position, then finally noticed us. Eve smiled. Val arched one brow and smirked.

"The bride and groom are ready to head out," Eve said. "If you two can press pause on the make-out session for a few minutes."

Damian peeled our bodies apart and straightened his tux jacket.

He and Val opened the main doors and held them, each leaning back against a door. Eve and I stood beside them.

The happy couple walked out of the reception hall hand in hand, grinning and whispering to each other, while their parents and Ollie's sister followed close behind. Once everyone exited through the main doors, the rest of us hurried down the steps after them, heading for the waiting limo. Sunset glowed pink and purple in the western sky, providing just enough light for the big goodbye.

Everyone hugged Mara and Ollie and wished them the best of everything.

When I hugged Mara, she whispered in my ear, "I know you and Damian will be the next to say 'I do,' and it won't be long at all." She drew her head back to aim a knowing smile at me. "Maybe he's already popped the question?"

How did she know? Maybe it showed on my face. "Don't worry about me and Damian. Go, have a fabulous honeymoon. I expect Ollie to be completely exhausted when you guys get home."

Val opened the limo door.

Ollie held out his hand to help Mara into the car.

While the limo drove away, and the ubiquitous tin cans rattled along behind it, I slipped an arm around Damian's waist and leaned my head against his shoulder. My throat went thick. Tears stung my eyes. Ollie and Mara, the two sweetest people on earth, had found their happily ever after, and so had I. Damian gave it to me.

And we were engaged.

Oh. My. God.

Damian kissed the top of my head. "Don't worry. We can get married tomorrow or wait five years. I don't care as long as I have you."

"Let's not wait five years, but tomorrow might be a bit too soon. I need to plan our wedding, you know. Plus, I've got my awesome new job."

"No rush. I'll wait forever for you."

God, I loved him.

After the limo drove out of sight, everyone went back inside to enjoy the party. Damian and I didn't run off to that closet after all. We stayed with our friends to celebrate. I wasn't disappointed at all because, hey, I loved a party. Everybody knew that. Maybe I hadn't let myself really cut loose in way too long, but tonight, I got back to being the old me—the real me. I partied hearty, doing every dance move I could pull off in this dress, and Damian joined me for every single silly thing I wanted to do. He came up with ideas of his own too, like juggling deviled eggs. Seriously, he did that. Damian called it "an old Ludar wedding tradition," but everyone knew he was making that up because he smirked and winked when he issued his proclamation.

That night, Damian and I slept in my room in the guest house.

After that, the days went by so fast. The families hung around for a couple more days to kick back, which gave us more time to spend with the Petrescus. Damian and I debated whether to tell them our happy news yet, but we finally decided they should hear it from us in person. So we took Damian's parents, his brother, his sister-in-law, and their two kids for a nature walk. Once we got well away from the resort, with no one else around, we stopped the group and faced them, hand in hand.

"We have some news," Damian said.

Monica raised her hands in a grand gesture and smiled. "You're engaged."

"Jeez, Mom, you could've at least let us tell you ourselves."

Adrian Petrescu chuckled. "Mothers always know these things."

Monica held two fingers to each of her temples and squinted. "I foresee children. Many children." She smiled and winked at us. "I foresee that happening soon."

Stefan grinned. "Better hope the kids look like Heidi, not my rat-faced brother."

"Uncle Damian is cute," said the niece of the man in question. "That's what my friends keep saying, anyway."

Damian rolled his eyes. "Is anybody going to congratulate us?"

"Of course, dear," Monica said. She threw her arms around both of us. "Congratulations. I knew from the moment I saw you two together that this would happen. You're destined for a long and happy life together. The spirits have assured me of that." Monica kissed Damian's cheek, then mine. "And your union will produce many grandchildren for me to spoil."

Damian half-scowled, half-smiled. "Mom, would you get off the 'many children' prophecy already? You're scaring Heidi."

"No, she's not," I said with a laugh. "Bring on the army of Ludar babies. I can handle it. They'll only be half Ludar, though."

"Nonsense," Monica said, patting my cheek. "You are one of us now. Ludar by desire, if not by blood."

"Thank you, Monica. That's so kind of you to say."

"Call me Mom. You're joining the family, after all."

My throat tightened. She wanted me to call her Mom. How would my actual mother feel about me marrying a gypsy and joining his family? I'd have to tell my parents, but just thinking about that made me slightly nauseous.

Damian's mother hugged me. "Don't worry, dear. Your parents will see the light one day."

The families went home the next day, but we hadn't shared our news with anyone other than Damian's family. When Ollie and Mara came home a week later, we knew it was time to break the news.

Damian being, well, Damian, he decided to make a big splash. He waited until everyone was gathered in the dining hall, including Val, Eve, Mara, and Ollie. We were seated at the same table with them. Our friends had gotten a touch suspicious when Damian insisted we all must eat in the dining hall tonight, but they went along with it.

Now, Damian jumped onto the table and hollered, "May I have your attention, please. Heidi and I have an announcement to make."

Everyone stopped talking. All eyes turned to us.

Damian bent to offer me his hand.

I accepted it and climbed onto the table with him.

He slipped his arm around me and announced, "We're getting married."

Cheers and whoops filled the hall, the noise almost deafening but filled with real joy.

Damian scooped me up in his arms and leaped off the table, landing flat on his feet inches behind the chairs we had occupied thirty seconds earlier. He kissed me, quick and hard. Then he hoisted me above his head. "The Ludar prince has claimed his mate."

When I glanced down at him, he winked at me.

Damian set me down amid even louder cheers and whoops.

At that moment, I knew our wedding would be one wild event. And I couldn't wait for that.

Chapter Thirty

Damian

A few days after we announced our engagement to our
friends and a crowd of naturists, Heidi and I got on a plane
to go visit her parents. She had suggested it. Though she was
keeping up a brave face, I knew she dreaded telling her mom
and dad about us, especially since she'd never mentioned me to
them. Heidi admitted to me she hadn't spoken to her parents in
months, not since they chastised her for dumping that douchebag cheater she'd kept going back to every time he begged her
to forgive him. Well, every time until the last time. Heidi had
found her inner strength at last.

We had one last hurdle to jump over. I was about to meet her
parents.

Heidi had told them she was bringing her new boyfriend, but
she'd wanted to hold off on sharing the engagement news until we
were there in person to tell them.

Ethan and Janice Mackenzie lived in Omaha, Nebraska, though
separately since they were divorced. Janice still lived in the same
cookie-cutter house inside the same cookie-cutter gated community where Heidi had grown up. Nothing wrong with that, but I
couldn't see Heidi feeling happy and free in a place like this. They
had rules for what people could do with their yards, how often

they had to mow and prune the bushes, what kind of Christmas lights they could put up, and lots more stuff. No wonder Heidi had needed to escape to the naturist resort.

I knew she'd been living in a small apartment in Omaha for years. She gave up that apartment a few days after we got engaged. Heidi Mackenzie belonged at the resort where everyone loved her, and where she could be herself without fear of offending anyone.

Yeah, I had a feeling her parents would be offended big time when they met me.

Heidi rang the doorbell and started wringing her hands.

I clasped her left hand, giving it a reassuring squeeze, and glanced at the engagement ring sparkling on her finger. Then I kissed her cheek. "Relax. If they act like dicks, you've got backup."

She smiled tightly. "I know. Thank you for coming with me."

"Just think of me as your Ludar knight, ready to defend your honor to the death."

The door opened, and a gray-haired man furrowed his brows at us. "You brought a man with you."

"Yeah, Dad," Heidi said. "I told you Damian was coming."

Ethan Mackenzie grunted. "Guess you better come inside. Not sure how your mother will react. You know she doesn't do well with the sorts of men you like to take up with. Whatever happened to Grant? He was the only good one."

I could see Heidi was clenching her jaw, but she maintained her polite demeanor.

Ethan led us inside and straight to the dining room where the table had been set up with places for four people. If they'd forgotten Heidi was bringing a guest, why had they set the table for us? I guessed Ethan and Janice just liked making their daughter feel as if she'd done something wrong.

Heidi's mom walked through the swinging door to the kitchen. She was carrying a roast on a platter, which she set down on the table. "At least you're here on time for dinner, Heidi."

As we got closer to the table, I saw name cards in front of each plate. I was supposed to sit across the table from Heidi.

Screw that.

I pretended not to notice the name cards and sat down in the chair next to Heidi's. She bit her lip for half a second, then settled onto the chair beside me, the one reserved for her. Ethan sat at the head of the table beside Heidi. His wife took the chair across from her daughter. I grabbed the place setting meant for me and moved it over to this side of the table.

Janice pursed her lips.

Neither of Heidi's parents had bothered with introductions.

I decided what the hell, I'd do it for them. "I'm Damian Petrescu, by the way. And you are Janice and Ethan Mackenzie. It's nice to meet you. Thank you for cooking such a nice meal for us."

The rest of the meal had already been laid out on the table before Janice brought in the roast. We had broccoli and cauliflower, mashed potatoes, and hot rolls. She really had made a nice meal, so I hadn't been lying when I thanked her for that. Now if she would only start acting like a decent human being, the night would be perfect.

"Petrescu," Janice said, pronouncing my last name as if she'd never heard anything so alien. "Is that Eastern European?"

"Romanian."

"How interesting." Her stiff tone and stiff posture suggested she didn't like having to converse with me. "Isn't that interesting, Ethan?"

"Yeah, it's damn fascinating." Heidi's dad shoved a forkful of meat into his mouth and talked while chewing, his gaze on me. "You one of those commies from the Eastern Bloc?"

"No, I'm descended from a long line of proud Ludar."

He paused in the middle of hacking off another piece of the roast. "Loo-what?"

"Ludar. My family, on both my mother's and my father's side, can trace our lineage back hundreds of years to the earliest Rom tribes."

"You're from Italy? Thought you said Romania."

I couldn't help smiling. Lots of people got confused when I talked about my heritage. "Rom is spelled R-O-M. It's not the city in Italy. It's who we are. The Ludar came from the Rom tribes, which most people call gypsies."

Janice's eyes flew wide. "Gypsies? Oh dear lord, what sort of man have you taken up with this time, Heidi?"

My fiancée slammed her fork down on her plate, making it wobble and smack back down. "Damian is a good man. The best I've ever met, way better than Grant, who you and Dad thought was the perfect match for me."

"He was. I'm sure he'd take you back if—"

"Grant cheated on me repeatedly. I kept taking him back, but never again. Damian is a thousand times the man Grant Busch will ever be."

"But this…gentleman is a gypsy." Janice spoke that word like it was the worst kind of swearing.

"Damian is a wonderful man." She raised her left hand, aiming that sparkling diamond toward her mom. "You guys didn't even notice this, did you? Damian and I are engaged."

Both her parents gaped at her.

I clasped her hand and kissed her ring.

"We know nothing about this man," Ethan said. "You can't marry a complete stranger."

"He's not a stranger to me," Heidi told him.

"Does he even have a job? Or will you be traveling around like hobos?"

"I'm the concierge at a resort," I said.

"What kind of resort?" Ethan asked.

Heidi and I glanced at each other, and I knew from her expression that she wanted me to tell them the truth, no matter how they reacted. "I work at Au Naturel Naturist Resort."

Janice contorted her face into an expression of genuine horror. "Isn't that the unseemly place where Heidi insists on taking her vacations? That's a nudist resort."

"Yeah, it is. We both work there now."

"My daughter cannot work at a place like that. Taking vacations there is bad enough, but—"

"Stop it, Mom," Heidi said. "I work there, and I'm marrying Damian. Get over it."

I was so proud of Heidi that I wanted to hug her.

But she wasn't done yet. The powerhouse hidden inside that easygoing exterior had lots more to say.

Chapter Thirty-One

Heidi

I pushed my chair back and got up, needing to stand tall while I told my parents all the things I should've told them a long time ago. Damian had helped me see how much I'd let my mom and dad affect my life and my choices, and he'd shown me I was done with that garbage. I loved him so much for getting the ball rolling, but now I needed to finish it.

"Yes, my favorite place on earth is a nudist resort," I said, my voice calmer than I could've hoped. I felt calm too, surprisingly so considering what I intended to do. "I feel more at home there than I ever did here with you two. The friends I've made at the resort have become like family to me. Honestly, they *are* my family now, more than my own parents have ever been."

"Heidi—"

I cut my mom off with a raised hand. "Let me finish. You're my parents, and I love you despite all the ways you've made me feel unworthy of your love. Every time you put me in the middle of one of your arguments, I thought it was my fault you couldn't get along. I thought it was my fault you got divorced. No boyfriend I ever had was good enough for you except for the creep who slept with every woman he met and told me it was my fault for not satisfying his needs."

My parents stared at me like I'd grown five extra heads.

But I had a bit more to say. "I should've told you all of this years ago, but I was afraid you'd never speak to me again if I did. Well, I don't care about that anymore. Cut me out of your lives if you want. You've pretty much done that already, but I'll keep the hope alive that one day you will take a hard look at your behavior and decide to end the cycle. When you do that, I'll welcome you back into my life."

They still stared at me.

Good. Maybe that meant I'd shocked them enough that they might actually think about what I'd told them.

"Let's go, Damian," I said. "I'm not hungry anymore."

He got up. "Neither am I."

From my purse, I pulled out the little pad of paper I always carried with me. After scribbling my new phone number and address on the pad, I tore off the page and set it on the table. "This is where you can find me. Good night, Mom. Good night, Dad."

Damian and I walked out of the house and drove to our hotel. We didn't get much sleep that night, though not because of stress or anxiety. He made love to me for hours, and in between each session, we talked and ate snacks and sipped wine. Confronting my parents should have been the most stressful thing I'd ever done, but instead, it had turned into a cathartic moment. The fears I'd lived with for so long melted away. Whether my parents ever wised up didn't matter. I was free.

The next morning, we flew home and got back to our life. And it was "ours" now, not mine or his. We shared a room in the guest house and wound up hunting for a house to buy in tandem with Ollie and Mara. Joint house hunting was a lot more fun than doing it by ourselves. Ollie and Mara found their dream house first, but then Damian and I realized we'd found ours too without even thinking about it.

We bought the house next door to theirs.

The two homes were separated by a few hundred feet, but it seemed appropriate to live so nearby considering that Ollie was Damian's best friend and Mara was mine. The houses sat on the outskirts of town, bordered by woods and fields on three sides, so it felt a lot like how we'd lived at the resort. The commute to work didn't bother us at all. The four of us carpooled.

A few weeks later, I handled my first event for a guest. I organized a birthday party for Ruth Norris. It was a hoot and a half, and it gave me more confidence in my ability to coordinate events for strangers since I'd managed to do two for my friends. My family. That's what they were. Not just friends, but the family I'd chosen for myself.

I still held out hope for my parents, but I didn't dwell on them. I had too much of my own life to keep me busy—and happy.

One day, Eve found me in the resort office. She marched straight up to the desk, where I was sitting while I plotted out a calendar of daily events for our guests. Eve bounced on her toes, biting her lip while she seemed to struggle not to grin. Her eyes shined with excitement too.

"What's up, Evie?" I asked. "You look like you've got amazing news. Are you pregnant?"

"No, not yet." She clasped her hands in front of her chest, bouncing even more. "We have a huge opportunity that could boost the resort's image and expand our demographics big time."

"That's amazing." I stood up. "What is this huge opportunity?"

"A wedding. Here at the resort." Though she still seemed excited, her almost grin turned slightly anxious as she bit down harder on her lip. "But it relies on you. I know you're still settling into your new job, and you haven't done anything this big yet, but..." She grabbed my hands and stopped bouncing. "Please don't say no until you've talked to him."

"Who?"

"The groom. He's British, and his fiancée is Scottish, and they have lots of relatives and friends in America and the UK." Eve gripped my hands tighter. "They have a *lot* of relatives on the bride's side. I mean a *lot*. They want to get married here, but we'll need to arrange for accommodations in town too since we don't have the capacity for this big a gathering. Then there will be events in the week leading up to the wedding, but the bride's sister wants to help out with that. The rest is up to us—and you."

The bride and groom had so many relatives and friends that we'd need to put some of them up in town. How many people would there be? Sheesh, it must be one enormous family.

"Um, well," I started, biting my lip much the way Eve had bitten hers, "you know I'm new at this event coordinator stuff. This sounds like a huge deal, and I don't want to screw it up. Maybe you should hire a professional."

"I have hired one. You." She grasped my shoulders. "You can do this, Heidi. We all believe in you. Plus, Mara and I can handle the logistics. The boys can help out too, with the heavy lifting and stuff. You will be the big boss, the one making the plans that we execute."

"Well… I don't know. What if I screw up our big chance to expand our demographics?"

"You won't. Talk to Damian. He'll convince you." Eve hugged me. "You can do this, Heidi. Trust me, you can."

How could I say no? Eve and Val had given me a job that I had no experience or training to do and trusted me to do it right. So far, I had. But a huge event like this ratcheted up my anxiety. Still, I refused to shy away from a challenge. And I had my new family to stand by me.

"Okay," I said. "I'll do it."

Eve, the level-headed resort owner, shrieked and leaped up and down. She dragged me into a bear hug, then bolted out the door.

Wow, this event must've been a doozy. Maybe it would flush the resort with cash so we could make even more improvements.

I found Damian at the gypsy wagon. He'd just finished up with a young couple and was standing outside the wagon shaking their hands and wishing them a good stay at the resort. When they walked away, I approached him.

"Did you hear about the massively huge event Eve set up?" I asked.

"Yeah, Ollie told me. You're nervous about coordinating the whole thing, aren't you?"

"Of course I am. But I'll do it anyway. I need to do it, to prove I can handle this job."

He slung an arm around my waist and tugged me close. "You can deal with anything, baby. After the way you stood up to your parents, I know there's nothing you can't handle."

"I really, really love you."

"Good. Because it's time to arrange our wedding."

Maybe I should've felt anxious about that since I had this other huge event to plan, but thinking about our wedding relaxed me. I couldn't wait to organize that. Couldn't wait to marry Damian.

Eve came running up from the direction of the guest house. She stopped a few feet from us, breathing hard. "Almost forgot. That British guy is coming tomorrow to check out the resort and talk to us in person about what events he and his fiancée would like to have here."

"We'll be ready," I said. "The Au Naturel Reserve Army is ready for action. And by that I mean me, Damian, Ollie, Mara, and Val."

"Guess that makes me the general."

I saluted her. "Yes, ma'am."

Eve grinned and sprinted for the caretaker's house.

"Ready to plan two weddings at once?" I asked Damian.

"Absolutely. I'm your slave, so order me to do anything you want." He bent his head until his nose bumped mine. "And I do mean anything. I'd love to be your personal masseur, strictly for stress relief."

"You are fantastic at relieving my stress."

We headed back to the office and got to work.

The next morning, we hosted our own little British invasion. Our guest didn't sing pop songs, but he was from that other country over there. He arrived in a rented car. Though Eve had offered to pick him up at the airport, he had declined their offer, saying he preferred to drive himself. His fiancée wasn't coming with him, Eve had said.

Val, Eve, Ollie, Mara, Damian, and I waited in the driveway as our guest parked and got out.

Wow, if all Brits were as hot as this guy, I'd have to drag Damian over to the UK for our honeymoon just so I could enjoy the eye candy. This Brit had a muscular body and a beautiful face, with whiskey-brown eyes and hair to match.

He strode up to our little army. "Which of you is Eve?"

"I am," our fearless leader said. She offered the man her hand. "Welcome to Au Naturel Naturist Resort, Dr. Thorne."

"Call me Alex." He shook her hand. "It's a pleasure to meet you, Eve, after the phone discussions we've had. Catriona would've loved to meet all of you too, but I haven't told her about this place yet. I wanted to see it for myself first and surprise her with the news."

"Let me introduce you to everyone." Eve turned sideways to us. "Guys, this is Dr. Alex Thorne. He's an archaeologist, and so is his fiancée. Alex, meet the Au Naturel team."

Eve introduced us one by one, starting with Val, and we had a group chat before Eve and Val took Alex Thorne on a tour of the grounds. That gave the rest of us a break before we would be asked to chat with our guest about what he and fiancée might like for their wedding and when that would be.

Since we had free time, Damian and I headed for the horse pasture. While I brushed the boys, Damian went over to the shed that held all the horsey stuff. I got engrossed in my grooming duties and didn't notice what he was doing until he came up beside me.

"Ready for a ride?" he asked.

I glanced at him. He was holding a saddle in his arms.

For two seconds, I panicked on the inside.

"You don't have to if you're not ready for it yet," he said. "But you've gotten comfortable with Lenny and Georgie. You lead them around and make them back up and stop. They love and respect you almost as much as I do, so I know you're ready for this. But it's up to you."

The panic had evaporated almost as quickly as it set in, and I knew one thing for certain. I was always safe when I was with Damian.

"Sure," I said. "It's about time I tried riding."

Damian put the saddle on Georgie and did up all the complicated doohickeys that held it in place. He would need to teach me about all that eventually, but for now, I just wanted to overcome my last remaining fear. I wanted to ride a horse.

Georgie nuzzled me when I approached him, like he wanted me to climb onto his back.

Damian half crouched and cupped his hands, linking his fingers. "I'll give you a boost."

I stepped into his waiting hands, and he pushed up while I grasped the saddle horn and swung my leg over. I slipped my boots into the stirrups and picked up the reins.

"How's it feel?" Damian asked.

"Good. A little weird, since I've never done this before. But mostly good."

"I'll lead him around until you get comfortable with everything."

Damian took hold of the reins and guided Georgie around in the paddock.

I was on a horse. Holy cow.

After a few minutes, Damian let go. He gave me advice on how to make Georgie do what I wanted, and I rode him around and around inside the paddock, feeling more at ease with every passing moment. Maybe I wasn't an expert rider, not yet, but I had the best teacher to guide me. And the sweetest horse too.

Whatever life threw at me now, I could handle it.

And as for the massive wedding... Yeah, I could deal with that too.

Chapter Thirty-Two

Damian

After Heidi's first ride, we returned to the resort for the big meeting with Alex Thorne. This was when we would all present our ideas for his wedding and listen to his thoughts so we could hash out the details. We had two months to get it done, but Eve wanted to have as much nailed down as possible before our guest flew home tomorrow. To accommodate all seven of us, we gathered in the dining hall and pushed two tables together.

Our guest sat at the head of the table. The ladies occupied one side while the guys took the other.

I'd never met a British person before, or a Scottish person either. But soon, I'd meet more Brits and a whole honking horde of Scots.

Eve and Heidi took the lead in our discussion.

Alex Thorne seemed to like that.

"Aren't I a lucky bloke?" he said. "Two beautiful women ready to cater to my every whim." He winked at me. "Don't worry. I have my hands full with a fiery Scots lass, so I don't have time to seduce your fiancée away from you."

"What about Eve?" I asked. "She's not your type?"

He chuckled. "Every woman is my type, but I'm strictly a window-shopper these days. I've waited fourteen bloody years to marry Catriona MacTaggart, and I won't bollocks it up. Not that I have eyes for anyone but her. She is my soul mate, which is something I used to think was rubbish."

"But now you're into it. I get that. Never believed in soul mates either until I fell for Heidi."

My fiancée glanced at me, her eyes widening briefly right before she smiled. "Yeah, I believe in that sappy stuff now too. Love changes your perspective on everything."

Alex sighed, his lips forming a soft smile. "Yes, it does. And to think I never would've found Cat again after all these years if her meddling family hadn't gotten involved."

"Is that the mob of Scots you mentioned earlier?" Ollie asked. "Can't wait to meet them. They sound like a crazy bunch."

"Oh yes, that they are," Alex said with what I could only describe as a devious smile. "Most of them want to murder me, but marrying Cat ought to keep their homicidal impulses at bay. She will beat to death anyone who lays a finger on me."

Were all Brits as weird as this guy? I kind of liked him, but damn, he had the most bizarre sense of humor. At least I thought he was kidding about Scots wanting to murder him.

Ollie seemed confused too. "You're joking, right? There won't seriously be Scottish people trying to off you while you're all here for the wedding."

"Yes, of course I'm joking," Alex said. "My parents did kidnap us recently, but Cat and I outwitted them. Now they're both locked up."

No one spoke. We all stared at Alex Thorne. Had that been another joke?

"I can see I've stunned the lot of you," Alex said. "It's true, though. My mother is in prison, and my father resides in a psychiatric facility."

Eve regained her ability to speak before the rest of us. "Do you tell everyone you meet about your, um, parents being…"

"Incarcerated? No, I don't spread that around." Alex clasped his hands behind his head. "But it was in the papers and on the telly a few months ago, at least in Scotland. So it's hardly a state secret these days."

"Telly?" I asked.

Val explained, "He means television. Brits call it the telly. I spent some time in England when I was on the Brazilian national football team."

"You're a footballer?" Alex said. "Have you ever tried shinty?"

"I have never heard of it."

"Not surprising. It's a Scottish game that I like to call the bastard child of lacrosse and field hockey."

The conversation continued from there, with Alex making strange jokes while he discussed the wedding preparations and the differences between the UK and America. We all got used to Alex's sense of humor and wound up laughing a lot. The wedding would take place in eight weeks, but when Eve told Alex we already had guests booked for that week, he offered to pay those people to take a vacation anywhere in the world they wanted to go, no matter the cost.

He wasn't kidding. He seriously would do that.

After the group confab, Eve and Val went into the caretaker's house to call those guests and tell them the plan. I had a feeling nobody would balk. I mean, Alex had vowed to spend "any amount of money" to send those people on "their dream holiday." Ollie and Mara went to the office to study the list of wedding guests Alex had given them.

Heidi and I took Alex out to the horse pasture. When I'd mentioned my pilot project, he had wanted to see it "purely for the sake of curiosity but potentially for more." I had no idea what he meant by "more," but hey, if the guy wanted to see the horse pasture, I'd show it to him. He was paying an obscene amount of money for a week-long "wedding extravaganza," as he called it.

We stood at the fence, petting the horses while we talked. He told us a bit about his life, and we shared funny stories from the resort.

"I saw a gypsy wagon out there," Alex said. "Is that owned by a guest or the resort?"

"The resort paid for it, but it's my thing."

"You would be the Ludar prince referenced on the sign."

"That's right."

Alex scratched under Georgie's chin. "Are you a genuine Ludar, or is that strictly an act for the tourists?"

My Ludar lidar was pinging, but in a good way. I had a feeling Alex knew about this stuff. "I'm descended from a long line of proud Ludar, that's what my mom likes to say. I've got Rom genes on both sides of the family tree."

"Your ancestors must've fled Eastern Europe in the late eighteen hundreds during the great migration."

"That's right."

"I'm not well-versed in the history of the gypsies, but it has always fascinated me. Everything historical interests me."

"Happy to give you a palm reading while you're here."

Alex raised one brow. "Don't think I'll risk finding out what the Fates have in store for me. I prefer to live in blissful ignorance believing only good things will come my way now that I have Catriona. The past is prologue, but it's not the denouement."

I had no idea what that meant, but it sounded cool.

Heidi cleared her throat. "Can I ask you a personal question, Alex?"

"Go on. I'm not at all shy. Shameless is more accurate."

The Brit and I had something in common. Who knew?

"Okay," Heidi said. She hesitated before asking, "How did you deal with having bad parents?"

Alex studied her for a moment, his head tipped to the side. "Am I sensing a bit of a kindred spirit in you, Heidi? Are your parents not the sweet, doting sort?"

"No. They're not as bad as yours, but they aren't ideal either. They've always made me the center of their arguments, even when I was a kid, and even after they got divorced."

I draped an arm around her shoulders. "Heidi told them off a while back. I think they're still recovering from the shock."

Alex braced his arm on the fence, tapping one finger on the board. "My best advice for dealing with rubbish parents is to pretend they don't exist. If your mother and father should ever want back in your life, you'll have to decide whether to let them in. Unless and until that happens, make your own family with the friends you have here. It seems as if they're already like family to you."

"Yeah, we're all super close. And you're not the first person who's told me family is what you make it, that blood isn't everything."

"That's true. I'm about to have parents-in-law, three brothers-in-law, and two sisters-in-law, not to mention an army of Catriona's cousins. Then there's my half-brother, though I had no idea he existed, and vice versa, until a few months ago. My brother has cousins too, and they've sort of adopted me." Alex smirked. "I'm positively swimming in family."

Heidi wasn't swimming in family yet, but she had plenty of people who loved her. I got why she'd asked Alex how he dealt with having jerks for parents, but I was also pretty sure she wouldn't have gotten upset if he'd told her he had never made peace with his past. Heidi had moved beyond all that too. I still hoped one day her mom and dad would get over their issues and start acting like adults. I wouldn't hold my breath, though.

We talked to Alex for a little while longer, then we returned to the resort to check in with what the rest of the gang had done in our absence concerning Alex's big wedding. Heidi went to the office to sort through all the ideas the gang had come up with and start formulating a plan. I had my concierge stuff to do, so I left Alex with Eve and Val.

Halfway through the afternoon, I stopped by the office to check on Heidi. She was poring over the information on several pieces of paper that were stapled together.

I settled onto the chair beside the desk. "How's it going?"

"Okay." She held up the stapled sheets so I could see the text printed on them. "This is the guest list. It's four pages long. Of course, some of that is explanations of how each guest is related to Alex or Cat or if they're just friends, plus details about their occupations and ages and how many kids they're bringing. This is more than a huge event. It's like Woodstock and the Super Bowl put together."

"You'll get it all sorted out. But if there's anything I can do to help, just ask." I spread a hand over her thigh. "The only payment I ask for is a blow job."

"Yeah, you're the easiest employee to handle."

"I'm not your employee, but I am your willing slave."

"Thanks, but I'm doing okay on my own." She leaned over to gaze into my eyes from inches away. "But I'll give you head anytime you want."

"Ditto." I slid my hand between her thighs. "Don't forget about our wedding plans. It's only two weeks away."

"I haven't forgotten. It's all sewn up."

"Seriously? Heidi, you are amazing."

"You know, I don't mind if you want to have a bachelor party."

"Got a better idea." I bent toward her to clasp her hands. "Let's ditch the traditional crap about not seeing each other the night before the wedding. I want to give you a full-body reading instead."

"Ooh, I'd love that. It's a date."

I rose and kissed her softly. "Don't work too hard."

Then I left Heidi to sort out the arrangements for the big event while I got back to work.

And in two weeks, I'd be married to that incredible woman.

Chapter Thirty-Three

Heidi
Two weeks later

I got married. Wow. The ceremony was mostly a blur of sounds and motion, but I remembered Eve and Mara fussing over my hair and my dress, then I walked down the aisle toward Damian—and I lost my breath. He looked gorgeous in a tux, but I'd already known that. What stole the air from my lungs wasn't his outfit. It was the expression on his face. He looked at me like I had a glowing golden aura around me and a sparkling halo over my head. When I reached the altar, I realized his eyes were glistening like he might cry any minute.

Yeah, I'd gotten choked up too, but I started crying the instant we faced each other and the minister started reciting the wedding spiel. I had only the haziest memory of speaking my vows and of exchanging the rings. The guests had clapped and cheered, and Sylvester Norris whistled, when Damian and I kissed. It wasn't a hot kiss, but we held our lips pressed to each other for a long moment, savoring the knowledge that we had bound our lives together. Euphoria had swept through me because I suddenly realized I had everything I'd always wanted.

Oh, did I forget to mention my parents showed up? Yeah, they had. My dad even asked if he could accompany me down the aisle and give me away. I said yes. I mean, my parents had gotten a lot better lately. Each of them had called me several times over the past two weeks, and they knew about the wedding. I'd sent them invitations, though I included a note saying I would understand if they didn't want to come.

Damian had bet me fifty bucks they would come.

He won. Was it thanks to Ludar lidar?

Mom and Dad arrived two days before the ceremony, and they hadn't argued once in all that time—at least, not so anyone heard or saw them. My parents were seeing a therapist, together and separately, to work through their issues. They had no plans to get back together, but they wanted to become better parents. All it took was for me to finally stand up and tell them how much they had hurt me over the years. Jeez, if I'd known that... I still wouldn't have done it any earlier. My parents were trying to change, but I'd had my transformation already, thanks to the amazing man I'd just married.

The reception was held at the resort since that was where we'd met and fallen in love. Damian and I stayed at the party for twenty minutes, just long enough for me to dance with my dad and my new husband. Then we retreated to the gypsy wagon. Sure, we had a Hawaiian honeymoon planned, but for tonight, my husband owed me a full-body reading.

I lay on the bed on my stomach, naked.

He straddled my legs and ran his hands over my body, starting with my shoulders, exploring my skin with his fingertips and painting a path of tingling warmth in their wake. I always got hot and bothered when Damian touched me. But the way his fingers trailed over my skin made me shiver too and suck in a breath. My nipples ached. Slick heat gathered between my thighs, and I knew I couldn't survive much longer without him inside.

"Your body tells me everything I need to know," he said while he skimmed his palms over my ass. "But I can't read you the right way unless I'm inside you."

"The whole body-reading thing was just a ploy to get me naked, then."

"I don't need tricks to do that." He dragged his tongue down my spine, swirling it as he moved. "All I have to do is look at you."

"Mm, that's true. For you, I'm the easiest lay on the planet."

"Ditto." He patted my hip. "Turn over, baby. I want to look into your eyes while we make love."

I flipped over, which took a little finagling since he was still straddling me. His dick waved above me, hard and thick, the crown damp. I couldn't resist lunging up to lick the moisture off it and flick my tongue across the slit underneath.

Damian hissed in a breath. "You can do that later. I need to be inside you now, baby."

He reached for a condom.

I grasped his wrist. "Skip that. Let's work on making a baby."

A grin slowly spread across his face. "Love to."

"We can skip foreplay too. I'm so damn ready."

"I can smell how ready you are." He knelt over me, pushing my thighs apart with his knee. "Let's make a rug rat tonight."

"You're supposed to say 'bundle of joy,' not rug rat."

"Right." He thrust into me with one long, swift stroke, filling me completely. "Might need to do this at least three times if we want to get you knocked up tonight."

"As long as it takes. I can't get enough of you, Damian."

He braced his hands at either side of my head and thrust in a measured rhythm, sucking in a breath every time he withdrew and blowing it out with a long groan when he pushed deep inside me again. I grasped his biceps and bent my knees, lifting my hips every time he plunged in. My gaze stayed riveted to his as our breaths quickened and his movements accelerated. The wet sound of our bodies merging mingled with our grunts and gasps and the groans that resonated in his chest. He punched into me faster and harder, making me bounce, and I latched my legs around him, clutching his arms, my neck arched and my back bowed, my mouth open though I couldn't draw in a breath, not anymore. The need to come bore down on me as every muscle in my body tensed.

Damian reached down to pinch my clit.

And I came. Thrashing, writhing, screaming his name, while my sex wrung his cock in wave after wave of pleasure. I was still climaxing when I felt his release pulse inside me. His back bowed too, and strangled shouts burst out of him.

He dropped onto the bed beside me. "That was—Holy shit."

"I know." I rolled over to cuddle up to him. "Imagine doing that over and over and over…"

"Gimme a few minutes, and I'll be ready for round two."

We did make love twice more, then Damian sneaked back to the reception to grab us some food and a bottle of champagne. Celebrating alone, in the wagon, seemed like the most appropriate way to start our marriage. The party continued for us even after the reception ended because we hopped on a plane the next morning to start our Hawaiian honeymoon. Though our honeymoon was fabulous, we were ready to come home after six days. Good thing we'd arranged to stay in Hawaii for only that long.

My parents visited the resort a few weeks later, and though they didn't go nude, they did see naked people. At first, they were freaked out, but they quickly got used to it and even made some new friends.

We still had the big wedding event to handle, but I wasn't worried at all. I had a blueprint for the entire week-long extravaganza, plus I had a bunch of amazing friends to help me. This event would prove to the world that a rural nudist resort could handle any kind of get-together. Alex Thorne had sent us a massive check that was way more than the contract for the wedding called for, but he included a note to explain.

"This is for the pilot project," he wrote, "and I fully expect to see more horses on the premises when I arrive for the wedding."

Damian was thrilled, but being a guy, he had to play it cool.

And the next day, we heard more good news. Eve was pregnant. Damian swore his Ludar lidar assured him I'd be a mom too, very soon. Having a baby would be amazing, but even if that never happened, I had everything I wanted. I had a real family—my parents, my friends, and all the other wonderful people who had come to mean the world to me. I'd been blessed. The future looked more than bright, it shined with the brilliance of a thousand stars. What else was there to say? Well, maybe just one more thing…

And we all lived happily ever after.

Did you love

Natural

Satisfaction?

Visit
AnnaDurand.com

to subscribe to her newsletter

for updates on forthcoming books

&

to receive free gifts for signing up!

nna Durand is a bestselling, multi-award-winning author of contemporary and paranormal romance. Her books have earned bestseller status on every major retailer and wonderful reviews from readers around the world. But that's the boring spiel. Here are some really cool things you want to know about Anna!

Born on Lackland Air Force Base in Texas, Anna grew up moving here, there, and everywhere thanks to her dad's job as an instructor pilot. She's lived in Texas (twice), Mississippi, California (twice), Michigan (twice), and Alaska—and now Ohio.

As for her writing, Anna has always made up stories in her head, but she didn't write them down until her teen years. Those first awful books went into the trash can a few years later, though she learned a lot from those stories. Eventually, she would pen her first romance novel, the paranormal romance *Willpower*, and she's never looked back since.

Want even more details about Anna? Get access to her extended bio when you subscribe to her newsletter and download the free bonus ebook, *Hot Scots Confidential*. You'll also get hot deleted scenes, character interviews, fun facts, and more including audio bonus chapters!